Mary W. S. Hawkins

Plymouth Armada Heroes

The Hawkins family - With original portraits, coats of arms, and other illustrations

Mary W. S. Hawkins

Plymouth Armada Heroes
The Hawkins family - With original portraits, coats of arms, and other illustrations

ISBN/EAN: 9783337195168

Printed in Europe, USA, Canada, Australia, Japan

Cover: Foto ©Andreas Hilbeck / pixelio.de

More available books at **www.hansebooks.com**

Plymouth Armada Heroes:

THE HAWKINS FAMILY.

WITH

Original Portraits, Coats of Arms, and other Illustrations.

BY

MARY W. S. HAWKINS.

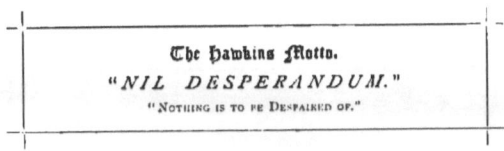

The Hawkins Motto.

"*NIL DESPERANDUM.*"

"NOTHING IS TO BE DESPAIRED OF."

"Bold let us follow through the foamy tides,
Where fortune better than a father guides,
'Avaunt, Despair!' when Teucer calls to fame,
The same your augur, and your guide the same."
—FRANCIS.

PLYMOUTH:
WILLIAM BRENDON AND SON, GEORGE STREET.
MDCCCLXXXVIII.

"'TIS opportune to look back upon old times,
    And contemplate our forefathers;
    Great examples grow thin,
    And to be fetched from the past world."
                    —SIR THOMAS BROWNE to THOMAS LE GROS.

1888 BEING THE TERCENTENARY of the defeat of the Great Armada of Spain, a Narrative of the lives of some members of the Hawkins family of Devon, intimately connected with the Town of Plymouth during the sixteenth century, may be of interest to all West-Country men, especially as three of them, Sir John Hawkins, his elder brother, Captain William Hawkins, and his son, Sir Richard Hawkins, commanded three ships—the *Victory*, the *Gryfyn*, and the *Swallow*—and greatly distinguished themselves in the several actions against the Spaniards. These three famous sailors may be justly considered the PLYMOUTH ARMADA HEROES OF 1588.

Sir John Hawkins.

"O! FAMOUS ANCESTOR, I boldly claim,
For thee and for thy deeds a foremost name.
In that great time three hundred years ago
When all our strength was taxed to ward the blow,
Of haughty Philip; thou to high command
Wert by thy Sovereign called, and from the land
Thy practised eye, quick glancing o'er the main,
Descried afar the galleons of Spain:
Then, as they proudly up the Channel sailed,
Not for a moment blanched thy cheek or quailed
Thy steadfast spirit, eager to pursue
Thine ancient foe and contests past renew :
See! Thou art slipped and eager for the fray—
The *Victory* bears exulting on their way
Thy gallant Seamen thirsting for the fight,
Which made them victors and thyself a Knight;
As *Santa Anna* fell a noble prize,
While rival squadrons looked with wondering eyes
On Hawkins, and begrudged him not his fame,
Or this fresh triumph added to his name."

J. L. H.

PREFACE.

OR some years I have been collecting information about the deeds of our ancestors, but without a thought of publication, until many friends suggested that I had enough matter—and much that had never been in print—to publish a book, which at this time particularly would be of public interest, and which will, I hope, repay those kind friends and subscribers who have been so ready with their support.

I am desirous of expressing my special thanks to the Countess of Rosebery for having a photograph taken for me of the jewel and miniature of Sir John Hawkins in her possession; also to the Marquis of Lothian for permission to have a photograph of the picture of Hawkins, Drake, and Candish; to the Governors of Sir John Hawkins's Hospital at Chatham for permission to reproduce the illustration of the chest containing the charter of incorporation granted by Queen Elizabeth, together with the hatchments of coats of arms; to Messrs. Macmillan for the use of their plates of the Armada sailing up Channel; to the Editor of the *Leisure Hour* and Mr. Wymper for the loan of the plate of the *Ark Royal;* to the Rev. Bradford R. J. Hawkins for the photograph of the ivory bust of Sir John Hawkins; to Mr. R. S. Hawkins for the photograph of the portrait of Sir Richard Hawkins; to the Hakluyt Society for permission to use their engravings of Slapton; to Mr. Clements Markham, C.B., F.R.S., for the loan of the block of a vessel of the Armada period, and kind help in many ways; and to Mr. R. N. Worth, F.G.S., for his able assistance.

I must also acknowledge the courtesy of many of the clergy of South Devon in allowing me to look over their Church Registers to obtain the necessary genealogical information.

Besides family and private papers, and manuscripts lent me, my chief authorities are: The State Papers at the Record Office; Wills at Somerset House, at Exeter, and the Heralds' College; the Plymouth Corporation Records; all the County Histories of Devon—Westcote, Risdon, Polwhele, Lysons, Moore, &c.; Worth's and Jewett's *Histories of Plymouth;* Hawkins's and Fox's *Kingsbridge;* Hasted's *Kent; Histories of Rochester;* Stow's *Survey and Annals;* Camden's *Britannia;* the Collections of Hakluyt and Purchas; Monson's *Naval Tracts;* Lidiard's *Naval History;* Abraham Darcie's *Annals;* Fuller's and Prince's *Worthies;* Barron's *Naval Worthies;* Pinkerton's *Voyages; Observations of Sir Richard Hawkins in his Voyage to the South Seas;* Payne's *Elizabethan Seamen;* Froude's *History of England;* Martin's and Duke Yonge's *Histories of England;* Creasy's *Battles;* Valentine's *Sea Fights;* Worth's *Sir John Hawkins;* Fox Brown's *English Merchants,* &c.

MARY W. S. HAWKINS.

HAYFORD HALL, BUCKFASTLEIGH,

     S. DEVON.

CONTENTS.

"HAILE then my native soile ! Thou blessed plot,
Whose equall all the world affordeth not !
Show me who can ? So many cristall rils,
Such sweet cloth'd vallies, or aspiring hills ;
Such wood-ground, pastures, quarries, wealthy mynes,
Such rocks in whom the diamond fairly shines,
And if the earth can show the like again,
Yet will she fail in her sea-ruling men.
Time never can produce men to ore-take
The fames of Greenvil, Davies, Gilbert, Drake,
Or worthy Hawkins, or of thousands more,
That by their powers made the Devonian shore
Mock the proud Tagus ; for whose richest spoyle
The boasted Spaniard left the Indian soyle
Bankrupt of store, knowing it would quit cost
By winning this though all the rest were lost."

   —Britannia's Pastorals (Book ii. Song 3).

    By WILLIAM BROWNE, poet, born 1590 at Tavistock.

The Illustrations to which the asterisks are prefixed are in the Superior Edition only.

" PLYM christneth that town which bears her noble name;
Upon the British coast, what ships yet ever came,
That not of Plymouth hears, where those brave navies lie
From cannons thund'ring flote, that all the world defy;
Which to invasive spoil, when the English list to draw,
Have checked Hyberia's pride, and kept her still in awe.
Oft furnishing our dames with India's rare devices,
And lent us gold and pearl, with silks and dainty spices."
                                    —DRAYTON'S *Polyolbion.*

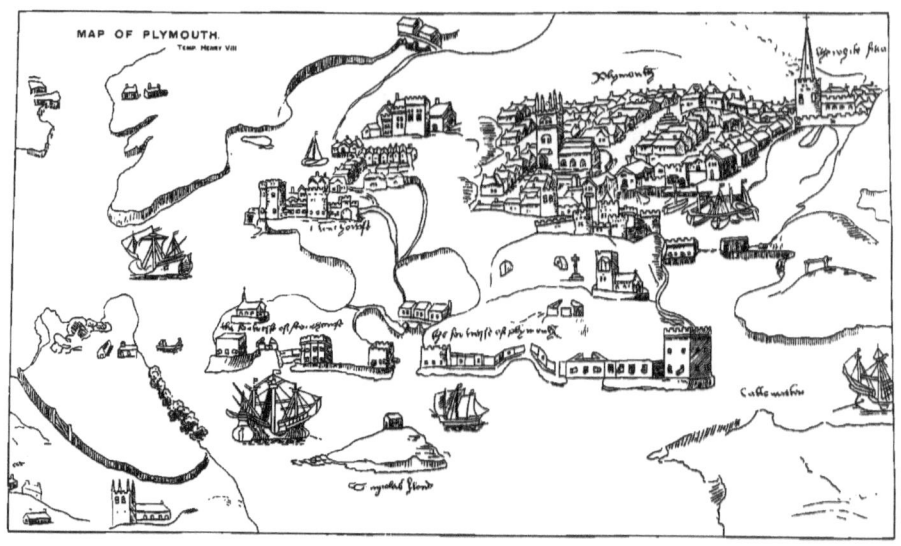

MAP OF PLYMOUTH.
TEMP HENRY VIII

MAP OF PLYMOUTH.

Temp. Henry VIII.

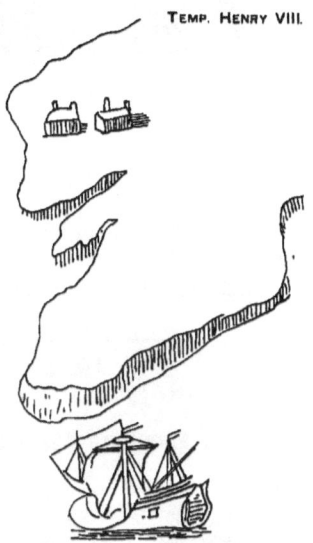

PLYMOUTH ARMADA HEROES:

THE HAWKINS FAMILY.

CHAPTER I.

William Hawkins the Elder.

PLYMOUTH in the sixteenth century was very different from the Plymouth of the present day. A chart, drawn in the time of King Henry VIII., shows that the whole town was then situated in the neighbourhood of Sutton Pool; that the Castle stood near where the Citadel now is, the site of which was partly occupied by bulwarks; and that a chain was thrown across the entrance of Sutton Pool: so that the old town of Sutton, or Plymouth, in appearance and size was something like Dartmouth now, with the houses rising one above another from the water's edge up the hill to St. Andrew's Church and the Castle.

The town was incorporated by Act of Parliament of King Henry VI., 1439-1440, "within these bounds" [there was an older corporation of some kind]; "namely, between the Hill called the Winnrigge and the back of Surpool, towards the North, unto the great ditch, and from thence to the North of Stoke Damerell fleet, by the shore of that fleet to Milbrooke bridge inclusively. From thence toward the East by the Middleditch of Houndscombe bridge to Thornhill Park, thence to Lipson bridge, and from thence by the sea-shore, continuing to the Lare and Catt of Hingston Fishtorre and East King, thence to the said hill of Winnrigge, as the bounds and metes there plainly showed." The Mayor and Commonalty were to hold the Borough of the King by 40s. paid yearly into the Exchequer, and to make stone towers and fortifications about the town for defence. William Kitherige was the first Mayor appointed by the King, and afterwards the Mayor was to be chosen every year upon St. Lambert's day and sworn on Michaelmas day before 11 o'clock. The Mayor and Commonalty to make Burgesses (or Freemen) as often as they pleased for the government of the town.

Plymouth was the home or birthplace, not of one distinguished sailor of the Hawkins family only, but of three generations in succession, of men who were celebrated as naval heroes for a period of one hundred years, extending over the reigns of Henry VIII., Edward VI., Queen Mary, Queen Elizabeth, and James I.

These Hawkinses were an extraordinary race—"gentlemen," as Prince quaintly phrases, "of worshipful extraction for several descents," but made more worshipful by their deeds. "For three generations they were the master spirits of Plymouth in its most illustrious days; its leading merchants, its bravest sailors, serving oft and well in the civic chair and in the House of Commons. For three generations too they were in the van of English seamanship; founders of England's commerce in south and west and east; stout in fight, of quenchless spirit in adventure—a family of merchants, statesmen, and heroes, to whom our country affords no parallel."

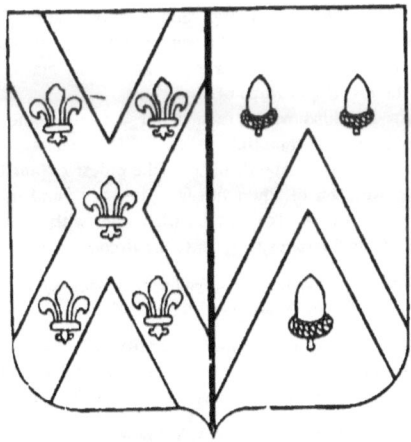

ARMS OF HAWKINS AND AMADAS.

The arms of Hawkins, as given above, were probably used from the time of Edward III. The castle of Manconseil was taken and garrisoned by three hundred men, under Rabigois of Derry, an Irishman, and Franklyn and Hawkins, two English esquires, in 1358. The origin of these arms is most likely from this expedition, the scaling ladder being represented by the saltire, and the fleurs-de-lis being on the standard of France, which was captured.

The name of Hawkins is derived from the village of Hawking, in the Hundred of Folkstone. Osbert de Hawking, in the reign of Henry II., was an ancestor of Andrew Hawkins of Nash Court, near Faversham, Kent, in the reign of Edward III.; which Andrew married Joan de Nash, an heiress, by whom the Hawkinses became possessed of Nash Court, and from whom are descended the Hawkinses of Devon.

A branch of the Hawkinses of Nash Court probably settled in Plymouth during the fifteenth century. John Hawkins held lands in the town under the Corporation before 1480, and was dead by or before 1490, when his heirs held them. This was before the Hawkinses were at Tavistock.*

William Hawkins, son of John Hawkins (who had lived at Tavistock), and Joan, daughter of William Amadas, of Launceston, was born probably at Plymouth towards the end of the fifteenth century. He was an officer in the navy of King Henry VIII. Being one of the principal sea captains in the West of England, he obtained a high and just reputation for his skill and experience, and was held in great esteem and favour by the King. He is thought to be the same Hawkins who in 1513 was master of the "Great Galley," one of the few Royal ships of that time.

This William Hawkins was a man of large fortune and estates, owning considerable property in Plymouth, and one of the richest (if not the richest) men in the town. His name stands fifth on the oldest extant list of Plymouth freemen. He was Receiver of Plymouth in 1524-1525; and in the Corporation books he is mentioned in 1527-1528, when he with others manned the bulwarks to defend the "arrogosye agcynst the ffrenchemen."

> Item received of tharrogosye† for defending their ship against the French-
> men that would have taken her, xvjli xivˢ ivᵈ.

Hawkins also sold to the town a quantity of gunpowder, 196 lbs. at 6d. a lb., and two brass guns, paid for in three annual instalments of £8.

The first voyage into the Southern Seas in which any Englishman was

---

* The family occur as holding property in Plymouth in a rent roll of 1485.

† The argosy ; probably a large Spanish merchantman.

concerned was that of Sebastian Cabot, from Seville to the River Plate, in April, 1527. This expedition was set forth by Spanish merchants; but one Robert Thorne and his partner advanced 1,400 ducats, "principally for that two Englishmen, friendes of mine,* which are somewhat learned in cosmographie, should goe in the same ships, to bring me certain relation of the situation of the country, and to be expert in the nauigation of those seas."

The voyage was intended for the Moluccas. We have no means of knowing who these two "cosmographical Englishmen" were; but the first independent expeditions, and the first to proceed from England, to the thereafter famous Spanish Main, sailed from Plymouth Sound, and were the private ventures of our Plymouth merchant, William Hawkins the elder, who was thus one of the earliest pioneers to Brazil in the reign of Henry the Eighth.

As William Hawkins made at least three voyages (the second and third in 1530 and 1532 respectively), his earliest can hardly have been later than 1528, when "he armed out a tall and goodlie ship of his own of 200 tons," called the *Paul of Plymouth;* his desire being to venture further than the ordinary short voyages made to the various coasts of Europe at that time. In this ship William Hawkins made his three long and famous voyages to Brazil—"a thing very rare in those days, especially for our nation"†—touching at the coast of Guinea, where he trafficked with the negroes, and procured elephants' teeth and other commodities, and then crossing the Atlantic to Brazil to exchange his cargo for other goods, with which he returned to England. In Brazil he behaved himself so wisely with the savage people that he grew into great familiarity and friendship with them; insomuch that on his second voyage, in 1530, one of their savage kings was contented to take ship and return with him to see the wonders of England; Captain Hawkins leaving Martin Cockeram, of Plymouth, behind as a pledge of their king's safe return.

They arrived safely in England, and the Brazilian chief was taken to Whitehall and presented to Henry VIII. On seeing him the King and Court were much astonished, and not, as was said, without cause; "for in his cheeks were holes made, and therein small bones were planted, standing an inch out from the said holes, which in his own country was reported for a great bravery. He had also another hole in his nether lip, wherein was set a precious stone about the bigness of a pease; all his apparell, behaviour, and gesture were very

* THORNE.   † HAKLUYT.

strange to the beholders "—as may be imagined ; he being the first savage chief. brought to England.

" Having spent nearly a year in this country, and the King with his sight fully satisfied, Captain Hawkins was returning with him to Brazil; but it fell out on the way that, by change of air and alteration of diet, the savage king died at sea, which was feared would be the cause of Martin Cockeram, his pledge, being put to death by the savages ; but they were persuaded of the honest dealing of our men with their prince, and restored the hostage to his friends, who with their ship freighted and furnished with the goods of the country, returned to England." Martin Cockeram lived at Plymouth for many years after this adventure.

William Hawkins made his third voyage in 1532, and on his return was chosen Mayor of Plymouth, 1532-3. In which year " King Henry VIII. married Anne Bollen, in November, 1532 ; Queen Katharine being divorced by Parliament. Queen Elizabeth was born 7th September, 1534."* In 1535 Hawkins lent money to the Corporation of Plymouth, receiving £4 a year until the loan was returned.

He was again Mayor in 1538-9, the year in which the King first established a Council for the West at Tavistock, and images in churches were pulled down. In 1539 he was elected " Burgess," or member of Parliament, with James Horswell.

Thus William Hawkins was one of the oldest members of the Plymouth Corporation, when, in 1540, he duly accounted for the proceeds of the "Church juells, plate, and furniture," taken by the Corporation at the Reformation, which had been delivered to him when mayor, and sold, apparently in London. A much larger quantity of Church plate and jewels was handed to him in 1543-4, "to by therw^th for the towne gunpowder, bowys, & for arrowys." These were purchased in London—10 barrels of gunpowder, 20 bows, and 30 sheaves of arrows.

Plymouth at this time, as would appear from the practical use thus made of the Church property as relics of Popery, had become strongly Puritan. During Queen Elizabeth's reign the local Puritan feeling, moreover, grew by the Huguenots making the port their head-quarters, and also by the frequent expeditions made from Plymouth against the Spaniards. William Hawkins himself was thoroughly imbued with the Reforming spirit.

In 1544, William Hawkins purchased the manor of Sutton Valletort, or

* *Plymouth Corporation Records,* in which it was the custom to enter the more remarkable events, local and national.

Vawter (which remained in the Hawkins family until 1637-8), of Sir Hugh Pollard, for 1000 marks; and his other property in Plymouth included quays and warehouses on Sutton Pool. Among the deeds entered in the Plymouth "Black Book" we find, "28th Henry VIII., Margery Pyne and others to Wm. Hawkins, merchant, conveyance of a tenement and garden in a certain venella, on the east of Kinterbury Street." In 1545, one between Peter Gryslyng and William Hawkyns; while 37th Henry VIII. a deed was registered in the "Black Book" transferring property in Plymouth from John Talazon, of North Petherwin, to William Hawkins.

In 1545-6, £4 was paid to Wm. Hawkins "for the Burgesses of the Parliament;" while in 1547 he was again chosen to represent the community, and in the following year received £14 for his services. He must have been very popular in Plymouth; for he was also elected member of Parliament in 1553, with Roger Budokeside (a connection of his through his mother, Joan Amadas). He died towards the close of the year.

A deed dated 8 February, 1554,* states that "Henry Hawkins clerk† (in orders), recently of Plymouth, brother and heir of William Hawkins Merchant *recently* deceased, for a sum of money gives up land in Plymouth to William Hawkins son of Joan Trelawny."

William Hawkins married Joan, sole daughter and heiress of Roger Trelawny, Esq., of Brightorre, third son of Sir John Trelawny and Blanche Pownde.‡

His two sons, William and John Hawkins, the distinguished seamen and naval heroes, entered the service with great advantages, owing to the wealth and experience of their father.

---

* The family of Hawkins of Cornwall also come from and bear the arms of Hawkins of Nash Court, Kent. The ancestor of the late Sir Christopher Hawkins, Bart., of Trewithan, settled in Cornwall in 1554. It is probable that he went into Cornwall from Plymouth, and was the Henry Hawkins mentioned above, who in this year 1554 describes himself as *recently* of Plymouth.

† Edmund Tremayne's father, in 1524, presented Henry Hawkins with the living of Lamerton.

‡ Over the west gate of the town of Launceston, now removed, were the arms and effigy of Henry V., below which was the following rhyme—

"He that will do aught for mee,
Let hym love well Sir John Tirlawnee."

Sir John Trelawny was with the King at Agincourt in 1415, and as a reward for his bravery had the three oak, or laurel leaves, added to the family arms, with a pension of £20 per annum.

ARMS OF HAWKINS AND TRELAWNY.

CHAPTER II.

The Second William Hawkins.

APTAIN WILLIAM HAWKINS, elder brother of Sir John Hawkins, was admitted to the freedom of Plymouth in 1553, where he held a most influential position, as extracts from the Corporation Records show. He was regarded as Governor of Plymouth; and had more to do with the affairs of the town than any man of his time.

In 1561 we have "Item paid to Mr Hawkins for money paid at Bristol for inrolling the Charter £1;" and also "paid to Mr Hawkins for fetching of the Ordynance from the Island to the Castle £2."

The Hawkinses owned considerable property in the vicinity of Sutton Pool; and in 1558 an Act of Parliament fixed Hawkins's Quay as the sole legal quay for landing goods. It was afterwards the property of Sir John, and then of his son Sir Richard Hawkins.

Captain William Hawkins was Mayor of Plymouth in 1567-8, when the earliest code of bye-laws extant for the regulation of Sutton Pool and the shipping therein was passed. Also "the wache on Midsummer night was renewed, which had not been used xx years before that time;" and the large sum (!) of 2s. 4d. was paid for the "newe cuttinge of the Gogmagoge, the picture of the Giant, at the Hawe." The last vestiges of this ancient memorial on the Hoe disappeared in 1671, no doubt to make room for the Citadel.

> In this year (1567-8) the war in the Low Countries began; and Mary Queen of Scots fled into England, and was imprisoned in the Castle of Carlisle.*

William Hawkins was a large shipowner, and in 1568 his Plymouth cruisers were the terror of Spain; and not only was he a wealthy shipowner and

* *Plymouth Corporation Records.*

If I may have any warrants, from his maiesty, or from your honor, I shall be glad to doe, for this my [...] of my [...] [...] presently I have already commyssion from the [...] Stattyllon, for one [...] to [...] for one [...] pleasures of naval and [...] but I may not pleasound, any forther, not out commyssyon / in this thynge I shall desyre your honor to be advertysed by my servant Frauncis Drake; and I shall Day by play for your longe [...] esealle / longe to indowed, from my mouthe the [...] of Janowary at nyght 1568
By your [...] always to Comande [...]

your honours most faythfully to comande John Hawkyns

your honors euer most humbly bounden
Richard Hawkyns

pretended to bring the information for which the town was longing, and dressed his tale to flatter the national pride and gratify Hawkins's friends and family. "Sir John had been in the enchanted garden of Aladdin, and had loaded himself with gold and jewels. He had taken a ship with 800,000 ducats, sacked a town, and taken heaps of pearls and jewels. A Spanish fleet of forty-four sail had passed a harbour where he was dressing his ships. On board this Spanish fleet a council of war had been held to consider the prudence of attacking him; but the admiral had said, 'For the ships that be in harbour I will not deal with them, for they being monstrous ships will sink some of us and put us to the worst, wherefore let us depart on our voyage.' And so they did. 'The worst boy in those ships might be a captain for riches;' and the Spaniard wished he had been one of them."

This story might have answered its end had there been time enough for it to work; but the wind which brought the fable brought the truth behind it. Two days later William Hawkins sent to Cecil the news of the real catastrophe.

The first rumour of the disaster at San Juan de Ulloa—where the treacherous Spaniards fell upon and massacred the English, in the fleet under John Hawkins, during peace between England and Spain—reached William Hawkins at Plymouth by the 3rd December, 1568, in a letter from Spain, written by Benedick Spinola, saying that the English fleet was totally destroyed. This was a declaration of the purposed treachery and intentions of Spain—there not being time enough for the news to have reached England from Ulloa at this date.

The report was enough for William Hawkins. He at once wrote to Cecil, asking that enquiry might be made, and recompense taken of "King Philip's treasure here in these parts." However, if the Queen would not "meddle in the matter," he asked no more than that her subjects should be allowed to do so. "Then I trust we should not only have recompense to the uttermost, but also do as good service as is to be desired, with so little cost. And I hope to please God best therein, for that they are God's enemies."

It was not until the 20th January, 1569, that there was full assurance of the evil tidings. That night the *Judith* reached Plymouth; and that night, without a moment's delay, William Hawkins sent a letter to the Privy Council, and one to Cecil, with such hasty details as he could bring together, sending also his "kinsman and servant," young Francis Drake, who had returned in the *Judith*, reporting that Hawkins and all with him were massacred by the treacherous Spaniards, as bearer of the news. What had become of his brother John he knew not. "My brothers safe return is very dangerous and doubtfull." But he knew very well that his brother and himself had lost at least £2000, and as the acting partner moved for recompense, either out "of those Spanyards goods here stayed," or what he thought still more satisfactory, by the Queen giving "me leave to work my own force against them." Four ships he was ready to set forth at once of his own, besides one already in commission.

William Hawkins to Sir William Cecil.

RIGHT HONORABLE,—My bownden dewtye alwayes had in Remembrance it may please your honor to be advertisyd that this present hour there is come to Plymouth one of the small barkes of my brothers fleat, and for that I have neither wrytynge nor any thing else from him I thought it good and moste my dewty, to send you the capetayne of the same barke, being our kinsman called Fransyes Dracke for that he shall thoroughly informe your honor of the whole proceedyngs of these affayres to the end the Quenes Matie may be advertisyd of the same, and for that it doth plainly appear of their manyfest injuries from time to time offered, and our losses only in this voyage two thousand pounds at at least, besydes my brothers absense, which unto me is more grefe than any other thing in this world, whom I trust, as god hathe preserved, wyll likewise preserve, and send well home in safety.

In the meane tyme my humble suit unto your honor is that the Quene's Majeste will when time shall serve see me, her humble and obedyent subjecte, partly recompensed, of those Spanyards goods here stayd.

And further if it shall please her grace to give me Leave to work my own selfe against them, to the end I may be the better recompensed, I shall be the more bownde unto her highnes which I pray god long to live, to the glory of god, and the comfort of her subjectes. If I may have any warrant from her Matie or from your honor I shall be glad to set forth four ships of mine own presently I have already commission from the Cardanal Shatyllyon for one ship to serve the princes of Navare and Conndye but I may not presume any further without commission in these things I shall desire your honors to be advertisyd by my servant Francis Dracke and I shall daily pray for your honors estate long to endure.

From Plymouth the xx^th of January at night 1568.

By your honors always to command

Wm HAWKYNS.

[Endorsed]   To the right honorable Sir Wm Cecil.*

* *Sta. Pa. Dom.* (Eliz.)

[This is No. 36, vol. 49; No. 37 is the same, with the following addition.]

AND for that my brothers safe return is very dangerous and doubtfull, but that it resteth in gods hands who send him well if it be his blessed will. . . . . .

By your honors always

W^M HAWKYNS.

[Endorsed] To the Right honorable and my singular good Lordes, the Lordes of the Privy Counsell.*

When William Hawkins was thus moving the Court to allow him to declare war on his own account, his brother—whose absence was to him "more grefe than any other thing in this world"—was near the English shores, reaching Mount's Bay with the *Minion* on the 25th January, 1568; whereupon "one of the Mount for good wyll came away immediately in poste" to Plymouth.

William Hawkins to Sir William Cecil.

RYGHT HONORABELL,—My bownden dewty alwayes had in Remembrance it may please your honor to be advertysed that I am credybly informyd of my brothers aryvall with the *Menyon* in Mounts bay in Cornwall not from hym nor any of his company but by one of the Mount for good wyll came immediately away in poste uppon the speache of one of his men who was sent a lande for help of men and also for cables and ankeres for that they had but one, and their men greatly weekened by reson he put ashore in the *Indyas* a C. [hundred] of his men for the salfe gard of the reste and also that he should caste overbowrde not v days before xlv men more and the rest being a lyve, were fain to live vij days uppon a noxe heyde [an ox head] who uppon the wind being esterly I sent away, for his sucker a barke with xxxiiij mariners store of flesh vytles two ankers iij cables and store of small warpes with other necessaries as I thought good. I am assured to hear from him self this night at the furthest and then I will certify your honor with spead agayne, and so for this tyme I leave to trouble your honor any further praying for the increase of your honors estate. From Plymouth the 27th of January 1568. . . . .

By your honors always to comande,

W^M HAWKYNS.

[Endorsed] To the right honorable Sir Wm Syssell Knt.*

William Hawkins did not neglect local affairs for national or personal. The New Conduit was built by him in 1569-70, and was apparently associated with the Market Cross, which stood in Old Town near the

* *Sta. Pa. Dom.* (Eliz.)

intersection of Treville Street. In 1578-9, while he was Mayor, "the Governor's House on the Barbican was builded;" and in 1579-1580 he had also the charge of procuring the patent which gave Plymouth authority over St. Nicholas Island with its fortifications.

> Itm p⁴ to Wᵐ Hawkins esquyre for money laid out in peuring the patent for the Ilonde, and for his charge in the suit thereof xxij*li.*

In 1580, he, together with Thomas Edmonds, was commissioned to seal with the common seal the necessary documents relating to the transfer of that island to the Crown.

> In 1580 the King of Spain seized the kingdom of Portugal, whose king came into England, and lay awhile at Mount Edgcumbe.

> 1580-1. The plague was so great in Plymouth that the mayor was chosen on Cat Down. 600 persons died; [a sign Plymouth was then but thinly peopled, and a small town].

> 1584-5. The Queen undertakes the protection of the Hollanders. The Barbican stairs built; the Queen gives a rent of £39 10*s.* 10*d.* for the maintenance of the Island.*

In 1581-2 Hawkins sailed on a voyage to the West Indies, taking with him his nephew, Sir Richard Hawkins.

During this voyage they visited the Margarita pearl fishery. "In anno 1583, in the island of Margarita, I was at the dredging of pearl oysters, after the manner we dredge oysters in England; and with my own hands I opened many, and took the pearls out of them, some greater, some less, and in good quantity."†

When Drake, in 1585, without opposition burnt San Jago, Cates, who wrote the account of the voyage, says, that none of the officials or the inhabitants came and asked the English that aught might be spared.‡ "The cause of their unreasonable distrust (as I do take it) was the fresh remembrance of the great wrong they had done to old Mr. William Hawkins of Plymouth, in the voyage he made four or five years before, when they did both break their promise, and murthered many of his men."

In 1588, the memorable year of the arrival of the Armada, William Hawkins was Mayor of Plymouth, and the great local preparations to meet

* *Plymouth Corporation Records.*
† *Observations of Sir Richard Hawkins.*
‡ BARROW'S *Life of Drake.*

the Spaniards were carried on under his direction. "Several great ships were being made ready for sea." We are also told that "Plymouth fitted out seven stout ships every way equal to the Queen's men of war," evidently owing largely to William Hawkins's experience, and chiefly owned by the Hawkinses. A letter written by William Hawkins from Plymouth, dated 17th February, 1587, gives a vivid description of the work. "The *Hope* and the *Nonpareil* are both graved and bottomed and the *Revenge* now aground. We have and do trim one side of every ship by night and the other by day. The ships get aground so strongly and are so staunch as if they were made of a whole tree. The doing of it is very chargeable [costly], being carried on by torchlights and cressets in the midst of a gale of wind, which consumes pitch, tallow, and furze abundantly." Captain William Hawkins commanded the *Griffin*, of 200 tons and 100 men, against the Armada.

During his whole life William Hawkins was thus employed in good works for, and improvements in, the town of Plymouth, and engaged in the greatest enterprises set forth by the port. No Plymouth merchant ever held such a position of trust and honour, or used it to such good account.

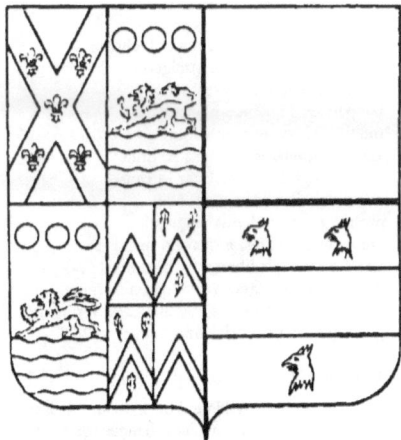

ARMS OF HAWKINS AND HALSE.

William Hawkins was married twice. By his first wife he had one son, William, also in the navy, who was afterwards ambassador at the Court of the Great Mogul, and three daughters—Judith, Clare, and Grace. By his second wife, Mary, daughter of John Halse, of Kenedon (by his second wife, Joan, daughter of William Tothill), he had four sons — Richard, Francis, Nicholas, and William, and three daughters—Frances, Mary, and Elizabeth. His widow survived him and became the first wife of Sir Warwick Hele, of Wembury. William Hawkins's three youngest sons were baptised at St. Andrew's Church, Plymouth, in 1582, 1584, and 1587. A daughter (Grace) was buried in 1582, and another daughter (Clare) was married there, in 1587, to Robert Michell.

There is a curious entry in St. Andrew's Church Register which is interesting, as another proof that William Hawkins, and not Humphrey Fownes,* was Mayor the Armada year. "Margarit Crumnell (servant ?) unto Mr. Hawkins, Mayor, was buried 5th July, 1588."

William Hawkins died on the 7th October, 1589, and was buried at Deptford, Kent.

Sir John Hawkins erected a monument to the memory of his brother in St. Nicholas Church, Deptford, which was in existence in Thorpe's time (it is now removed), with this inscription :

> "Sacræ perpetuæque memoriæ Gulielmi
> Hawkyns de Plimouth armigeri ;
> qui veræ religionis verus cultor,
> pauperibus præcipue naviculariis
> munificiis, rerum nauticarum
> studiosissimus, longinquas instituit
> sæpe navigationes : arbiter in causis
> difficilissimis æquissimus, fide,
> probitate, et prudentia singulari.
> Duos duxit uxores, e quarum una 4 ex
> altera 7 suscepit liberos. Johannes Hawkyns
> eques auratus, classis regiæ quæstor, frater
> mæstissimus posuit. Obiit spe certa resurgendi
> 7 die mensis Octobris anno domini 1589."

The following is a translation :

"To the ever living memory of William Hawkyns of Plymouth esquire ; who was a worshipper of the true religion ; a munificent benefactor to poor mariners ; skilled

* Humphrey Fownes is represented as Mayor in Lucas's picture of the game of bowls.

· in navigation; oftentimes undertaking long voyages; a just arbiter in difficult cases; and a man of singular faith, probity, and prudence. He had two wives, four children by one, and seven by the other. John Hawkins, Knight, Treasurer of the Queen's Navy, his brother, most sorrowfully erected this. He died in the sure and certain hope of resurrection, on the 7th day of October, in the year of our Lord 1589."

Will of William Hawkins.

I WILLIAM HAWKINS of Plimouth Esq. 6ᵗʰ Oct. 1589

My body to be buried in place & sort as my brother Sʳ John Hawkins Knt. & my wife Marie Hawkins shall think most convenient

Concerning my said wife & the children I have now living as well by her as by my former wife, & all my lands I dispose of them as follows :—an annuity of £40 to William Hawkins my eldest son for life out of my lands in Plimouth

I give all my lands so charged & all my other lands whatsoever to my wife Marie for life, with remainder to Richard Hawkins my eldest son by the said Marie, & to his heirs male, with remainder respectively in tail mail to Francis my 2ⁿᵈ, Nicholas, my 3ʳᵈ, William my 4ᵗʰ son & my own right heirs for ever

To Judith Whitakers one of my daughters "all that my bargayne of Hindwell "

To William Whitakers her eldest son, my grandchild £10 & to every of her other children £5.

To Clare Michaell my daughter £40

[Several legacies to servants.]

All the rest of my goods to be divided into 3 equal parts, one 3ʳᵈ part to be divided among all my Children by my wife Marie, another 3ʳᵈ part to my wife Marie, & the remaining one to my brother Sir John Hawkins

I constitute my wife my sole Executrix, and my brother Sir John Hawkins & Anthony Halse gent. my brother in law my Supervisors

Read, signed & sealed in the presence of Edward Combes, Robert Peterson, Wᵐ Hales, Thos. Nun, James Finche, Ric. Wood, Ric. Hawkins, Ric. Collyns, Charles Fenton.

Proved in London 20ᵗʰ Oct. 1589 by Marie the relict. [*Leicester*, 78.]

CHAPTER III.

Sir John Hawkins.

AWKINS was the patriarch of the great sea-dogs of Elizabeth's reign. Frobisher, Drake, Gilbert, Candish, Ralegh, and others, who subsequently made voyages of discovery, were but boys when he was a man of mark (with the exception perhaps of Frobisher), learning to profit by the wisdom and experience of John Hawkins, the pioneer of English seamen across the Atlantic.

Edmund Spenser, in his "Colin Clout's Come Home Again," speaks of Sir John Hawkins as Proteus.

> "And Proteus eke with him does drive his herd
> Of stinking seals and porcpises together ;
> With hoary head and dewy-dropping beard,
> Compelling them which way he list and whether."

Admiral Sir John Hawkins was one of the most distinguished men of his time : closely connected with the history of our navy, for forty-eight years a gallant commander at sea, and an able administrator on shore. He was the second son of William Hawkins the elder, by Joan Trelawny. Born at Plymouth in 1532, as a youth—like the rest of his family—he made mathematics and navigation his study, and soon began to acquire knowledge, and to make good use of his skill and learning.

Hakluyt tells us that "Master John Hawkins," previous to his first long voyage in 1562, had made several voyages to Spain, Portugal, and the Canary Islands, where he obtained information about the state of West India. Amongst other things he learnt that negroes were in demand at Hispaniola (St. Domingo), and that they could be easily procured upon the coast of Guinea. He resolved to make trial of this, and communicated his plan to his friends, the greatest traders in London—namely, Sir Lionel Ducket, Sir Thomas Lodge, Mr. Gonson (his father-in-law), Sir William Winter,

D

Mr. Bronfield, and others—who were pleased with and contributed largely to the enterprise. Three good ships were immediately provided—the *Solomon*, of 120 tons, with Hawkins himself as "General" in command; the *Swallow*, of 100 tons, Captain Thomas Hampton; and the *Jonas*, a bark of 40 tons, "wherein the master supplied the captain's room, in which small fleet M. Hawkins took with him not above 100 men, for fear of sickness and other inconveniences;" and "this little squadron was the first English fleet which navigated the West Indian seas. This voyage opened those seas to the English."

Hawkins sailed on his first long voyage in October, 1562, and in his course touched first at Teneriffe, where he received friendly entertainment. Thence he went to Sierra Leone, where he stayed, and got possession of 300 negroes, with other merchandise. With this cargo he sailed "over the ocean sea" to St. Domingo, where he peaceably exchanged the negroes at the ports of Isabella, Port Plata, and Monte Christi for such a quantity of merchandise, that besides his own three ships, which were laden with hides, ginger, sugars, and some quantity of pearls, he also freighted two hulks with goods, which he sent to Spain, in command of Captain Hampton, to dispose of the merchandise at Cadiz. This cargo was confiscated, and Hawkins lost half his profits. The loss was estimated by him at 40,000 ducats. "Fearless of man or devil, he thought of going in person to Madrid, and taking Philip by the beard in his own den."[*] Also an order was sent to the West Indies, by the Spanish Government, that for the future no English ship should be allowed to trade there.

Having dispatched the hulks for Spain, Hawkins departed from St. Domingo and sailed for England, where he arrived in September, 1563.

John Hawkins is often stigmatised as the first Englishman engaged in the slave trade. He was not, as his first voyage to Guinea and the West Indies was in 1562, while nine years previously, "in 1553, John Lok was tempted to the African shores by the ivory and gold dust; and he (first of Englishmen), discovering that the negroes were a people of beastly living, without God, law, religion, or commonwealth, gave some of them opportunity of a life in creation, and carried them off as slaves. It is noticeable that on their first appearance on the West Coast of Africa the English visitors were received by the natives with marked cordiality. The slave trade had hitherto been a monopoly of the Spaniards and Portuguese. It had been established in concert with the native chiefs, as a means of relieving the tribes of bad subjects,

* FROUDE.

who would otherwise have been hanged. Thieves, murderers, and suchlike were taken down to the depôts and sold to the West Indian traders."*

"No blame attaches to the conduct of John Hawkins in undertaking a venture which all the world in those days looked upon as legitimate, and even as beneficial. It was in 1517 that Charles V. issued royal licences for the importation of negroes into the West Indies, and in 1551 a licence for importing 17,000 negroes was offered for sale. The measure was adopted from philanthropic motives, and was intended to preserve the Indians. It was looked upon as prudent and humane, even if it involved some suffering on the part of a far inferior race. The English were particularly eager to enter upon the slave trade; and by the treaty of Utrecht, in 1713, England at length obtained the 'asiento,' giving her the exclusive right to carry on the slave trade between Africa and the Spanish Indies for thirty years. So strong was the party in favour of this trade in England, that the contest for its abolition was continued for forty-eight years, from 1759 to 1807. It is not therefore John Hawkins alone who can justly be blamed for the slave trade, but the whole English people during 250 years, who must all divide the blame with him."†

"To himself," as Mr. Worth observes, "as to all but a very few among his contemporaries, his deeds were not only allowable, but praiseworthy. The Queen and many men of name shared in the expeditions. The sea-dogs of those days were neither slavers nor buccaneers; they regarded themselves 'as the elect, to whom God had given the heathen for an inheritance.' Now we are content with the heathen land only; but

> ' You take my life
> When you do take the means whereby I live.'"
> *Merchant of Venice*, Act IV., Scene 1.

"It is interesting to note that in all the early narratives of the slave trade there is no intimation that it involved cruelty or any form of wrong."

On the 18th October, 1564, Captain John Hawkins sailed from Plymouth on his second long voyage in command of the Queen's famous ship the *Jesus of Lubek*,‡ of 700 tons, and as "General" of the *Solomon*, 140 tons, and her two barques the *Tiger* of 50, and the *Swallow* of 30 tons, with 170 men. His sailing orders concluded with the quaint advice from Queen Elizabeth, to "serve God daily, love one another, preserve your victuals, beware of fire, and keepe good companie." § This expedition was on a much larger

---

* FROUDE. † CLEMENTS MARKHAM, Introduction to *Hawkins' Voyages.*
‡ *Sta. Pa. Dom.* (vol. xxxvii. No. 61). § HAKLUYT.

scale than the previous one, and was prolonged so as to become an important voyage of discovery. The Earls of Pembroke and Leicester were among the adventurers.

John Sparke, who sailed with Hawkins, wrote a most interesting account of the voyage, with details respecting the various places in Africa and the West Indies touched at, including an account of Florida. It is the first narrative of a Plymouth expedition that was written and published in England by an eye-witness. Sparke was subsequently Mayor of Plymouth, in 1583-4 and 1591-2. The little fleet departed from Plymouth with a fair wind, but on the 21st October were overtaken by a severe storm which obliged them to put into Ferrol, where they remained a few days, then proceeding on their voyage. Arrived at the Isle of Palmes, Teneriffe, Canaries, at first the inhabitants were unwilling to make friends, but afterwards Pedro de Ponte, Governor of Santa Cruz, entertained Hawkins most kindly. Thence they sailed to the Cape Verde Islands, to Sambula, and to Bymba, where the assault of the town brought disaster; for the Portuguese told Hawkins that this place contained great quantities of gold, and that it would yield one hundred slaves, which determined him to attack. Meeting with unexpected and considerable resistance, the English were driven to their boats, having procured ten negroes only, with the loss of seven of their best men, including Field, Captain of the *Solomon*, besides twenty-seven wounded. Hawkins felt this loss deeply, although he in "a singular wise manner carried himself, with countenance very cheerful outwardly, as though he did little weigh the death of his men, nor yet the great hurt of the rest; although his heart inwardly was broken in pieces for it." The chief blame for this misadventure was laid to the Portuguese, who were "not to be trusted."

From Bymba they departed to Taggarin. Here the *Swallow* sailed up the river Casseroes to traffic, and they saw great towns of the negroes, and canoes that held sixty men apiece. "On the 18th January, at night, we departed from Taggarin, being bound for the West Indies," writes John Sparke; but just before they sailed, "the King of Sierra Leona had made all the power he could, to take some of us, partly for the desire he had to see what kind of people we were that had spoiled his people at the Idols, whereof he had news before our coming, and also upon other occasions provoked by the Tangomangos; but sure we were that the army was come down, by means that in the evening we saw such a monstrous fire, made by the watering place. If these men had come down in the evening, they had done us great displeasure, for that we were on shore filling water."

Sailing towards the West Indies they were becalmed for twenty-one days, at intervals having contrary winds and some tornadoes. This delay shortened the supply of victuals and water, and after some inconvenience they arrived at Dominica, where, and in the adjacent islands, "the cannibals are the most desperate warriors that are in the Indies by the Spaniards' report, who are never able to conquer them." None of the natives appeared, and departing thence Hawkins sailed for Santa Fé, where there was a good watering place, and the natives presented them with "a kind of corn called maize, in bigness of pease, the ear whereof is much like to a teasel, but a span in length, having thereon a number of grains. Also they brought down to us hens, potatoes, and pines," which were exchanged for beads, knives, whistles, and other trifles. "These potatoes be the most delicate roots that may be eaten, and do far exceed their parsnips or carrots."

Potatoes * were first imported into Europe, in 1565, by Hawkins, from Santa Fé, in Spanish America; planted first in Ireland by Sir Walter Ralegh, who had an estate there. A total ignorance of what part of the plant was proper food had nearly prevented any further attention to its culture ; for the green apples on the stem were supposed to be the eatable part ; and these being boiled, and found unpalatable, the idea of growing potatoes was abandoned. Accident discovered the real fruit, owing to the ground being turned over through necessity that season, when a plentiful crop was discovered *underground*, which, being boiled, proved good to the taste, whereupon the cultivation of potatoes was continued. Some authors say that Sir John imported potatoes in 1563, in September, on his return from his first voyage to America.

Departing from Santa Fé, they directed their course along the coast to the town of Burburata, where, having ended their traffic without disturbance, they set sail for Curaçao. Here they "had traffic for hides, and found great refreshing both of beef, mutton, and lambs. The increase of cattle in this island is marvellous, which from a dozen of each sort brought thither by the Governor, in twenty-five years had a hundred thousand at the least. We departed from Curaçao being not a little to the rejoicing of our Captain and us, that we had ended our traffic ; for notwithstanding our sweet meat we had sour sauce by reason of our riding so open at sea, and contrary winds blowing."

Passing a little island called Aruba, they came to Rio de la Hauche, so called from the first Spanish settlers giving the natives a hatchet, to show

* These were sweet (convolvulus) potatoes.

them where water might be found. Here they landed, and met with some
difficulty about exchanging goods, on account of the order sent from Spain
to have no dealings with the English. On hearing of this order, "our Captain
replied, that he was in an Armada of the Queen's Majesty of England,"
and driven by contrary winds to come into those parts, where he hoped
to find such friendship as he should do in Spain, in that there was amity
betwixt their princes." But seeing that "contrary to all reason they would
withstand his traffic," Hawkins ordered a cannon to be fired to summon the
town, and with a hundred men in armour went ashore; whereupon the people
came to the shore in battle array. Hawkins, "perceiving them so brag,"
discharged two guns from his boats, "which put them in no small fear
. . . at every shot they fell flat to the ground, and as we approached near
unto them they broke their array, and dispersed themselves for fear of
the ordinance." Hawkins was putting his men in order to march forward
and encounter the enemy, when they sent a messenger with a flag of truce
—and a friendly traffic was agreed to.

"In this river we saw many crocodiles of sundry bignesses, but some
as big as a boat, with four feet, a long broad mouth, and a long tail, whose
skin is so hard that a sword will not pierce it." Hawkins and his sailors
disliked the alligators, or crocodiles as they called them. John Sparke
writes, "His nature is ever, when he would have his praie, to crie and sobbe like
a Christian bodie to provoke them to come to him, and then he snatcheth
at them; and thereupon came this proverbe that is applied unto women
when they weepe Lachrymæ Crocodile, the meaning whereof is that as
the crocodile when he crieth goeth then about to deceive, so doth a woman
most commonly when she weepeth."

"Shakspere, who was about this time writing his 'King Henry VI,'
apparently borrowed from Sir John Hawkins this story, and introduced it."

> " As the mournful crocodile
> With sorrow snares relenting passengers."
> *2 Henry VI.* iii. 1.

They now departed for St. Domingo and Jamaica, and on the 20th June fell
in with the western end of Cuba. With a north-east wind they ranged along
the coast of Florida, at that time supposed to be an island, the captain in
the ship's pinnace going into every creek to enquire of the Floridians where
the French colonists dwelt. Sailing up the May river, they discovered three
French ships, and obtained information that M. Laudonnière with his soldiers

were some miles higher up the river, in a fort which they had built. Here Hawkins found and greatly relieved the distressed Frenchmen, giving them provisions and other necessaries, and to help them to return home, "we spared them one of our barks of 50 tons."

"The Floridians when they travel have a kind of herb dried [tobacco], which with a cane, and an earthen cup in the end, with fire, and the dried herbs put together; do suck through the cane the smoke thereof, which smoke satisfieth their hunger, and herewith they live four or five days without meat or drink, and this all the Frenchmen used for this purpose : yet do they hold opinion withall, that it causeth water and phlegm to void from their stomachs." *

Sir Richard Hawkins observes, in his *Voyage to the South Sea*, that "with drinking [smoking] of tobacco it is said that the *Roebucke* was burned in the range at Dartmouth."

The introduction of tobacco into England is attributed to Sir John Hawkins, on his return from his third voyage in January, 1569, by Stow; and also by John Taylor, the Water Poet, in his *Prosaical Postcript to the Old, Old, Very Old Man*, &c. (4to., 1635). Another account says that Sir John introduced tobacco into England in 1564, which seems the more likely, as tobacco is mentioned in the account of this second voyage.

The Floridians did not esteem gold or silver, being ignorant of their value. They wore flat pieces of gold as ornaments. "As for mines, the Frenchmen can hear of none, and how they come by this gold and silver they know not. The Frenchmen obtained pearls of them of great bigness, but they were black, by means of roasting them." From hence Hawkins departed, on the 28th July, navigating the coasts of Virginia and Newfoundland, upon his homeward voyage, after taking leave of the French, who were to follow with all diligence. Contrary winds, however, prolonged the voyage "in such manner that victuals scanted with us, so that we were divers in despair of ever coming home . . . after which with a good large wind the 20 of September we came to Padstow in Cornwall God be thanked, in safety, with the loss of 20 persons in all the voyage, and profitable to the venturers of the said voyage, as also to the whole Realm, in bringing home both gold, silver, pearls, and other jewels great store. His name be praised for ever more. Amen. The names of certain gentlemen that were in this voyage : M. John Hawkins; M. John Chester, Sir William Chester's son; M. Anthony Parkhurst; M. Fitzwilliam; M. Thomas Woorley; M. Edward Lacy, with divers others." †

* SPARKE. † HAKLUYT.

WHEREAS the Quene's Matie did of late at the petition and desier of the right honorable The Erle of Pembrock and the Erle of Leyceter graunte vnto their honors her Maties shipp called the *Jesus* with ordinance tackle and apparell, beinge in sorte able and meete to serve a voyage to the Costes of Affrica and America, which shipp with her ordinance tackle and apparell was praysed by ffowre indifferent persons to be worth ij^mxij^li xvs. ij*d.* [£2012 15*s.* 2*d.*] for the answeringe wherof to the quenes Matie the said Erles did become bounde to her Highnes either to redeliver the said shipp the *Jesus* at Gillingham before the feast of Christmas next comynge with her ordnance tackle and apparell in as good and ample manner as the same was at the tyme of the recevinge, or els to paie unto her Highnes the foresaid £2012 15*s.* 2*d.* at that daie. And nowe forasmuche as we do understand that the said shipp the *Jesus* is returned into this realme in savetie from the viadge aforesaid pretended, and presentlie remayneth in the west countrie in a harborowgh called Padstowe, from whence she cannot be convenyently browght abowt to Gillingham before the springe of the next yere, and that the said Lordes are contented to allowe unto her Matie as well for the wearing of the said shipp her ordinance tackle and apparell As also for the chardges which may be sustayned for the bringinge abowt of the said shipp to the harborowgh of Gillingham the some of v^cli [£500] readie monney to be paid into her Highnes office of the Admyraltie to Benyamyn Gonson her graces Treasorer whiche some of £500 we her Highnes officers whose names are underwritten do thinke the same sufficyent for the repayringe and furnyshinge of the ordinance tackle and apparell with the said shipp in as ample manner as the same was delivered to the said Erles. Written the xxiij^th of October 1565.

W. WYNTER.   WILLM. HOLSTOCK.

BENJAMIN GONSON.   G.(?) WYNTER.*

Hawkins is the name of a county of Tennessee, U.S. (area 750 square miles), commemorating the discoveries of Hawkins during this voyage.

In the account of "*The Arrival and Courtesy of M. Hawkins to the Distressed Frenchmen in Florida*, recorded both in French and English in the history of Laudonierre, written by himself, and published in Paris 1586," M. Laudonierre speaks of Hawkins's great kindness to the French, "wherein doubtless he hath won the reputation of a good and charitable man, deserving to be esteemed as much of us all as if he had saved our lives."

These voyages obtained for Hawkins a great reputation as a seaman, and also gained for him, to a large extent, the confidence of Queen Elizabeth and the Government.

Hawkins thought it prudent to make light of his victory over the King of Spain. "I have always," he said in a letter to Queen Elizabeth, "been a help

* *Sta. Pa. Dom.* (Eliz.)

to all Spaniards and Portugals that have come in my way, without any form or prejudice offered by me to any of them, although many times in this tract they have been under my power."* "I met him in the palace," wrote the Spanish Ambassador in London to King Philip, in November, "and invited him to dine with me. He gave me a full account of his voyage, keeping back only the way in which he had contrived to trade at our ports. He assured me, on the contrary, that he had given the greatest satisfaction to all the Spaniards with whom he had had dealings, and had received full permission from the governors of the towns where he had been. The vast profit made by the voyage had excited other merchants to undertake similar expeditions. Hawkins himself is going out again next May, and the thing needs immediate attention. I might tell the Queen that, by his own confession, he had traded in ports prohibited by your Majesty, and require her to punish him, but I must request your Majesty to give me full and clear instructions what to do."†

"Accidents delayed the equipment of Hawkins's fleet until October. Meanwhile the remonstrances of Philip had their effect; and just as Hawkins was on the point of starting, a letter arrived at Plymouth from Cecil, forbidding him in the Queen's name to traffic at places privileged by the King of Spain, and requiring from him a bond in £500 to this effect before his vessels started. Hawkins executed the bond 31 Oct., 1566, and dispatched the ships, himself remaining at home." Of this expedition no detailed record exists, but in all probability it was a successful voyage, and paved the way for his third famous expedition.

In the early part of the year 1567 Hawkins sailed to the relief of the French Protestants. On returning from France, while awaiting the Queen's orders with the fleet at Plymouth, an amusing incident happened, of which Sir Richard Hawkins writes an account. "I being of tender years, there came a fleet of Spaniards of above 50 sail, bound for Flanders, to fetch the Queen, Donna Anna de Austria, last wife to Philip II. of Spain, which entered betwixt the island and the main without vayling their top-sayles, or taking in of their flags: which my father, Sir John Hawkins (admirall of a fleet of her majesties ships, then riding in Cattwater), perceiving, commanded his gunner to shoot at the flag of the admiral, that they might thereby see their error: which, notwithstanding, they persevered arrogantly to keep displayed; whereupon the gunner at the next shot lact the admiral through and through, whereby the Spaniards finding that the matter began to grow to earnest, took in their flags and top-sayles, and so ran to an anchor. The general presently sent his

* *Cambridge MS.* † *Simancas MS.*

boat, with a principal personage to expostulate the cause and reason of that proceeding; but my father would not permit him to come into his ship, nor to hear his message; but by another gentleman commanded him to return, and to tell his general, that in as much as in the Queen's port and chamber, he had neglected to do the acknowledgment and reverence which all owe unto her majestie (especially her ships being present), and comming with so great a navie, he could not but give suspicion by such proceeding of malicious intention, and therefore required him, that within twelve hours he should depart the port, upon pain to be held as a common enemy, and to proceed against him with force. Which answer the general understanding, presently in the same boat came to the *Jesus of Lubek*, and craved licence to speak with my father, which at first was denied him, but upon the second intreaty was admitted to enter the ship, and to parley." The Spaniard then demanded if there was war between England and Spain, and was answered "that his arrogant manner of proceeding, usurping the queen his mistresses right, as much as in him lay, had given sufficient cause for breach of the peace, and that he [Hawkins] purposed presently to give notice thereof to the queen and her council, and in the mean time, that he might depart. The Spanish admiral replied that he knew not any offence he had committed, and that he would be glad to know wherein he had misbehaved himself. My father seeing he pretended to escape by ignorance, began to put him in mind of the custom of Spain, and France, and many other ports, and that he could by no means be ignorant of that which was common right to all princes in their kingdoms; demanding if an English fleet should come into any port of Spain (the kings majesties ships being present), if the English should carry their flags in the top, whether the Spanish would not shoot them down and if they persevered, if they would not beat them out of their port. The Spanish general confessed his fault, pleaded ignorance not malice, and submitted himself to the penalty my father [Hawkins] would impose; but intreated that their princes (through them) might not come to have any jar. My father a while (as though offended), made himself hard to be intreated, but in the end, all was shut up by his acknowledgement, and the ancient amity renewed, by feasting each other aboard and ashore. The self-same fleet, at their return from Flanders, meeting with her majesties ships in the Channel, though sent to accompany the aforesaid queen, was constrained during the time they were with the English, to vayle their flags, and to acknowledge that which all must do that pass through the English seas."

Immediately before his third voyage, efforts being made to restrain his actions, Hawkins protested that it would be the ruin of himself and others if his expedition was prevented, and addressed the following letter to his sleeping partner, the Queen:

John Hawkins to the Queen.

MY SOVERAIGNE GOOD LADY AND MYSTRES,—Your Highnes may be advertised that this daye being the xvj[th] of September the Portyngales who should have dyrected us this pretended enterpryse have fledd and as I have certayne under-standing taken passadge into France, havinge no cawse for that they had of me better entertaynement then appertayned to suche mean persons, and an army prepared sufficient to doe any resonable enterpryse, but it appeared that they could by no meanes performe their lardge promises, and so having gleaned a piece of money to our merchantes are fledd to deceive some other. And although this enterpryse cannot take effecte (which I think God hath provided for the best) I do ascertayne your highnes that I have provision sufficient and an able army to defend our chardge and to bring home (with gods help) fortye thowsand markes gaynes without the offence of the lest of any of your highnes alyes or friends It shall be no dishonor unto your highnes that your owne servante and subjecte shall in suche an extremitie convert such an enterpryse and turn it both to your highnes honor and to the benefit of your whole realme which I will not enterpryse withowt your highnes consent, but am ready to do what service by your Ma[tie] shall be commaunded yet to shew your highnes the truth I should be undone if your Ma[tie] should staye the voyadge wherunto I hope your highnes will have some regard. The voyadge I pretend is to lade negroes in Genoya [Guinea] and sell them in the west Indyes in troke [truck] of golde perrels and Esmeraldes wherof I dowte not but to bring home great abondance to the contentation of your highnes and to the releife of a nomber of worthy servitures reddy nowe for this pretended voyadge which otherwise would shortly be dryven to great misery and reddy to commit any folly. Thus having advertysed your highnes the state of this matter do most humbly praye your highnes to signifye your pleasure by this bearer which I shall most willingly accomplish. From Plymouth the xvj[th] daye of September 1567.

Your highnes most humble servante

JOHN HAWKINS.

To the quenes most excellent Ma[tie].*

This third voyage of Sir John Hawkins, of which he wrote a brief account, was made in the years 1567 and 1568. He sailed from Plymouth on the 2nd October, 1567, with a fleet of six ships—the *Jesus of Lubek*,

* *Sta. Pa. Dom.* (Eliz.)

the *Minion*, the *William and John*, the *Judith*,[*] the *Angel*, and the *Swallow*.
The *Jesus* and the *Minion* were "the Queen's Maiesties," the other four
ships were Hawkins's private venture.[†] The fleet were caught in a severe
storm a few days after they had departed, in which they lost all their large
boats, and the ships were separated, but met again at the Canary Islands,
and sailed for Cape Verde Islands, arriving 18th November. Here they
landed one hundred and fifty men to procure some negroes, but succeeded in
obtaining very few, and those with great loss to the Englishmen from
poisoned arrows; "and although in the beginning they seemed to be but
small hurtes," says Hawkins, "yet there hardly escaped any that had blood
drawen of them, but died in a strange sort, with their mouths shut, some
ten days before he died, and after their wounds were whole, where I myself
had one of the greatest wounds, yet, thanks be to God, escaped."

From thence they sailed to the coast of Guinea, searching the rivers
from Rio Grande to Sierra Leone till the 12th January, without getting
more than 150 negroes, when the lateness of the season, and the
sickness of their men, obliged them to leave. Not having sufficient
cargo for the West Indies, they thought to go to the coast of Myne to
obtain some gold for their wares; but meanwhile a negro arrived, sent from
his king, "oppressed by other kings his neighbours," desiring aid from
Hawkins against these other tribes, with a promise that the negroes obtained
during the war should be at the pleasure of the English. Whereupon
120 men were sent, who on the 15th January assaulted a town of
the negro ally's enemies, in which there were 8000 inhabitants; "but
it was so well defended, that our men prevailed not, but lost six men,
and forty hurt, so that our men sent forthwith to me for more help: . . .
I went myself, and with the help of the king on our side, assaulted the
town both by land and sea, and very hardly with fire (their houses being
covered with dry palm leaves) obtained the town, and put the inhabitants
to flight, where we took 250 persons, and by our friend the king of our
side, there were taken 600 prisoners, whereof we hoped to have our choice;
but the negro (in which nation is seldom or never found truth) meant nothing
less; for that night he removed his camp, and prisoners, so that we were
fain to content us with those few which we had gotten ourselves." Having

---

* A bark of 50 tons, commanded by young Francis Drake. "He was born in 1545 son of one
Edmund Drake sailor being the eldest of 12 brethren and was brought up at the expense and under the
care of his kinsman Sir John Hawkins. At 18 he was purser of a ship trading to Guinea, at 20 made a
voyage to Guinea and at 22 sailed with Hawkins."—So STOW's *Annals*, p. 807.

† *Hist. Gen.* (lib. xix. cap. 8).

obtained between 400 and 500 negroes they set sail for the West Indies, where they experienced some difficulty in exchanging them for merchandise, owing to the order from Spain forbidding dealings with the English; but notwithstanding this order they had a reasonable trade, and courteous entertainment.

From the Isle of Margarita to Cartagena, without anything greatly worth the noting, saving "at Capo de la Vela, in a town called Rio de la Hauche, from whence came all the pearls," where the Governor would not agree to any trade, or let them take in water; he had "fortified his town with divers bulwarks in all places where it might be entered," and so thought "by famine to have enforced us to have put a land our negroes."

Seeing this, Hawkins with 200 men broke in upon their bulwarks, and entered and took the town, "with the loss of two men only, and no hurt done to the Spaniards, because after their volley of shott discharged they all fled." Thus having possession of the town, and the Spaniards desiring the negroes, by the friendship of the Governor they obtained a secret trade, the Spaniards coming by night, and buying 200 negroes. At Cartagena the Governor would not traffic; so, without losing more time, the trade being so nearly finished, they departed 24th July, hoping to escape the time of their storms called "Furicanos." Towards the coast of Florida they were overtaken by a dreadful storm which lasted four days, and "so beat the *Jesus* that we cut down all her higher buildings." Her rudder was also shaken, and having sprung a big leak she was on the point of being abandoned, they finding no haven because of the shallowness of the coast; thus being in "great despair, and taken with a new storm which continued other three dayes, we were enforced to take for our haven the port which serveth the city of Mexico, called St. John de Ulloa. In seeking of which port we took in our way three ships which carried passengers to the number of 100, which passengers we hoped would be the means of our obtaining victuals for our money, and a quiet place to repair our fleet. Shortly after, 16th September, we entered the port of Ulloa, and in our entry, the Spaniards thinking us to be the fleet of Spain, the chief officers of the country came aboard us, which being deceived of their expectation were greatly dismayed; but immediately when they saw our demand was nothing but victuals, were recomforted. . . . .

"I found also in the same port twelve ships which had in them by the report, 200,000 li. in gold and silver, all which, being in my possession, with the King's Island, as also the passengers before in my way thitherwards stayed, I set at liberty, without the taking from them the weight of a grote : only because I would not be delayed of my dispatch, I stayed two men of estimation, and sent post immediately to Mexico, 200 miles from us, to the Presidents and Council there, showing them of our arrivall there by the force of weather, and the necessity of the repair of our ships and victuals, which wants wee required as friends to King Philip to be furnished of for our money." Also stating that the Presidents and Council should give orders that on the arrival of the Spanish fleet, which was daily expected, there might be no cause of quarrel.

This message being dispatched the day of the arrival of the English fleet, the next morning, the 16th, they "saw open of the Haven thirteen great ships." Understanding them to be the Spanish fleet, Hawkins immediately sent to advertise the "General of the fleet" of his being there, giving him to understand that before he would allow the Spanish fleet to enter the port, conditions must pass between them for the maintenance of peace, and the safety of the English fleet of six ships. "Now it is to be understood that this Port is a little Island of stones not three foot above the water in the highest place, and but a bow shot of length any way. This Island standeth from the mainland two bow shots or more, also that there is not in all this coast any other place for ships to arrive in safety, because the north wind hath there such violence that unless the ships be very safely moored with their anchors fastened upon the Island, there is no remedy for these north winds but death : also the place of the Haven was so little, that of necessity the ships must ride one aboard the other, so that we could not give place to them, nor they to us : and here I began to bewail that which after followed, for now said I, I am in two dangers, and forced to receive the one of them. That was, either I must have kept out the fleet from entering the Port, that which with God's help I was very well able to do, or else suffer them to enter in with their accustomed treason, which they never fail to execute, where they may have opportunity, or circumvent it by any means : if I had kept them out [Sir John says], there had been present shipwarke [shipwreck] of all the fleet which amounted in value to six millions, which was in value of our money 1,800,000 li. which I considered I was not able to answer, fearing the Queens Maiesties indignation in so weighty a matter . . . therefore as choosing the least mischief I proceeded to conditions." The first messenger now returned from the Spanish fleet reporting the arrival of a Viceroy "who sent us word that we should send our conditions, with many fair words; how passing the coast of the Indies he had understood of our honest behaviour . . . . "

Hawkins's requests were acceded to; namely, that he required victuals for his money; that on either side there might be twelve gentlemen hostages; and that the island, for their better safety, might be in the possession of the English, with the ordnance thereon (eleven pieces of brass), during the stay of the English; also that no Spaniard might land on the island with any kind of weapon.

"These conditions at the first, he somewhat misliked, chiefly the gard of the Island to be in our own keeping, which if they had had, we had soon known our fate: for with the first north wind they had cut our cables and our ships had gone ashore: but in the end he concluded to our request, bringing the twelve hostages to ten, with a writing from the Vice Roy signed with his hand and sealed with his seal, of all the conditions concluded." A trumpet was then blown, with a command that the peace was not to be violated upon pain of death; "further that the two generals of the fleets should meet and give faith each to the other for the performance of the promises which was so done. . . . .

"Thus at the end of three days all was concluded, and the Spanish fleet entered the port, saluting one another as the manner of the sea doth require."

The English fleet had entered the port on Thursday. On Friday they saw the Spanish fleet, which on Monday (at night) also entered the port. Two days were taken up in "placing the English ships by themselves, and the Spanish ships by themselves, the captains of each part and inferior men of their parts promising great amity of all sides;" but the treacherous Spaniards "had furnished themselves with a supply of men to the number of 1000, and meant the next Thursday, being the 23 of Sep^t, at dinner time, to set upon us on all sides." On the Thursday morning some appearance of treason was shown, "as shifting of weapons from ship to ship, planting and bending of ordnance from the ship to the Island where our men warded, passing to and fro of companies of men more than required for their necessary business, and many other ill likelihoods which caused us to have a vehement suspicion, and therewithal sent to the Vice Roy to inquire what was meant by it, who sent immediately straight commandment to unplant all things suspicious, and also sent word that he in the faith of a Vice Roy would be our defence from all villanies. Yet we being not satisfied with this answer because we suspected a great number of men to be hid in a great ship of 900 tons which was moored next unto the *Minion*, sent again to the Vice Roy, Robert Barret, the master of the *Jesus*," who spoke Spanish, and required to be satisfied.

The Viceroy, seeing that the treason must now be discovered, kept the master, blew a trumpet, "and on all sides set upon us ; our men which warded ashore being stricken with sudden fear, gave place, fled, and sought to recover succour of the ships. The Spaniards being before provided for the purpose landed in all places in multitudes from their ships, which they might easily do without boats and slew all our men ashore without mercy." A few of them escaped aboard the *Jesus*. The great ship with 300 men hid in her, immediately fell aboard the *Minion*, but the English suspecting their design half an hour previously, in that short time, "the *Minion* was made ready to avoid and so leesing her hed fastes, and hayling away by the stern fasts she was gotten out : thus with God's help she defended the violence of the first brunt of these 300 men. The *Minion* being past out they came aboard the *Jesus*, which also with very much ado and the loss of many of our men were defended and kept out. Two other ships assaulted the *Jesus*, so that she escaped hardly." After the *Jesus* and the *Minion* had got two ship's lengths from the Spanish fleet, the fight began hotly on all sides. Within an hour the "Admiral" of the Spaniards was supposed to be sunk, their "Vice Admiral" burned, and another principal ship supposed to be sunk, "so that the ships were little to annoy us. But all the ordinance on the Island was in the Spaniards hands which did us so great annoyance, that it cut all the masts and yards of the *Jesus* that there was no hope to carry her away : also it sunk our smaller ships, whereupon we determined to place the *Jesus* on that side of the *Minion* next the battery to be a defence for the *Minion* till night, then after taking victual and other necessaries from the *Jesus* as time would allow, to leave her. When the *Minion* had been thus sheltered from the shot of the land, suddenly the Spaniards had had set on fire two great ships which were coming directly to us and having no means to avoid the fire, great fear spread among the men, some saying 'Let us depart with the *Minion*,' others said 'Let us see if the wind will carry the fire from us.' But the *Minion* men who had always their sails in readiness, thought to make sure work, and so without consent of the captain or master cut their sail, so that verily," says Hawkins, "hardly was I received into the *Minion*. Most of the men that were left alive in the *Jesus* made shift and followed in a small boat, the rest were forced to abide the mercy of the Spaniards ; so with the *Minion* only and the *Judith* (a small bark of 50 tons) we escaped, which bark the same night forsook us in our great misery."

The *Judith* was commanded by young Francis Drake, and it does not say much in his favour that he forsook his admiral in distress. It is also remarkable that Hawkins never once mentions Drake's name throughout the narrative; perhaps to shield his young kinsman from censure.

The *Minion* lay that night two bowshots from the Spanish ships, and next morning recovered an island a mile off, where she was overtaken by a north wind, and being left with only two anchors and two cables (having lost two anchors and three cables in the conflict) they thought to have lost the ship during the storm. The weather improving, the Saturday they set sail with a great number of men and little victuals, and with small hope of life wandered in an unknown sea fourteen days, till hunger forced them to seek land, for "rats, cats, mice, and dogs were thought very good meat—none escaped that might be gotten."

On the 8th October they sighted land in the same bay of Mexico, where they hoped to procure victuals and repair the ship, "which was so sore beaten with shot from our enemies and bruised with shooting of our own ordinance that our weary and weak arms were scarce able to defend and keep out the water." But they found nothing except a dangerous place, wherein a boat might be landed. Some of the men, forced with hunger, desired to be set on land, about 94 in all, the remaining 100 desiring to go homewards. Having landed the men who wished to remain, the next day Hawkins, with fifty men, went ashore to bring off water, when a storm arose, so that for three days they could not return to the ship, which was in such peril that every hour they looked for shipwreck. However, fair weather returning, they departed 16th October, with prosperous weather till 16th November, on which day they were clear of the coast and out of the Gulf of Bahama. After this, nearing the cold country, together with famine, the men died continually. Those left were so weak that they could scarce manage the ship, the wind being always against their direction for England, which determined them to go to Galicia, in Spain, to relieve their distress.

On the 31st December, at Ponte Vedra, near Vigo, the men with excess of fresh meat got miserable diseases, and a great part of them died; and by access of the Spaniards the feebleness of the English became known, whereupon they tried to betray them; but with all speed the English departed to Vigo, where some English ships helped them, and with twelve fresh men they sailed 20th January, 1568, and arrived in Mount's Bay, Cornwall, the 25th of the same month. Thence Hawkins wrote the following letter:

F

RIGHT HONORABLE

My dewty most humbly consydered : yt may please your honor to be
advertysed that the 25th day of Januarii (thanks be to God) we aryved in a
place in Cornewall called Mounts bay, onelie with the *Minyon* which is left us
of all our flet, and because I wold not in my letters be prolyxe, after what
manner we came to our dysgrace, I have sent your honor here inclosed some
part of the circumstance, and althoughe not all our meseryes that hath past yet
the greatest matters worthye of notynge, but yf I shold wryt of all our
calamytyes I am seure a volome as great as the byble wyll scarcelie suffyce ;
all which thyngs I most humblie beseeche your bonour to advertyse the Queens
Majestie and the rest of the counsell (soch as you shall thinke mette).

Our voyage was, although very hardly, well achieved and brought to
resonable passe, but now a great part of our treasure, merchandyze, shippinge
and men devoured by the treason of the Spanyards.

I have not moche or any thynge more to advertyse your honour, nore the
rest, because all our business hath had infelycytye, mysfortune, and an unhappy
end, and therefore wyll troble the Queens Majestie, nor the rest of my good
lords with soch yll newes. But herewith pray your honours estate to impart
to soch as you shall thynke mete the sequell of our busyness.

I mynd with Gods grace to make all expedicyon to London myselfe, at
what tyme I shall declare more of our esstate that ys here omytted. Thus
prayinge to God for your Honours prosperous estate take my leave : from the
Mynion the 25th day of Januarii 1568.

Yours most humbly to command

(Signed)   JOHN HAWKINS.

To the Ryght Honorable Sir Wᵐ Cycylle Knighte, and Principall Secretarie
to the Queen's Majestie, gyve this.

So ends Hawkins's sorrowful narrative.* How he escaped at all is
marvellous ; and the Spaniards must have thought that they had "Achines
de Plimua" caught in their trap at last !

Hakluyt quotes a brief summary of the affair at St. Jean de Ulloa by Job
Hartop, one of the sufferers who returned to England, December 2nd, 1590 :

"From Cartegena, by foule weather, wee were forced to seeke the port of
Saint John de Ulloa. In our way thwart of Campecke we met with a Spaniard,
a small ship who was bound for Santo Domingo ; he had in him a Spaniard
called Augustine de Villa Neuva ; him we took and brought with us into the

---

* *Sta. Pa. Dom.* (Eliz.) Vol. LIII. of this collection is occupied with reports of Hawkins's case.

port of Saint John de Ulloa. Our Generall made great account of him, and used him like a nobleman; howbeit in the ende he was one of them that betrayed. When wee had mored our ships and landed, wee mounted the ordinance that wee found there in the Ilande, and for our safeties kept watch and warde. The next day after wee discovered the Spanish fleete, whereof Luçon, a Spanyard, was Generall: with him came a Spaniard called Don Martin Henriquez, whom the King of Spain sent to be his viceroy of the Indies. He sent a pinnesse with a flag of truce into our Generall, to knowe of what countrie those shippes were that rode there in the King of Spaine's port; who sayd they were the Queene of England's ships which came in there for victuals for their money; wherefore if your Generall will come in here, he shall give me victuals and all other necessaries, and I will goe out on the one side the port, and he shall come in on the other side."

Hawkins, during the pretended friendship of the Spaniards in the port of Ulloa, nearly lost his life by assassination. Some of the Spanish officers were dining on board Hawkins's ship, when Augustine de Villa Neuva was detected with a dagger, "which he had privily hid in his sleeve," while sitting at table, and with which he intended to have killed his host, "which was espyed and prevented by one John Chamberlayne, who took the poynarde out of his sleeve. Our General hastily rose up and commanded him to be put prisoner in the steward's room."* This confirmed Hawkins's idea of the treachery of the Spaniards, who to the number of 300 then boarded the *Minion;* "whereat our general with a loud and fierce voice called unto us, saying, 'God and St. George! Upon these traitorous villains, and rescue the *Minion!* I trust in God, the day shall be ours!'" Nearly 600 Spaniards fell in that day's unequal fight.

And here again Hawkins had a second narrow escape; for "when the *Minion* stood off," says Hartop, "our general courageously cheered up his soldiers and gunners, and called to Samuel, his page, for a cup of beer; who brought it to him in a silver cup: and he drinking to all the men, willed 'the gunners to stand to their ordinance lustily like men.' He had no sooner set the cup out of his hand but a demi-culverin shot struck away the cup and a cooper's plane that stood by the mainmast and ran out on the other side of the ship; which nothing dismayed our general, for he ceased not to encourage us, saying, 'Fear nothing! For God, who hath preserved me from this shot, will also deliver us from these traitors and villains!'"†

"The disaster in the harbour of Ulloa, was made the subject of inquiry

* Hartop.   † *Hist. Gen.* (Book xix. c. 18).

in the English Admiralty Court, with a view to assess the amount of damage, and the depositions made are still preserved. They are those of Hawkins himself; of Thomas Hampton, captain of the *Minion ;* William Clarke, supercargo; John Tommes, Hawkins's servant; Jean Turren, trumpeter in the *Jesus ;* Humphry Fownes, steward of the *Angel* (afterwards Mayor of Plymouth); and of William Fowler, a merchant trading with Mexico, to give independent testimony as to prices. Drake was not called. The loss was very heavy. Fitting out the expedition cost £16,500; and making allowance for the profits in the traffic antecedent to the fight, the claims put in amounted to about £29,000.

"Incidentally we get here an indication of the wealth and style of Hawkins, who was very far indeed from being the rough, old, 'tarry-breeked,' sea-dog described by Kingsley (in *Westward Ho !*). His personal apparel and furniture were set down as worth at least £440, which would be little if at all short of £3000 now. And supercargo Clarke deposed that he saw Master Hawkins wear during the voyage 'divers suits of apparel of velvets and silks, with buttons of gold and pearl.' His cabin was hung with tapestry said to be worth £100; and his 'instruments of the sea, books, and other things' were put at £60."*

The Spaniards, after this breach of treaty at Ulloa, turned a deaf ear to all expostulations, and vindicated the injustice of the Viceroy, or at least forbore to redress it.

The fate of the 100 men landed in the Bay of Mexico was most cruel. Some were killed by the natives; others were sent to the capital, where they suffered in the most inhuman way at the hands of the Inquisition. Robert Barrett, the master of the *Jesus,* was burnt at the stake in Seville, which was the fate of several; others were left to die of hunger in the dungeons. Three men only out of the 100 escaped—Miles Philips and Job Hartop, who returned to England, the one after sixteen years', the other after twenty-three years' captivity; and David Ingram, who found his way among the savage tribes to Cape Breton, coming home in a French ship the next year, when he visited Hawkins. The narratives of these men are extant,† and no one who reads them can wonder at the extreme hatred of the English against the Spaniards.

"The Spanish treachery at San Juan de Ulloa, by which means this voyage ended so disastrously, resulted in the mightiest issues. Plymouth declared war against Spain, and no opportunity was missed of harassing the Spaniards, which culminated in the invasion and destruction of the Spanish Armada.

* WORTH ; from the depositions.   † HAKLUYT, vol. iii.

For every English life then lost, for every pound of English treasure then taken, Spain paid a hundred and a thousand fold. John Hawkins led the way with one of the boldest acts of Machiavellian statesmanship on record. The plain blunt sailor set his wits against those of King Philip and all his Court, and bent them to his will like puppets."*

Hawkins had great affection for his seamen, and he was extremely anxious about the fate of his 100 unhappy men who were put on shore in Mexico. "Hawkins promised," says Hartop, "if God sent him safe home, he would do what he could, that as many of us as lived should by some means be brought into England." He intended to go out again, but the news soon became known that most of his men were in the hands of the Inquisition, where entreaty was hopeless, and force also. What could be done? "Hawkins could not rest until they were rescued. They owed their captivity to Spanish treachery; they should owe their deliverance to English pretence. With Burleigh's permission, and the consent of the Queen, he complained bitterly to the Spanish ambassador of the way in which he had been treated by Elizabeth; that he was deeply penitent for his evil deeds; that he was broken-hearted at the progress of heresy; that he would do his utmost to place the Queen of Scots upon the throne. He offered to go over to Spain with his ships and men. The bait took. Having thus paved the way, he applied to Philip himself, by sending George Fitzwilliam, one of his officers, to Spain with full powers to arrange matters. Philip at first could not believe such good news that the redoubted 'Achines,' the terror of the Spaniards, the simple occurrence of whose name in a dispatch made the Spanish King splatter the margin with exclamation-marks of horror and dismay, would turn traitor."

Hawkins even succeeded in taking in Dr. Lingard, who mistook pretence for earnest, but never was there a more absurd calumny than that Hawkins had consented to betray his country for a bribe with Spain. Lingard quotes an agreement made at Madrid, 10th August, 1571, between the Duke of Feria, on the part of Philip II., and George Fitzwilliam on the part of John Hawkins, by which the latter was to transfer his services to Spain, with sixteen of the Queen's ships fully equipped with 420 guns, in return for pardon for past offences, and 16,987 ducats monthly pay. This agreement is indeed amongst the Spanish archives. The calumny lies in Dr. Lingard's conclusion from it, and in his statement —"The secret was carefully kept, but did not elude suspicion. Hawkins was summoned, and examined by order of the Council. Their lordships were, or pretended to be, satisfied, and he was engaged in the Queen's service." Lingard adds that Hawkins tendered hostages to Spain for his fidelity. All these supplementary statements are untrue. The simple fact was that Hawkins was trying to deceive and entrap the Spaniards, with the full knowledge and approval of the English Government from the first. This is proved beyond doubt by Cecil's correspondence. A more loyal and devoted subject never lived. His whole life was one of zealous devotion to the service of his Queen. His Spanish intrigue was undertaken with the object of rescuing his unfortunate men by a resort to guile, as he could not do so by force.

Fitzwilliam returned from Spain, and with Burleigh's help he had an interview with the Queen of Scots. He returned to Philip with credentials from her on Hawkins's behalf;[*] who wrote to Burleigh that he had no doubt three "commodities" would follow: "First. The practices of their enemies will be daily more and more discovered. Second. There will be credit gotten hither for a good sum of money. Third. The same money, as the time shall bring forth cause, shall be employed to their own detriment; and what ships there shall be appointed (as they shall suppose to serve their turn) may do some notable exploit to their great damage."

The King of Spain was thoroughly taken in. To show his good faith in the proposals made he set the remaining imprisoned sailors free, and gave ten dollars to each man; granted Hawkins a full pardon, and made him a grandee of Spain. Hawkins sent a copy of the pardon to Burleigh—"large enough! with very great titles and honours from the King: from which may God deliver me!" and alluding to the Spaniards, he adds, "Their practices be very mischievous, and they be never idle; but God, I hope, will confound them! and turn these devices upon their own necks."[†]

The plot, wrote Hawkins to Burleigh, was, "that my power should join with the Duke of Alva's power, which he doth secretly provide in Flanders, as well as with the power which cometh with the Duke of Medina out of Spain, and so altogether to invade this realm and set up the Queen of Scots."

This scheme of 1571 was identical with that which was in 1588 attempted with the Armada.

The next move made by Hawkins was to ask Philip for two months' pay for 1600 men, to man the fleet of sixteen ships with which he was to join him. "The Spanish Ambassador paid Hawkins; and the money was at once laid out in works of defence! There was no immediate danger; the Spanish plans had been unravelled, and England saved, by the statecraft of a Plymouth sailor."

* *Sta. Pa.* (Scot.), vol. vi.　　　† *Sta. Pa. Dom.* (Eliz.)

For some years John Hawkins appears to have made no long voyages—though still occasionally serving afloat—and resided in Plymouth. In 1571 and 1572 he was twice elected to represent the town in Parliament.

While the Duke of Feria, and other Spanish grandees, were assuring Hawkins of their friendship, Elizabeth was urged through Walsingham by Count Ludovici, to license Hawkins to serve him "underhand" against the Spanish power in Flanders. It was said that no Spaniard could land there while Hawkins kept the seas. No English sailor at this time bore so famous a name. In 1572 we find the Dutch Admiral, de la Marck, complaining that Hawkins, either Sir John or his brother William, had done some damage to one of his captains.

The great occupation of Plymouth seamen, however, was to defend the Protestant cause, and their own interests, together with those of the nation, by attacking any of the Catholic powers, such as the Spaniards or Portuguese. The Huguenots were under the protection of the English, and in 1573 Charles IX., in a letter to La Motte Fénélon, dated 23rd February, complained that M. Haquin (Hawkins) had joined with certain of his rebels near the Isle of Wight, with twelve or thirteen ships, with which they carried munitions and stores from England to Rochelle, and had taken several French ships. Two years later a St. Malo ship was captured by a vessel belonging to the Hawkinses, called the *Castle of Comfort.*

"The accursed doctrine of the Inquisition, that no faith was to be kept with heretics, proved a dangerous doctrine for Spain when the heretics were such men as Hawkins, Candish, and Drake."[*]

Sir Thomas Smith to Lord Burleigh.

My very good Lord,— .... I shewed also her Majestie Hawkyns letter. .... Her Majestie willed me further to tell you, that Conte Montgomerie and Vidame were here with her Highnes, and wold that her Majestie should send Hawkyns or some other, by some colour with some munition of powder to Rochelle as driven thither by tempest or contrary winds. But she saith, she cannot tell how to do it, especially being already spoken to by the French ambassador not to aid. Her Majestie praies you to think of it, and devise how it may be done, for she thynks it necessary. .... Thus I commit your Honor to Almighty God. From Hampton Court the 8th of January, 1572,[†] by English account.

Your Lordships alwais at commandement,

T. Smith.[‡]

[*] Justin Winsor's *Hist. of America.*   [†] The dates of the quoted documents are Old Style.
[‡] *Sta. Pa. Dom.* (Eliz.)

In 1573 Sir John Hawkins was very nearly being murdered, as he was going to Court, by an assassin who mistook him for Sir Christopher Hatton. The man who made the attempt was one Peter Burchet, of the Inner Temple, a fanatical Puritan, who, as Hatton was a Papist, thought there was merit in putting to death a man to whom his party had an implacable hatred. Hawkins, after receiving one dangerous wound (probably from behind), managed to defend himself, and seized the would-be murderer. This is referred to in the following letter:

Sir Thomas Smith to Lord Burleigh.

MY VERY GOOD LORD,—I moved the Quenes Majestie yesternight, as sone as I came to the Courte, touching the advertisement of the Vidame. Her Majestie thynketh, that neither it is possible nor likely for the French to attempt anything now, they are so well occupied otherwise, and it were so unprofitable for themself now to provoke displeasure of their neighbors. I perceive her Highnes is *multum secura;* yet she lyketh well the sending away of the man into France, and not much mislyketh the sending of some bark or pynnes to discover. Her Majestie taketh heavily the hurting of Hawkyns* and sent her own Surgeons to hym and Mr. Gorges to visite and comforte hym. It will sone appeare whether he can escape or no. Neither her Majestie, nor allmost any one here can thynke otherwyse, but that there is some conspiracie for that murder, and that Burchet is not indeede mad. It is said here that divers tymes, within this fortnight, both by wordes and writings, Mr. Haddon hath bene admonished to take hede to hymself; for his life was laide in waite for. Mr. Garret told me that he hath bene with one or two gentlemen that came out of the west countrey to London with Burchet, who declareth that he had many phantasticall speeches and doings whereby they might perceive that he was not well in his witts all the whole journey hitherwards.

. . . . Thus I commit your Lordship to Allmighty God, the 15th of October, 1573.

Your Lordships at commandement,

T. SMITH.†

The Queen and her ministers now availed themselves of Hawkins's skill and experience to employ him in the service of the public, by appointing him Treasurer of the Navy, a post in those days not only of great honour, but also of considerable trust.

---

* The Queen, it seems, was so enraged, that she would have had Burchet executed immediately by martial law, but the Earl of Essex showed her that it was contrary to the laws of the country. When Burchet was committed to the Tower, he killed his keeper with a billet that lay in his prison. He was hanged.

† *Sta. Pa. Dom.* (Eliz.)

Queen Elizabeth,

The Founder of our Colonial Empire.

"In 1573 Hawkins succeeded his father-in-law (Benjamin Gonson) as Treasurer of the Navy, and commenced a useful but very anxious and laborious administrative career on shore. But he still occasionally served afloat. . . . . Besides the Treasurership of the Navy, Hawkins was also Treasurer of the Queen's Majesty's Marine Causes; and in the same year he succeeded Mr. Holstock as Comptroller of the Navy. He was a keen reformer of Dockyard abuses, and Sir William Monson says that he introduced more useful inventions and better regulations into the navy than any of his predecessors."

DECLARATION of the accompte of John Hawkins Esq. Treasurer of the Marine causes thereunto appointed with Benjamin Gonson Esq. since lately deceased by Letters Patent dated 18th Nov. 20 Eliz. [1577], to have & occupy the said office of Treasurer to Benjamin Gonson & John Hawkins for their natural life, with all fees wages & allowances thereunto belonging; also an annuity of 100 marks sterling, and for two clerks under them 8*d.* sterling by the day, together with the allowance of 6*s.* 8*d.* for every day that the s[d] Ben Gonson & J. Hawkins shall travail & by occupied either by sea or land, only for such business as shall be needful to be dispatched concerning the same office, and £8 sterling by the year for their boatehier. The said Benjamin and John shall have full allowance for all and every such sums of money as they shall disburse about the said Marine causes, they having the hands of 2 or 3 of the officers of the same Marine causes subscribed to the books of account or reckoning, the shewing of such books to be a sufficient warrant to all and every Auditor. Further the said Benjamin Gonson & John Hawkins to have the costs & charges of their clerks when & as often as they shall send them for the payment or receipt of any money for the said Marine causes. By the death of Benjamin Gonson the said office has wholly fallen upon John Hawkins.†

[Then follows the account of John Hawkins for one year from 1st Jan. 20 Eliz. to 31st Dec. 21 Eliz.]

"Sir John Hawkins recommended forming accommodation at the Isle of Wight, Weymouth, Dartmouth, Plymouth, and Falmouth, to save ships the time and expense of coming round to the river and the Downs." ‡

Stow tells us that Hawkins was the inventor of the cunning stratagem of boarding nettings early in the Queen's reign, which he introduced into the fleet to protect ships in action. Also that he was the author of chain-pumps for ships, which were of excellent use. Besides these he brought in many

* *Hawkins' Voyages.*   † Audit Office. Declared Accounts. Bale 1684. Roll 13.
‡ HASTED'S *Kent.*

G

inventions from time to time, and was indefatigable in labouring to bring all things as near as might be to perfection.

He was thus chosen by Queen Elizabeth as the "fittest person in all her dominions to manage her naval affairs," and never had she a more faithful, devoted servant. "Endowed with huge capacity for work, Hawkins toiled terribly in the discharge of his manifold official duties. All that is now carried out by the executive department of the Admiralty fell upon his shoulders. His office was no mere matter of accountancy. It involved the whole management and maintenance of the fleet. He had to estimate the cost of all expeditions, to keep the stores, to build the ships, to provide and pay the crews, to report on harbour works. Every disbursement was made through him, and he had to render the strictest account of each item of expenditure. The office demanded the exercise of all his sea-craft, required the possession of distinguished abilities as a financier, and proved an incessant drain on all his energies. Driven nearly to his wits' end by the parsimony of Elizabeth, perpetually harassed by rivals whose pilferings he stopped, or whose useless offices he abolished, and who in return insinuated that he was turning the public money to private account; he did for England then what no other man had equal technical skill, energy, and dogged perseverance to perform."* Faithful in the least, as well as in the greatest, when the moment of trial came "he sent her ships to sea in such a condition that they had no match in the world." The royal vessels that sailed out of Plymouth Sound to beat the Armada were perfectly equipped to the minutest detail, though Hawkins bitterly felt the straits to which he had been put.

As time went on the need of weakening the strength of Spain became apparent. The English expeditions kept the Spaniards in check, but stronger measures were required for the safety of England. In November, 1577, the Queen received a remarkable letter, in which the writer declared his readiness to deal a blow, to be the means of putting an end to the naval power of Spain, Portugal, and France. The proposal was to clear out of England's way some 25,000 sailors belonging to the Catholic powers by attacking the Newfoundland fisheries, the great nursery of European sailors, "the best [ships] to be brought away, the rest to be burned." Who the writer was is unknown; the signature has been erased. Froude hesitates to assign what he considers its guilt to anyone, but doubtfully hints at the possibility that it may have been Drake. Less cautious authorities have been positive it was Hawkins. "But the letter is unlike anything Drake or Hawkins ever wrote, and I," says

* WORTH.

Mr. Worth, "feel little doubt that it came from the pen of Ralegh's half-brother, Sir Humphry Gilbert, famous through all time as he who went down to his death with the brave words, 'Heaven is as near by water as by land.'"

In 1581 Hawkins had a severe illness,* but he had recovered in 1583, when he was busily investigating reductions of naval expenses, in which he met with great opposition. The officers at Chatham during fifteen months "took hardness and courage to oppose themselves against him," yet he saved there a sum of over £3200, while adding to the efficiency of the navy. "His correspondence with Sir Julius Cæsar, the Judge of the Admiralty, shows that he paid close attention to all branches of naval expenditure, detecting and putting a stop to many abuses. This good service naturally made him enemies. Mr. Borowe who was ousted made a book against him." And in 1583 there were articles drawn up "against the injuste mind and deceitful dealings of John Hawkins." Among those whom he found out conniving at abuses were Sir William Winter and the Master Shipwright Baker, who of course became his bitter enemies; and he had a controversy with "Peter Pett, the shipwright," touching his accounts. Winter wrote: 'When he was hurte in the Strande, and made his will, he was not able to give £500. All that he is now worth hath been drawne by deceipte from her Majesty.' These calumnies received no credit, and Hawkins never lost the confidence of his Government." Among his other duties he was Surveyor of the Queen's Lands in Kent.†

---

* *John Hawkins to Mr. Bolland.*

I have received your letter of the 19th of this present, together with a letter inclosed from Sir Fr Drake of the 14th of the same. I would be glad my ability and state were such that I might be an adventurer in this journey; but I assure you I had so great a burden layd upon me in this last preparation, that with all the means that I can make I am hardly able to overcome the debt I owe her Majestie and keep my credit. It is well known to you, Mr Bolland, to whom I did at large declare my losses and burdens, besides the shipping and other dead provisions which lay upon my hands. My sickness doth continually abide with me, and every second day I have a fit; if I look [a ?]broad *e* in the air but one hour, I can hardly recover it in six days with good order, so as I am heartily sorry that I cannot attend upon my very good Lord [Leicester], whom I am desirous to satisfy according to my ability, if I had strength, for I am more like to provide for my grave than encumber me with worldly matters.

There cannot lack neither adventurers nor anything that is good, to the furtherance of so good an attempt, which enterprise I have had always a very good liking unto for the farther benefiting of our country, which God, I hope, will send to a good and prosperous end, and so I heartily take my leave.

From Chatham, the 20th Octr 1581

Your assured and loving friend

JOHN HAWKYNS.

† HASTED'S *Kent.*

John Hawkyns to Lord Burleigh.

My bounden duty in right humble manner remembered unto your good Lordship. I have briefly considered upon a substantial course and the material reasons that by mine own experience, I know (with God's assistance) will strongly annoy and offend the King of Spain, the mortal enemy of our religion and the present government of the realm of England.

And surely my very good Lord, if I should only consider and look for mine own life, my quietness and commodity, then truly mine own nature and disposition doth prefer peace before all things. But when I consider whereunto we are born, not for ourselves but for the defence of the church of God, our prince, and our country, I do then think how this most happy government might with good providence, prevent the conspiracies of our enemies.

I do nothing at all doubt of our ability in wealth, for that I am persuaded that the substance of this realm is trebled in value since her Majesty's reign. God be glorified for it!

Neither do I think there wanteth provisions carefully provided, of shipping, ordinance, powder, armour, and munition, so as our people were exercised by some means in the course of wars.

For I read when Mahomet the Turk took that famous city of Constantinople, digging by the foundations and bottoms of the houses, he found such infinite treasure, as the said Mahomet condemning their wretchedness, wondered how this city could have been overcome, or taken, if they had in time provided men of war and furniture for their defence, as they were very well able; so I say there wanteth no ability in us, if we be not taken unprovided, and upon a sudden.

And this is th' only cause that hath moved me to say my mind frankly in this matter, and to set down these notes enclosed, praying th' Almighty God, which directeth the hearts of all governours, either to the good or benefit of the people for their relief and deliverance, or else doth alter and hinder their understanding to the punishment and ruin of the people for their sins and offences. Humbly beseeching your good Lordship to bear with my presumption in dealing with matters so high, and to judge of them by your great wisdom and experience how they may in your Lordship's judgment be worthy of the consideration, humbly taking my leave.

From Deptford the 20th July 1584

Your honourable Lordship's ever assuredly bounden

JOHN HAWKYNS.

The enclosure alluded to is as follows :

The best means how to annoy the King of Spain, in my opinion, without charge to her Majesty, which also shall bring great profit to her Highness and subjects, is as followeth. First, if it shall be thought meet that the King of

William Cecil, Lord Burghley.

OB. . 1598.

Portugal may in his right make war with the King of Spain, then he would be the best means to be the head of the faction.

There would be obtained from the said King of Portugal an authority to some person that should always give leave to such as upon their own charge would serve and annoy the King of Spain as they might both by sea and land, and of their booties, to pay unto the King of Portugal, five or ten of the hundred.

There would be also some person authorized by her Majesty to take notes of such as do serve the said King of Portugal, and to that party with her Majestie's consent to give them leave and allowance to retire, victual, and sell in some port of the West Countrye, for which liberty they should pay unto their Majesty five or ten of the hundred.

None should have leave to serve the said King of Portugal, but they should put in surety to offend no person, but such as the said King had war with, but should be bound to break no bulk but in the port allowed, where would be commissioners appointed to restore those goods as are belonging to friends in amity with the King of Portugal, and to allow the rest to the taker.

There would be martial law for such as committed piracy, for there can be none excuse, but all idle seamen may be employed.

If these conditions be allowed, and that men may enjoy that which they lawfully take in this service, the best owners and merchant adventurers in the river will put in foot, and attempt great things.

The gentlemen and owners in the west parts will enter deeply into this party.

The Flushingers will also be a great party in this matter.

The Protestants of France will be a great company to help this attempt.

The Portuguese in the Islands, in Brazil, and in Guinea, for the most part will continually revolt.

The fishings of Spain and Portugal, which is their greatest relief, will be utterly impeded and destroyed.

The islands will be sacked, their forts defaced, and their brass ordinance brought away.

Our own people, as gunners (whereof we have few) would be made expert, and grow in number, our idle men would grow to be good men of war both by land and sea.

The coast of Spain and Portugal in all places would be so annoyed, as to keep continual armies there would be no possibility; for that of my knowledge it is trouble more tedious and chargeable to prepare shipping and men in those parts than it is with us.

The voyage offered by Sir Francis Drake might best be made lawful to go under that licence also, which would be secret till the time draw near of their readiness.

All this before rehearsed shall not by any means draw the King of Spain to offer a war, for that this party will not only consist of Englishmen, but rather of the French, Flemings, Scotts, and such like, so as King Phillip shall be forced by great entreaty to make her Majestie a mean to withdraw the forces of her subjects and the aid of her Highness' ports, for otherwise there will be such scarcity in Spain, and his coast so annoyed, as Spain never endured so great smart. The reason is that the greatest traffics of all Phillip's dominions must pass to and fro by the seas, which will hardly escape intercepting.*

In 1584 Hawkins held a consultation with Peter Pett with regard to improving Dover Harbour. In 1585 he submitted books to Lord Burleigh with lists of her Majesty's ships, their tonnage, and estimates for outfit, at the same time sending in a statement of the management of the Navy from 1568 to 1579, with his scheme for its future government by commissioners.

Hawkins was the British sailors' first friend; for by his advice their pay was raised, in 1585, from 6s. 8d. a month to 10s., holding that this would bring the service better and more capable men, so that fewer would do the same work. "Such as could make shift for themselves, and keep themselves clean without vermin." As well as raising the quality of the men he improved the ships. The finest vessels in the English fleet against the Armada were built with Hawkins's improvements; he lowered the sterns and forecastles, made the keels longer, and the lines finer and sharper, thus anticipating the main principles of improvement which have been continued down to the present time.

His health at this time was very bad, but ill or well he never gave up his work. In January, 1586, he had a fit every other day. Vast sums of money passed through his hands, his jealous enemies asserting that he was enriching himself; but such malicious reports were treated with the contempt they merited.

Writing to Burleigh, November 13th, 1587, Hawkins speaks of the improvements during his office through money spared from the ordinary warrant —"the refitting of sail, cordage, bolts, hulks, pullies, forges, warfs, storehouses, an much more," ending with

> For myne owne parte I have lived in a very mean estate since I came to be an officer [Treasurer], neither have I vainly or superfluously consumed Her Majestie's treasure, or myne owne substance, but ever been diligently and carefully occupied to prepare for the danger to come, and whatsoever hath been or is maliciously spoken of me, I doubt not but your Lordshipes wisdome is such that ye may discern and judge of my fidelity, of which Her Matie and your Lordships have had long trial, and hereafter I will speak little in mine own behalf.

* *Sta. Pa. Dom.* (Eliz.)

John Hawkins to Sir F. Walsingham.

My duetie humblie remembred unto your honour, havinge of longe tyme seen the malycious practises of the Papists combined generally throughout Christendome to alter the government of this Realme and to bring it to Papisterie, and consequently to servitude, povertie and slaverye, I have had a good will from time to time to doe and set forward something as I could have credit to impeach their purpose, but it hath prevailed little, for that there was never any substantiall ground laid to be followed effectually and therefore it hath taken bad effect and bred great charge, and we still in worse case, and less assurance of quietnes.

I doe therefore now utter my mind particularly to your Honour howe I doe conceave some good to be done at last; I do see we are desirous to have peace, as it becometh good Christians, which is best for all men and I wish it might any way be brought to that passe, but in my poor Judgment the right way is not taken. . . . . .

Therefore in my mind our profit and best assurance ys to seek our Peace by a determyned and resolute Warre, which no doubte would be both less charge, more assurance of safetye, and would best discern our friends from our foes, both abroad and at home, and satisfy the people best generallie throughout the whole Realme.

In the continuance of this Warre, I wish it to be ordered in this sorte, That first we have as little to doe in forrayne Countries, as may be, but of meere necessitie, for that breedeth great charge and no profit at all.

Nexte that there be always Six principal good shipps of her Maties upon the Coast of Spain, victualled for some months & accompanied with some six small vessels, which shall haunt the Coast of Spain and the Islands, And be a sufficient company to distress any thing that goeth throughe that seas. And when these must return, there would be other six shipps likewise accompanyed, to keepe the place, So should the seas be never unfurnished, But as one company at the four monethes ende doth return, the other company should be always in the place. . . . . .

For these 6 ships we shall not break the strength of our Navie, for we shall leave a sufficient company always at home, to front any violence that can be any way offered unto us. I do herewith send a note how the shipps may be fitted, and what they are, and what will be left at home. In open and lawfull warrs God will help us, for we defend the chief cause, our religion, Gods own cause, for if we would leave our profession and turn to serve Baal (as god forbid, and rather to die a thousand deaths) we might have peace but not with God. . . . . .

From aborde the *Bonaventure* the first of Feb. 1587.

Your Honours humbly to command

JOHN HAWKYNS.

[Endorsed] To the right honorable Sir Francis Walsingham Knt.*

* *Sta. Pa. Dom.* (Eliz.)

The Treasurer had a house for his office at Deptford; but Hawkins resided in the parish of St. Dunstan's in the East, and also at his house in Plymouth. In December, 1587, Sir William Wynter and William Holstock reported that Hawkins's duties had been satisfactorily performed.

Masses of State papers remain to bear testimony of his labour, industry, and zeal in carrying out this dry detail business. Still he never lost his love of adventure, and often longed for the sea to escape from the vexations of his land service. Hence his offer in November, 1587, to undertake, with seventeen ships and pinnaces (the real germ of the Armada fleet), to oppose the landing of any foreign power on any part of the West coast.

But he had other work to do on land. With keen foresight he scented the struggle from afar. Hence we find him writing that it was impossible things could remain as they were. "The only way to gain a solid peace was by a determined and resolute war." When the intention of Spain to invade England became manifest, a Council, consisting of Lord Charles Howard, Hawkins, Drake, and Frobisher, got the English fleet in readiness to meet its formidable adversary. Hawkins was appointed Vice-Admiral, hoisting his flag on board the *Victory*, and received the highest reward, a mark of the highest distinction in those days, the honour of knighthood, during the action on the 26th of July! *

The following despatch from Sir John, detailing the circumstances of the defeat of the Armada, shows the practical business side of his character to the life:

To the Honble Mr Sec Walsingham

July 31—1588

My bounden duty humbly remembered unto your good Lordship I have not busied myself to write often to your Lordship in this great Cause for that my Lord Admiral doth continually advertise the manner of all things that doth pass, so do others that understand the state of all things as well as myself. We met with this fleet somewhat to the westward of Plymouth upon Sunday in the morning being the 21st July where we had some small fight with them in the afternoon. By the coming aboard one of the other of the Spainards a great ship a Biscane, spent her formast & bowsprit which was lost by the fleet in the Sea and so taken up by Sir Francis Drake the next morning.

The same Sunday there was by a fyer chancing by a barrel of powder a great Biscane spoiled and abandoned which my lord took up and sent away.

The Tuesday following athwart of Portland we had a sharp & long fight

* For the account of the defeat of the Armada and the part of Hawkins therein, see Chapter IV.

Sir Francis Walsingham.

OB., 1590.

with them, wherein we spent a great part of our powder & shot, so as it was not thought good to deal with them any more till that was releived .

The Thursday following by the occasion of the scattering of one of the great ships from the fleet which we hoped to have cut off, there grew a hot fray where in some store of powder was spent & after that little done till we came near to Calais where the fleet of Spain anchored & our fleet by them, and because they should not be in peace there to refresh their water or to have conference with those of the Duke of Parmas party, my lord admiral with firing of shipes determined to remove them as he did and put them to the seas in which broil the chief galliasse spoiled hir rother [rudder] and so rowed ashore near the town of Calais where she was possessed of our men but so aground as she could not be brought away

That morning being Monday 29 July we followed the Spaniards and all that day had with them a long and great fight wherein there was great valor shown generally of our company in that Battile. There was spent very much of our powder & shot and so the wind began to grow westerly a fresh gale and the Spaniards put them selves somewhat to the northward where we follow & keep company with them, in this fight there was some hurt done among the Spaniards. A great ship of the galleons of Portugal spoiled her rother and so the fleet left her in the sea. I doubt not but all these things are written more at large to your Lordship (then I can do but this is the substance and material matter that hath passed)

Our ships God be thanked have received little hurt and are of great force to accompany them and of such advantage that with some continuance at the seas and sufficiently provided of shot and powder we shall be able with Gods favour to weary them out of the sea and confound them.

Yet as I gather certainly there are amongst them so forcible and invincible ships which consist of those that follow viz 9 galleons of Portugal of 800 Tons apiece saving 2 of them are but 400 Tons apiece 20 great Venetians and argosies of the seas within the Straight of 800 apiece one ship of the Duke of Florence of 800 Tons 20 great Biskanes of 500 or 600 tons 4 galliasses where of one is in France There are 30 hulks and 30 other small ships whereof little account is to be made. At their departing from Lisbon being the 19th May by our account they were victualled for 6 months, they stayed in the Groyne 28 days and there refreshed their water, at their coming from Lisbon they were taken with a flawe and 14 hulks or thereabouts came near Ushante and so returned with contrary winds to the Groyne and there met, and else there was none other company upon our coast before the whole fleet arrived and in their coming now a little flaw took them 50 leagues from the coast of Spain where one great ship was severed from them and 4 gallies which hitherto have not recovered their company

At their departing from Lisbon the soldiers were 20,000 the mariners and others 8000 so that in all they were 28000 men. Their commission was to

II

confer with the Prince of Parma (as I learned) and then to proceed to the service that should be there concluded.   And so the Duke to return into Spain with these ships and mariners, the soldiers and their furniture being left behind. Now this fleet is here and very forcible and must be waited upon with all our force which is little enough. there would be an infinite quantity of powder & shot provided and continually sent aboard without the which great hazard may grow to our country for this is the greatest and strongest combination to my understanding that ever was gathered in Christendom, therefore I wish it of all hands to be mightily and diligently looked unto and cared for.

The men have been long unpaid and need relief I pray your Lordship that the money that should have gone to Plymouth may now be sent to Dover.

August now cometh in, and this cost [coast] will spend ground tackle, cordage canvas and victual, all which would be sent to Dover in good plenty, with these things and Gods blessing our kingdom may be preserved which being neglected great hazard may come.   I write to your Lordship briefly and plainly, your wisdom and experience is great, But this is a matter far passing all that hath been seen in our time or long before.

And so praying to God for a happy deliverance from the malicious and dangerous practice of our enemies I humbly take my leave from the sea aboard the *Victory* yᵉ last of July 1588.

The Spaniards take their course for Scotland My Lord doth follow them. I doubt not with Gods favor but we shall impeach their landing, there must be order for victual and many powder and shot to be sent after us.

Your Lordships humbly to command

JOHN HAWKINS

This is copy of the letter I send to my Lord Treasurer whereby I shall not need to write to your honour help us with furniture and with Gods favour we shall confound their devyse.

Your Honours ever bounden

JOHN HAWKINS

I pray your honour bear with this for it is done in haste and bad weather.*

But the defeat of the Armada was child's play for Hawkins in comparison with the subsequent rendering of his accounts, which he was called upon to do. For years the whole burden of the navy had lain upon his shoulders; and when the money of the State had failed, he had freely spent his own.   The Queen insisted that every item should be vouched ; Hawkins, more careful of results than book-keeping, held himself a ruined man.   Howard defended him from the unjust aspersions of his enemies; but Burleigh wrote him so severely, that in reply Hawkins says, "I pray God I may end this account to her Majesty's

* *Sta. Pa. Dom.* (Eliz.)

and your Lordship's liking, and avoid mine own undoing, and I trust God will so provide for me as I shall never meddle with such intricate matters more."

The following correspondence from the State Papers will show better than any mere description the nature of the work Sir John had to do, and the difficulties he had to overcome:

Sir John Hawkins to Lord Howard of Effingham.

THE QUEENES SHIPPES.

The *White Beare*
The *Victorye*
The *Nonperely*
The *Hope*
The *Swiftsure*
The *Foresight*
The *Moone*
The *White Lyon*
The *Disdaine*

THE SHIPPES OF LONDON.

The *Mynyon*
The *Golden Lyon*
The *Tho: Bonavent*
The *Hercules*
The *Redde Lyonn*
The *Royall Defence*
The *B. Burre*

The Gallion *Leicester*
The Gallyon *Dudley*
The *Teigar* of Plymouth
The Barque *Bonner*
The *Samaritane* of Dartmouth
The *Delight*
The *Eliz. Bonaventure*
The *Diamonde* of Dartmouth
The *Mynyon* of Plymouth
The *Jacob* of Lyme
The Barque *Hawkins*
The *Chaunce* of Plymouth
The *John* of Barstable
The *Acteon*
The Barque *Fleminge*
The *Sallomon* of Alborow
The *Pellicane* of Lee
The *Katherine*
The *Ratte*

MY VERIE GOOD LORD,—This Thursdaie beinge the viij^{th} of August we came into Harwiche with these shippes that are above noted. We are in hande to have out the Ordenance and Ballast of the *Hope* and so to grounde her. With the nexte faire wynde we mynde with those shippes that are here to follow your Lordshippe into the Downes, or where we maye heare of your Lordshippe, and to bring all the victuallers with us.

There are three of the wholes here alreddye with Beere and bread and the rest being seven more, have order to come hither. We will relyeve such as be in necessitie, and bringe awaie the rest with us.

The *Beare* hath a leake which is thought to be verie lowe, yet my Lord will follow your Lordship.

The *Elizabeth Jonas* and the *Trynmphe* drave the last stormie night being Mondaye, since which time we have not heard of them. But this faire weather I hope your Lordshippe shall heare of them at the Forelande. As I wrote this letter more of the Victuallers are come. There is xiiij daies victuall in them

for the shippes under your Lordshippes charge as I learne. And so praying to
God to sende us shortly to meete with your Lordshippe I humbly take my
leave from Harwich the 8ᵗʰ of August 1588.

Your honorable Lordshippes most bounden

JOHN HAWKYNS

THIS is the coppy of the letter sent to my Lord Admyrall which I send to yor
Honour, that ye may see in what state we are & what we pretend.   the wynd
is now bad for us to ply to my Lord but we will lose no tyme.

Your Honours most bounden

JOHN HAWKYNS.*

Sir John Hawkins and Lord Howard to Lord Burleigh.

RIGHT honorable myne especyall good Lord this day my Lord Admyrall called
Sʳ William Wynter and me aboard his Lordships ship and shewed unto us
your Lordships letter of the 24th of August wherby your Lordship required
to bee advertised what numbers of maryners and soldiers there were in the
ships that are here with my Lord.   Since I came down the weather hath been
such as our fleet hath been divided part in Dover rood and part at Margate &
goorend and never could come either of us to other and those at the Margate
can hardly row ashore or gett aboard when they were ashore.

Sʳ Francis Drake and I discharged & sent away many of the westerne &
coast ships before my Lord came down which upon some news that Sʳ Edward
Norys brought, my Lord was somewhat displeased & misliked it.

I am not able to send your Lordship a better particular of the numbers
that are & were in her Majesties certain pay then that which I sent from
Plymouth wherein was demaunded about xix thousand pounds to bring the pay
to the 28 of July wherein there was no condoctes demanded for that no
discharge was then thought of, neither was there any ships of the coast spoken
of, or voluntary ships but those of Sʳ Richard Graynfylds & those taken into
service by Sir Francis Drake then, over & above his warrant yet by order from
the counsell as Sʳ Richard Graynfyld & he hath to shew.

Your Lordship may think that by death, by discharging of sick men &
such like, that there may be spared somethinge in the generall pay, first those
that die their friends require their pay   in place of those which are discharged
sike & insufficient which indeed are many there are fresh men taken, which
breedeth a far greater Charge by mean of their condoct in discharge, which
exceedeth the wages of those which were lastly taken in, & more lost by that
then saved.   We do pay by the poll & by a Check book wherby if anything be
spared, it is to her Majesties benefit only.   The ships that I have paid of those

* *Sta. Pa. Dom.* (Eliz.)

which were under Sr Francis Drakes Charge, I find full furnished with men & many above their numbers. Those ships that are under my Lord Seemour, Sir Wm Wynter doth assure my Lord they have their full numbers besyde there were sent aboard 500 soldiers by Sir John Norys and others which stood them in little stede for that they were imperfect men. but they kept them not above viij days. The weather continueth so extreme & the tides run so swift that we cannot get any victuals aboard but with trouble & difficulty we go from ship to ship, but as weather will serve & time to gather better notes your Lordship shall be more particularly informed of all things.

And so I humbly take my leave from the *Arke Rawley* in Dover roode the 26th of August 1588.

Your good Lordship humbly to command

JOHN HAWKYNS.

[Appended to the same letter]

My good Lord this is as much as is possible for Mr Hawkyns to do at this time. There is here in our ship many Lieutenants and Corporals which of necessity we were and are driven to have. Your Lordship knoweth well how services be far from what they were, and assure your Lordship of necessity it must be so. God knoweth how they shall be paid except her Majesty have some consideration on them. The matter it is not great in respect of the service I think 500^{li} with the help of my own purse will do it, but howsoever it fall out I must see them paid and will for I do not like to end with this service, and therefore I must be solved here after. My good Lord look but what the officers had with Sir Francis Drake having been 4 of her Majesty's ships I do not desire half so much for all this great fleet.

My good Lord it grieveth me much to hear of my Lord Chamberlains sickness. The Almighty God help him. The Queens Majesty and the Realm should have as great a loss as of any one man that I do know. God send the next news to be of his Amendment. God send you health my good Lord.

Your Lordships most assured to Command

HOWARD.*

Sir John Hawkins to Lord Burleigh.

MY HONORABLE GOOD LORD,—I am sorry I do live so long to receive so sharp a letter from your Lordship considering how carefully I take care to do all for the best & to cease charge. . . . .

It shall hereafter be none offence to your Lordship that I do so much alone, for with Gods favour I will & must leave all. I pray God I may end this accompt to her Majesties & your Lordships liking & avoid myne own

* *Sta. Pa. Dom.* (Eliz.)

undoing, & I trust you will so provide for me as I shall never meddle with such intricate matters more, for they be importyble for any man to please & overcome it; if I had any enemy I wolde wish hym no more harme then the course of my troublesome and painfull liffe; but hereunto, & to Gods good providence we are born.

I have shewed your Lordships letter to my Lord Admiral & Sir William Wynter who can best judge of my care & painfull travail & the desire I have to cease the charge.

Since we came to Harwyche the Margett & Dover our men have much fallen sick whereby many are discharged which we have not greatly desired to increase because we always hoped of a generall discharge, yet some mariners we have procured to divers of the ships to redress them. And so I leave in haste to trouble your Lordship. From Dover the 28 of August 1588.

Your Honorable Lordships humbly to command

JOHN HAWKYNS.*

Sir John Hawkins to Secretary Walsingham.

. . . . . My Lord Treasurer I understand hath not been pleased for that I could not send his Lordship the certain number of such men as were in her Majestys pay. The truth is, the weather was such & so cruel as I cold not ferry from ship to ship a long time & the fleet was dispersed some at Dover, some at Margate & some to seek out the great Spaniard upon the coast of France. but now the vth of September all the fleet met in the Downs & presently within two hours I sent my Lord a perfect note which was near about 4300 men that remained in pay.

I would to God I were delivered of the delyng for money & then I doubt not but I should as well deserve & continue my Lords good liking as any man of my sort. but now I know I shall never please his Lordship two months together for which I am very sorry, for I am sure no man living hath taken more pain, nor been more careful to obtain & continue his Lordships good liking & favour toward him then I have been.

My pain & mysery in this service is infinite, every man would have his turn served though very unreasonable yet if it be refused then adieu friendship. I yield to many things more than there is whereof, and yet it will not satisfy many. God I trust will deliver me of it ere it be long for there is no other help.

I devise to ease charge & shorten what I can for which I am in a general misliking but my Lord Treasurer thinketh I do little but I assure your Honour I am seldom idelle.

I marvel we doubt the Spaniards. surely there can be no cause & we put our ships in great peril for they are unfitted of many things & unmeet for

* *Sta. Pa. Dom.* (Eliz.)

service till they pass a new furnishing both of men grownding & reforming of a world of provisions as it will be felt when we shall set forth again. The discourse which I wrote your honour in December last must take effect & so her Majesties charge shall cease, the coast of Spain & all his traffiques impeached & afflicted, & our people set awork, contented & satisfied in conscience & there is no other way to avoid the misery that daily groweth among our people, & so being over "fattygatyd" with a number of troubles I humbly take my leave from the Downes aboard the *Victory* the 5th of Sept. 1588.

Your Honours ever assured & bounden

JOHN HAWKYNS.[*]

So anxious and troublesome a time had Sir John, in paying off the fleet after the defeat of the Armada, owing to the frequent engaging and discharging of the men by the Queen's orders in the spring of 1588 ! So many changes too added greatly to the expense, independently of the large amount of money required to fit out the fleet for the extraordinary sea service during that year. In December, 1588, at Hawkins's request, Edward Fenton, his brother-in-law, who commanded the *Mary Rose* against the Armada, was appointed his deputy for a year, to enable him to finish his great and intricate accounts.[*] Hawkins set to his task with accustomed energy; and by the following September the accounts for eleven years—some had been previously sent in— were made up complete to December, 1588, and he was able to "clear himself with credit. The office was not one of profit; although an unscrupulous man might have made a fortune. Hawkins did not find in his time any fees or vails worth 20s. besides his ordinary fee and diet which he consumed in attending his office." Instead of profit his post was a great loss.

According to the original accounts, Sir John Hawkins, while Treasurer of the Navy, had paid out of his own pocket for thirteen years up to 1590 the sum of £9659 5s. 4d. This sum in the present day represents about £30,000. So he prayed to be delivered from this "continual thraldom," but in vain. "Elizabeth knew when she had a good servant, though she did not know how to treat him." His work increased. The yearly payment in 1590 for keeping and repairing vessels in harbour was advanced to £8973 12s. 10d., now equal to £50,000.

In 1588, after the defeat of the Armada, Sir John Hawkins and Sir Francis Drake instituted that useful fund long known as the "Chest at Chatham," for seamen and shipwrights voluntarily to set apart every month a portion of their pay, for the perpetual relief of such as were maimed or wounded in the service

[*] *Sta. Pa. Dom.* (Eliz.)

of the Crown. Probably the distress of the men after the fight of 1588 suggested the idea. This fund is now removed to and incorporated with Greenwich Hospital, of which it was the forerunner.

"In this Hundred of Blackheath, moreover, which contains two royal dockyards intimately associated with their names, and that noble institution Greenwich Hospital, both Hawkins and Drake deserve especial mention, since they were the first to make provision for disabled seamen."[*]

But it is not in this instance alone that seafaring men employed in the Queen's service have reason to gratefully commemorate the good deeds of Sir John Hawkins; for, not satisfied with having promoted the excellent scheme of the "Chest at Chatham," this noble and public-spirited officer founded and endowed during his lifetime, entirely at his own cost, a hospital at Chatham for poor decayed mariners and shipwrights. From an old inscription cut in the wall, the building was finished in 1592. And on the 27th of August, 1594, Queen Elizabeth, at the request of Sir John, granted a charter (which is in fine preservation, and still kept in the chest belonging to this charity) of incorporation, by the name of "the governors of the hospital of Sir John Hawkins, Knight, in Chatham. The society were always to consist of twenty-six governors, recited as follows in the charter: The Archbishop of Canterbury; the Bishop of Rochester; the Lord High Admiral; the Lord Warden of the Cinque Ports; the Dean of Rochester; the Treasurer, Comptroller, Surveyor, and Clerk of the Accounts of the Navy; six principal Masters of Mariners; two principal Shipwrights; the Master and Wardens of Trinity House, for the time being, and their successors," &c. [†]

"It reflects a lasting honour on the character of this worthy Knight, that he in his lifetime, and while he was blessed with health and vigour, to have enjoyed his fortune, conveyed to this house of charity the lands and tithes which he intended for the poor inhabitants of it." During his life Sir John had the sole power of appointing the poor men who were received into his hospital. After his death the right devolved upon the governors. Twelve pensioners were settled in the hospital, and a weekly stipend of two shillings was to be paid to each poor seaman; and no person was eligible who, while in the service of the Royal Navy, had not been maimed, disabled, or brought to poverty. In 1722 this hospital was put in thorough repair, by order of the governors, and the original inscriptions were continued. On the outer side, over the gate, "The poor you shall always have with you: to whom y⁵ may do good yf y⁵ wyl;" and on the inner side, "Because there shall be ever some poor

<hr>

[*] HASTED's *Kent*.   [†] *History of Rochester.*

CHEST AND HATCHMENTS IN SIR JOHN HAWKINS'S HOSPITAL, CHATHAM.

in the land, therefore I command thee, saying, Thou shall open thyne hand unto thy brother that is needy and poor in the land." *

"It is evident that the founder by fixing in a conspicuous part of the walls these admonitions to charity, intended to awaken in the minds of passengers sentiments of pity and compassion, and to excite those of his own profession, at least, who had been successful in the world, to enlarge and improve upon a plan calculated for the support, in the decline of life, of a body of men useful to the community, and to whose laborious and perilous assistance they were chiefly indebted for the wealth they had acquired. But if this was the expectation and laudable aim of Sir John Hawkins, they have been in a great measure ineffectual. For though, since the establishing of this institution, very ample—nay, noble—fortunes have been made by naval officers in the service of the Crown, the name of Robert Davis is almost the only one who stands recorded as a benefactor, and it was by the direction of Dame Elizabeth Narborough (afterwards Shovel), whom he appointed his sole executrix."†

Sir John, after settling his accounts with regard to the navy in 1590, requiring a relief from his arduous office work, suggested an expedition to Cadiz and the South Seas, "the sea calling him, and feeling there was good work to be done."‡ As usual he was vexed by delays, but towards the end of the summer of 1590 the fleet of fourteen ships, commanded by himself in the *Mary Rose* and Sir M. Frobisher in the *Revenge*, set sail, with orders to do all possible mischief on the coast of Spain.§ In September Hawkins was Admiral at Flores, waiting for the

* Twelve pensioners are still living in Sir John Hawkins's Hospital at Chatham, but during this century the old gate has disappeared. In the Council Room, over the fireplace, is a portrait in oils of the founder, also two hatchments, one with the arms of Sir John Hawkins, and the other with the arms of Trelawny impaling Arg. on a chev. sable three cross crosslets of the first, likewise a huge oak chest with three locks, in which the charter is kept. On the lid of the chest are the arms of Sir John Hawkins.

† *History of Rochester.*

‡ 1590. May 2. Westminster. Commission of Queen Elizabeth to Sir John Hawkins, authorising him to press and take up men for her service to the furnishing of such ships as are committed to his charge, viz. the *Mary Rose, Hope, Nonpareil, Rainbow, Swiftsure,* and *Foresight,* in any place upon the coasts of England and Ireland any mariners, soldiers, &c. Provided that Sir John, and those who accompany him in the voyage, shall not willingly attempt anything that may give just cause of offence to such princes as are in good amity and league with England.—*Second Report of the Historical Manuscripts Commission. Duke of Northumberland's MSS.*

§ Sir John Hawkins and Sir Martin Forbusher, their voyage to the Coast of Spain and Islands Anno 1590.

The *Revenge* .	. Sir Martin Fobisher	The *Hope* .	. Captain Bostock
The *Mary Rose*	. Sir John Hawkins	The *Crane* .	. Captain [Richard] Hawkins
The *Lion* .	. Sir Edward Yorke	The *Quittance*	. Captain Burnell
The *Bonaventure*	. Captain Fenner	The *Foresight* .	
The *Rainbow* .	. Sir George Becston	The *Swiftsure* .	

MONSON's *Naval Tracts.*

1

Spanish fleet. Says Sir Richard, in his *Voyage to the South Seas*, "In the fleet of her Majesty, under the charge of my father Sir John Hawkins anno 1590, upon the coast of Spain the Vice-Admiral [Frobisher?] being ahead one morning, where his place was to be astern, lost us the taking of eight men of war laden with ammunition, victuals, and provisions, for the supply of the soldiers in Brittany [the Spaniards sent assistance of troops and stores to the Duc de Mercœur in Brittany, in his war against Hen. IV., which was not concluded until 1598], and although they were 7 or 8 leagues from the shore, when our Vice-Admiral began to fight with them, yet for that the rest of our fleet were some 4, some 5 leagues, and some more distant from them, when we began to give chase, the Spaniards recovered into the harbour of Mungia [14 miles N. of Cape Finisterre] before our Admiral [Sir John Hawkins] could come up to give direction ; yet well beaten, with loss of above 200 men, as they themselves confessed to me after. And doubtless, if the wind had not over-blown and that to follow them I was forced to shut all my lower ports, the ship I undertook [chased] doubtless had never endured to come to the port ; but being double fli-boats, and all of good sail they bare for their lives, and we did what we could to follow and fetch them up,"* and to intercept the Spanish fleet.

"But the Plate fleet was warned in time, and remained in the Indies. None of the enemy's ships appeared, and the expedition came back without any results."

The English in this year were seven months without taking a ship, as the Spaniards did not come out of port, but the English fleet succeeded in stopping trade with Spain. Not taking the eight men of war on their way to Brittany was no fault of Sir John, who, however, had to bear the blame. For when he returned and reminded Elizabeth that "Paul doth plant, Appollo doth water, but God giveth the increase," "God's death!" exclaimed the Queen, "this fool went out a soldier and is come home a divine."†

Sir John Hawkins to Lord Burleigh.

MY MOST HONORABLE GOOD LORD,

. . . . I ame many wayes burdenyd & brought behinde hande and especyally by the overthrow of this Jorney which I had with great care & cost brought to passe, hopinge as your Lordship dyd see an orderly & a sparyng begynnyng so yf yt had pleased God that yt shold have procyded ther shold have byne sene with Gods favour a rare example of governement, wherin matter of great moment might have byne performyd, but seying yt ys thus I can but saye, the wyll of god be done.

<hr>

* This proves that Sir Richard Hawkins was in this expedition of 1590.   † *Sta. Pa. Dom.* (Eliz.)

I ame many wayes to be an humble sewter to your good Lordship to looke favourably to me, ells I shall be utterly cast downe, for many thynges are now owt of my handes wherein I have streched my abyllytye & many of my fryndes, & especially this late Jorney intendyd.

The remayne of the warrant of the 27 of March 1588 .	2147	10	o
the consideracon for my ship the *repentance* . .	714	o	o
my porcyon with S^r francys Drake which her Matie promysed me long syns beynge . . .	7000	o	o

all which I thought shold have byne small matters in comparyson of that which God wold have blessyd me with yf I had procyded, but now beynge owt of hope that ever I shall performe any royall thynge, I do put on a meane mynde, & humbly pray your Lordship to be good lord to me, to whome onely I wylbe beholdynge, & wyll be dysposed of and all that I have by your Lordship & ever thankfull.

From London the first of Marche 1589.

Your Lordships ever bownden

JOHN HAWKYNS.

[Endorsed] To the Ry^t Honorable my synguler good Lord the Lord High tresorer of Ingland.*

We subsequently find :

Sir John Hawkins to Lord Burleigh.

My bownden dewty Humbly remembryd unto your good Lordship. We aryvyd by Dover with fowre of her Maties good shipes and the *Daynty* in good saffety god be thankyd the viiith day of Desember, & mynd to plye into chattham with all spede possyble. . . . .

The pryse at Dartmouthe ys dyschargyd there and a perfytt inventory sent unto your Lordship of all that was fownd in her by the costomer or collectour Mr Blaccoller to which inventory bothe he and I have subscrybed, & lest the same may not come so soone to your Lordships hands by land as now by me I have sent your Lordship a coppy of it word for word.

I have delyveryd the cochenyle to those your Lordship and the rest of the Lordes wrot for even at my beyng under sayle I gave order for it.

The ryalls of platt & the matters of worthe I have here with me in the *Mary rose* which I wyll bryng to your Lordship, so have I other things wherin your Lordship shall see I have demynyshed nothing.

From the *Mary rose* nere Dover the 8th of Des. 1590.

Your Honorable Lordships ever bounden

JOHN HAWKYNS.

[Endorsed] To the Ry^t Honorable my synguler good Lord The Lord Heigh Tresorer of Ingland.*

* *Sta. Pa. Dom.* (Eliz.)

The character of the disputes that arose in the division of the spoil is indicated by the annexed curious official report:

> MOST worshippful Sir, having traveled about your affaires conserning the goods of yours brought into Plimouth by Sir John Hawkins and Sir Martin Frobisher Knights at my coming to Plimouth aforesaid your factors and I fownde in sundrye warehowses by ther markes the said goodes mentioned in scedules geven us. And by virtue of letters from the right honourable the Lords and others of her Majesties Privie Councell your factors receyved them and transported them according to your directions, saving fortie bagges of Cochinille and one smale barrell delivered me by waight by Humferye Founes in this manner, viz. x bagges and a smale barrell in his owne keeping, as allotted out for his share, and so he commanded from one Phillipps Goddard and Mr Hawkins as their share also x bagges a piece more, All which commodities after the possession for my discharge being goodes of great vallewe called some honest persons to viewe them And fownd the said goodes to be mingled with grimy (?) graynes and coldust &c. And after roade to the Commissioners viz. Sir John Gilbert Knt. &c. to shew them how the forenamed persons together with Mr Richard Hawkins had misused (?) the said goodes in manner as is aforesaid. . . . .
>
> Uppon the 26th of October past Sir John Hawkins being sent unto by the said commissioners, and a coppie of Her Maties warrant, desiering him to be a meane that his kinsman Richard Hawkins might restore the rest of the said goodes, which he refused to do, but wrote his warrant unto the Mayor of Plimouth to take the same goodes again from us. . . . .
>
> Sir John sent to the number of 50 or threescore mariners, with a man or twoe of his own well weaponed the xxixth of October and with great violence took the same goodes from us. . . . .
>
> CAR. ATKINSON.*

There was still sharper controversy when the *Madre de Dios* was captured, in 1592, after a hot engagement. This great caracke, or seven-decked ship, of 165 feet from stem to stern, manned by 600 men, was the largest prize that had ever been brought to England. The Queen, who had contributed little towards the expenses of the enterprise, nevertheless engrossed the largest share of the profits, which were estimated by Ralegh and Sir John Hawkins, who had joined him in this expedition, at £500,000. The officers and sailors, however, had previously secured for themselves the jewels and other valuable effects, and thus obtained considerable booty. This vessel was brought into the port of Dartmouth. Ralegh's share of the profits is said to have exceeded £30,000; but he complains that he had back less than his own.

We find under date, October 28th, 1594:

GRANT to Sir John Hawkins, Sir John Hart, Hen. Colthurst, John Moore, and other merchants of London, of a prohibition for two years against the bringing in of pepper, with proviso that they sell the pepper which they have bought of the Queen at not more than 3*s.* the pound.*

Sir John Hawkins's career was now drawing to a close. His health became affected from the strain of a continuance of service afloat, combined with the performance of responsible and laborious duties on shore. Hence he writes, in January, 1594, begging again to be released from his labours. He had grown grey in the service of his country, and now required the much-needed rest. "His second wife, Margaret Vaughan, was weak, and could not be removed. His brother William had died and been honoured by a monument in Deptford Church. There was to be no other rest for him."

As his life had been heroic so was his death. In 1593 his only child, Richard Hawkins, had sailed on his adventurous voyage to the South Sea. Then came the news that his son was a prisoner in the hands of the Spaniards; and his brave father determined to put to sea once more, broken-hearted as he was, to attempt the rescue of his son, hoping that during the enterprise an opportunity might offer to procure his freedom.

An expedition to sail to the West Indies was planned by Hawkins, who as usual directed all the preparations himself. Sir Thomas Gorges reported, from Plymouth to Cecil, of this his last service, "Sir John Hawkins is an excellent man in all these things; he sees all things done orderly."

The fleet was under the command of Sir John Hawkins and Sir Francis Drake. The Queen was to bear a share of the expenses, and to have a third of the profits. Hawkins was to victual the fleet at his own cost. "As a matter of fact the chief outlay fell upon Sir John," who expended £18,661 18*s.* 6*d.*, and Drake £12,842 9*s.* 10*d.* If required the Queen would have found £20,000; but Hawkins and Drake paid £1504 8*s.* 5*d.* above their proportion.

Carew notes: On the 23rd July, 1595, four Spanish galleys arrived off the Cornish coast near Penzance, where they landed, and set the town on fire. A messenger was sent by post to Sir Francis Drake, and Sir John Hawkins, then at Plymouth with a fleet bound for the Indies, &c.

The following letter will be read with interest:

Sir F. Drake and Sir J. Hawkins to Lord Burleigh.

Our duty in most humble manner remembered, it may please your Lordship, we have answered her Majestys letter we hope to her Highness contentment, whom we would not willingly displease.

* *Sta. Pa. Dom.* (Eliz.)

We humbly thank your Lordship for your manifold favours which we have always found never variable, but with all favour, love, and constancy, for which we can never be sufficiently thankful, but with our prayers to God long to bless your good Lordship with honour and wealth.

We think it be true, that some small men of war be taken upon the coast of Spain, but they are of very small moment; they be for the most part such small carvels as was before this taken from the Spaniards. Some small number of our men are yet in Spain, which is the only loss, but as we learn, there be not above one hundred left in Spain of them, but many returned already into England. And so looking daily for a good wind, we humbly take our leave. From Plymouth the 18th of August, 1595.

Your Lordships ever most bounden,

Fra. Drake,
John Hawkins.*

Their force consisted of 27 ships and 2500 men. Of all the expeditions against the Spaniards there was none that promised so much success, and which ended with less.

This fleet of six royal ships, the *Bonaventure, Garland, Defiance, Hope, Foresight,* and *Adventure,* with twenty-one other vessels, was detained by reports of a Spanish invasion, which proved without foundation. The ships sailed from Cawsand Bay on the 29th April, 1595, to execute their plan of burning Nombre de Dios, marching to Panama, and there seizing the treasure which had arrived from Peru. The first mishap that occurred was to the *Hope.* She struck on the Eddystone, but was got off again. A few days before they sailed, the Queen sent to say that the Plate fleet had arrived in Spain, with the exception of one galleon, which had lost a mast and was obliged to return to Porto Rico, and advised their taking this vessel. When they were at sea the "generals" in a very short time differed. Hawkins was for executing the Queen's command; but Drake, instead of seconding the wise judgment of his kinsman and early patron, succeeded in persuading him to make an attack on the Canaries. But the attempt of reducing these islands proved as dishonourable as it was unsuccessful, and they set sail for Dominica, where they spent too much time in refreshing the crews and building pinnaces, remaining at Guadaloupe until the 4th November; thus giving the Spaniards so much insight into their design that, having heard of the departure and force of the English squadron, they dispatched five stout frigates to bring away the galleon from Porto Rico.

* Sta. Pa. Dom. (Eliz)

Sir John Hawkins having left St. Dominica, the same day the *Francis*, of thirty-five tons, and the sternmost of his ships, fell in with the five Spanish ships despatched to observe the English, and to convoy the Plate fleet from Porto Rico. The Spaniards, by putting the master and mariners of the *Francis* to the torture, obliged them to confess all they knew with regard to the expedition. This loss so deeply affected Sir John Hawkins that, on hearing the news, the consequence of which he had foreseen, and knowing that their whole scheme must be discovered, he was thrown into a fit of sickness, of which (or rather of a broken heart) he died, on the 21st November, 1595, the very day the fleet anchored before Porto Rico. Hawkins's death had a great effect upon those whom he commanded, because what he predicted had come only too true. This was so mortifying to Drake, he being greatly to blame, that he too fell ill, and died a few weeks later.

"His younger colleague and pupil soon afterwards followed him, and shared the same watery grave."*

Anticipating the arrival of the English fleet, the Spaniards had sunk a great ship to prevent the English entering the haven, where there were five Spanish vessels well armed for defence. Directly the English came to an anchor, they played their great guns upon them, doing much damage. Sir Nicholas Clifford and Brute Brown were mortally wounded. Baskerville, however, with twenty-five boats, ventured within the Roads, burning and doing much harm to their ships, and the fight was obstinately contested on both sides.

The English then proceeded to Nombre de Dios, whence Sir Thomas Baskerville, with 750 soldiers, began the march to Panama; but was repulsed, and returned, after they had gone halfway to the South Seas, with his half-starved and harassed men.

After the death of Sir Francis Drake, before the fleet reached Porto Bello, the command devolved upon Baskerville; and he, with the advice of the other officers, set sail for England, and, after a severe fight with a Spanish fleet off Cuba, arrived home in May, 1596, with very little booty, which was but a poor recompense to the nation for the loss of the two greatest sea officers then in Europe; and was much regretted and remembered for many years as a public calamity.

Sir John Hawkins was graceful in his youth, and of a grave and reverend aspect as he advanced in years. "Every inch a sailor," with a thorough understanding of maritime affairs; a skilled mathematician, and a shrewd

* BARROW.

tactician, with a keen insight into the characters of men; of an almost
boundless capacity for work; an able and upright administrator, who for
forty-eight years was employed in the active service of his country. He was a
man of undaunted personal courage, and never-failing presence of mind, which
enabled him frequently to deliver himself and others out of the most imminent
dangers. He formed his plans judiciously, and executed the orders he received
with the utmost punctuality. Submissive to his superiors, and courteous to
inferiors; extremely affable to his seamen, and remarkably beloved by them:
"merciful," says Maynard, "and apt to forgive, and faithful to his word;"
placing the sufferings of his men far before his own private disasters. "Not
only the ablest seaman of his day, but the best shipwright that England had
ever seen; often entering upon what in modern eyes are questionable ways, but
never false to his own conscience and the moral standard of his time; 'a very
wise, vigilant, and true-hearted man,' as Stow speaks of him in his *Chronicle*—
Sir John Hawkins, of all the Elizabethan galaxy, seems to me most nearly
to approach the typical Englishman. The very solidity of his virtues, the
very greatness of his deeds, have caused them to be inadequately esteemed."*

He was not without failings, and these were exaggerated by such people
as found it easy to censure a man whom it would have been difficult to
imitate.

An anonymous letter, of doubtful authenticity,† quoted by Prince, dis-
paraging Hawkins, bears the marks of bias, and was in all probability written
by one of the men Hawkins detected in abuses, and who thus owed him a
grudge, and wrote the letter in retaliation.

In spite of objections, it is made evident from facts that Sir John Hawkins
was one of the principal supports of the English navy, in a reign when its glory
was very conspicuous, in consequence of which he received many testimonies
of honour, favour, and reward. His merit was not only understood by the
Queen and her ministers, but by the country also, since Sir John was so
popular, that he was twice elected member of Parliament for Plymouth, and a
third time for some other borough.

He was a pious man, as appears from his recorded sayings and letters,
and from his having erected and endowed during his lifetime the hospital at
Chatham.

* WORTH.

† The writer has carefully omitted his name. It has been stated, but on unreliable authority, that
Sir Wm. Monson wrote this letter. This is incorrect, as Sir Wm. Monson speaks in the highest terms
of Hawkins.

That he was a man of education, and able to handle the pen to good purpose, is proved by his narrative of the voyage to San Juan de Ulloa, and many letters still extant.

His contemporary, John Davis, in his *World's Hydrographical Description,* says, "The first Englishman that gave any attempt on the coasts of West India, was Sir John Hawkins, Knight: who there and in that attempt, as in many others sithens, did and hath proved himself to be a man of excellent capacity, great government, and perfect resolution. For before he attempted the same it was a matter doubtful and reported the extremest limit of danger to sail upon those coasts. . . . How then may Sir John Hawkins be esteemed, who being a man of good account in his country, of wealth and great employment, did notwithstanding for the good of his country, to procure trade, give that notable and resolute attempt."

Admiral Sir John Hawkins was married twice. About 1558 he married Katherine, daughter of Benjamin Gonson, Esq., of Sebright Hall, Great Badow, near Chelmsford, by Ursula, daughter of Anthony Hussey, Judge of the Admiralty. Benjamin Gonson, and his father William Gonson before him, were Treasurers of the Navy in the reigns of Henry VIII., Edward VI., Mary, and Elizabeth. In 1573 Benjamin Gonson resigned in favour of his son-in-law, John Hawkins, who held the office of Treasurer of the Navy until his death, in 1595—a period of twenty-two years. Sir John's first wife, Katherine Gonson, was the mother of Sir Richard Hawkins, his only child. She died in 1591, and was buried in St. Nicholas Church, Deptford. Katherine's sister, Tomasine Gonson, married first Captain Edward Fenton, Squire of the body to Queen Elizabeth, and commander of the *Mary Rose* against the Armada. He died in 1603, and a monument commemorates his memory in St. Nicholas Church, Deptford. His widow married, secondly, Christopher Browne, Esq., of Sayes Court, Deptford.

Sir John Hawkins's second wife was Margaret, daughter of Charles Vaughan, Esq., of Hergest, by Elizabeth, daughter of Sir James Baskerville, of Eardisley Castle, Co. Hereford. Lady Hawkins was bedchamber woman to Queen Elizabeth. Lady Hawkins is mentioned, in 1594, as attending the funeral, as "chefe morner," of her aunt, Lady Katherine Gates, widow of Sir Henry Gates; and again in the Carew MSS., 1601–1603. She survived her husband twenty-six years, and died in 1621.*

His skill and success had given him such a reputation, that by way of augmentation to his arms (Sable, a golden lion walking over the waves),

* Sir John Hawkins's two wives were allied to Roger Boyle, Earl of Cork.

K

Mr. Harvey, then Clarencieux King-at-Arms, granted to John Hawkins, by patent, for his crest, on his return from his voyage of 1564, a demi-Moor proper bound captive, with annulets on his arms and in his ears, for his victory over the Moors.

"2nd augmentation for John Hawkins exploits at Rio de la Hauche, and in honour of his great action at Ulloa, and to preserve the memory of his other noble achievements, Mr Cooke then Clarencieux added to his arms—on a canton or an escallop between two palmer's staves sable. This patent is [in 1779] still in existance."

The terms of the first grant of augmentation are worthy of note. Sir John is described as "gentleman," and as the second son of William Hawkins, of Plymouth, and Joan his wife, daughter of "Edmund" Trelawny, of Cornwall, who was son of John Hawkins, of Lawnstone, Cornwall, esquire, by Joane his wife, daughter and heir of William Amidas, of Lawnstone aforesaid. There is no record of the original grant of arms, which according to the augmentation were borne by his immediate ancestors.

In 1616 the Corporation of Plymouth placed the arms of Sir John Hawkins, and those of Sir John Hele, in the Guildhall windows, at a cost of 33s. 6d., protecting them the next year with a "small grate of wire" costing 13s. 10d. In the new Guildhall windows Sir John is represented, but his arms have been omitted.

Sir John Hawkins's grave lies far away in the depths of the Western Ocean; but a handsome monument erected to his memory on the north side of the chancel of St. Dunstan's-in-the-East, which was his place of worship during many years, gave his age as "six times ten and three."[*] This would make his birth in 1532; the date usually given is 1520, but on no authority. This cenotaph was destroyed in the great fire of London in 1666. The present church was built by Sir Christopher Wren; and the tomb has disappeared. The monument bore the following inscription :

> Johannes Hawkins, Eques Auratis, clariss. Reginæ Marinarum causarum Thesaurarius. Qui cum xliii annos muniis bellicis et longis periculosisque navigationibus, detegendis novis regionibus, ad Patriæ utililatem, et suam ipsius gloriam, strenuam et egregiam operam navasset, in expeditione, cui Generalis præfuit ad Indiam occidentalem dum in anchoris ad portum S. Joannis in insula Beriquena staret, placide in Domino ad cœlestem patriam emigravit, 12 die Novembris anno salutis 1595. In cujus memoriam ob virtutem et res gestas Domina Margareta Hawkins, Uxor mæstissima, hoc monumentum cum lachrymis posuit.

[*] The same date is given on Sir John's original portrait, in the possession of C. Stuart Hawkins, Esq.

ARMS OF SIR JOHN HAWKINS,
Impaling Gonson and Vaughan.

Stow, in his *Survey of London*, tells us that his widow hung a "fair table" by the tomb, "fastened in the wall, with these verses in English:"

Dame Margaret,
A widow well affected
This monument
Of memory erected,
Deciphering
Unto the viewer's sight
The life and death
Of Sir John Hawkins, Knight;
One fearing God
And loyal to his Queen,
True to the State
By trial ever seen,
Kind to his wives,
Both gentlewomen born,
Whose counterfeits
With grace this work adorn.
Dame Katherine,
The first, of rare report,
Dame Margaret
The last, of Court consort,
Attendant on
The chamber and the bed
Of England's Queen
Elizabeth, our head
Next unto Christ,
Of whom all princes hold
Their scepters, states,
And diadems of gold.
Free to their friends
On either side his kin
Careful to keep
The credit he was in.
Unto the seamen
Beneficial,
As testifieth
Chatham Hospital.
The poor of Plymouth
And of Deptford Town
Have had, now have,
And shall have, many a crown.
Proceeding from
His liberality
By way of great
And gracious legacy,
This parish of
St. Dunstan standing east

(Wherein he dwelt
Full thirty years at least)
Hath of the springs
Of his good will a part,
Derived from
The fountain of his heart,
All which bequests,
With many moe unsaid,
Dame Margaret
Hath bountifully paid.
Deep of conceit,
In speaking grave and wise,
Endighting swift
And pregnant to devise.
In conference
Revealing haughty skill
In all affairs,
Having a worthie's will;
On sea and land,
Spending his course and time,
By steps of years
As he to age did climb.
God hath his soul,
The sea his body keeps,
Where (for a while)
As Jonas now he sleeps;
Till he which said
To Lazarus, Come forth,
Awakes this Knight,
And gives to him his worth.
In Christian faith
And faithful penitence,
In quickening hope
And constant patience,
He running ran
A faithful pilgrim's race,
God giving him
The guidance of His Grace,
Ending his life
With his experience
By deep decree
Of God's high providence.
His years to six times
Ten and three amounting,
The ninth the seventh
Climacterick by counting

Dame Katherine,
His first religious wife,
Saw years thrice ten
And two of mortal life,
Leaving the world the sixth,
The seventh ascending.
Thus he and she
Alike their compass ending,
Asunder both
By death and flesh alone,
Together both in soul,
Two making one,
Among the saints above,
From troubles free,
Where two in one shall meet
And make up three.
The Christian Knight

And his good ladies twain,
Flesh, soul, and spirit
United once again;
Beholding Christ,
Who comfortably saith,
Come, mine elect,
Receive the crown of faith.

L'ENVOY.

Give God, saith Christ,
Give Cæsar lawfull right,
Owe no man, saith St. Paul,
ne mine, ne mite
Save love, which made
this chaste memoriall,
Subscribed with
Truths testimoniall.

An epitaph on Sir John Hawkins and Sir Francis Drake was written by Richard Barnfield, in an address "To the Gentlemen Readers" preceding *The Encomium of Lady Pecunia; or, The Praise of Money* (1598). He writes: "The bravest Voyages in the World have been made for gold: for it Men have venterd (by sea) to the furthest parts of the earth: In the pursute whereof, England's Nestor and Neptune [Hawkins and Drake] lost their lives. Upon the Deathes of the which two, of the first I write this:

"The waters were his Winding Sheete, the Sea
was made his Toombe;
Yet for his fame the Ocean Sea, was not
Sufficient roome.

Of the latter this:

"England his hart ; his Corps the waters have,
And that which raysd his fame, became his grave."

The frontispiece represents an original portrait on panel of Admiral Sir John Hawkins. On the left side are the arms, and on the right, "Ætatis SVÆ LVIII Anno Dōmi 1591." This portrait is now in the possession of Christopher Stuart Hawkins, Esq., whose father, Admiral Abraham Mills Hawkins, about 1850, obtained the picture from Richard King, Esq., of Bigadon, into whose hands it came after having been sold with the "old lumber" referred to on page 70, on the death of Mrs. William Creed (relict of William Creed, a descendant of Admiral Sir John Hawkins), who was the grandmother of Admiral Abraham Mills Hawkins, as well as of John Luscombe, Esq., late of Coombe Royal, near Kingsbridge.

The accompanying illustration represents a miniature of Sir John Hawkins, and the jewel given to him by Queen Elizabeth, after the defeat of the Armada, together with a lock of her Majesty's hair.*

The miniature is in an ivory case, and beautifully preserved, with a blue background. These relics were given to Sir Henry Seale, Bart., by Miss Mary Southcote about 1845. A few years later Baron E. Rothschild came into Dartmouth in his yacht, and purchased the miniature and pendant from Sir Henry, and they are now in the possession of his daughter, the Countess of Rosebery.

The following extract is taken from a letter:

> THE miniature is a very good resemblance of Sir John Hawkins, painted by Peter Oliver, considered the first English artist in Queen Eliz[ths] day. Sir John Hawkins was one of the admirals of Queen Eliz[ths] fleet which took and dispersed the Spanish Armada in the year 1588, for which service the Queen presented him with the accompanying jewel, and which at that time was suspended by a handsome gold chain. The whole coming into the possession of two sisters,† they agreed to a division—the younger, Mary, taking the picture and jewel, the elder, Harriet, keeping the chain, all trace of which is now lost, but John Luscombe, Esq', of Coombe Royal near Kingsbridge, Devon, says he well remembers to have seen amongst some old lumber of his grandmother's, M[rs] W[m] Creed, a portrait of Sir John Hawkins wearing this jewel and the chain round his neck. After his grandmother's death the old lumber was sold, and with it this portrait.
>
> Nearly 50 years since I remember to have heard my Father say that he had been offered £500 for this relic but which he had refused!
>
>   MARY SOUTHCOTE.‡

The Marquis of Lothian has in his possession a picture of Hawkins, Drake, and Candish. "It is ascribed to Mytens, and it has been at Newbattle for about 250 years at least."§ The portrait of Hawkins in this picture is a *fac-simile* of the one that belongs to Mr. C. Stuart Hawkins.

---

* This lock of Queen Elizabeth's hair was carefully preserved and given to Henry Southcote, who changed his name to Aston, second son of John Henry Southcote, by his second wife Priscilla Aston. He unfortunately lost the hair a few years since.

† Daughters of John Henry Southcote, ob. 1820 aged 73, of Buckland-tout-Saints, which he sold to the Clarkes in 1793, and of the manor of Stokefleming, High Sheriff of Devon.

‡ Mary Southcote, ob. 1849, daughter of John Henry Southcote, by his first wife Margaret Luttrell. This heirloom came to John Henry Southcote through his mother Joan Creed, and to the Creeds from Judith, daughter of Thomas Hawkins, Esq., of Stokefleming, who married Peter Creed.

§ Letter from the Marquis of Lothian.

Admiral Sir John Hawkins

In the Council-room of Sir John Hawkins's Hospital at Chatham is a portrait in oils of the founder, apparently taken at a younger period of his life.

The basso-relievo ivory bust of Sir John Hawkins is in the possession of the Rev. Bradford R. J. Hawkins, of Crowfield Parsonage, Needham, Suffolk, who believes the bust came from Dr. Deane, Archdeacon of Rochester and Rector of Lambeth, through Bishop Bradford, whose niece William Hawkins, of Westminster, married. The said William Hawkins was great grandfather of the Rev. Bradford R. J. Hawkins, the present owner of the bust.

Will of Katherine Lady Hawkins.

BE it known to all men by these presents that whereas I Sir John Hawkins Knt. am possessed of one house with one garden & appurtenances thereunto belonging in Deptford And whereas I am also possessed of certain other lands in Deptford aforesaid within [*sic*] Katherine my wellbeloved wife is in the remainder to dispose to her & her heirs knowe ye that I the said Sir John Hawkins in consideration of my great good will borne to my wife aforesaid and in consideration of the great care & travels she hath alwaies borne towards the increasing & maintenance of my estate have licensed and do by these licence and give libertie to the said Katherine my wife to make her last will & testament and therein to dispose & give & bequeath at her good pleasure and liking to anie person or persons & their heirs not only the possession & reversion of the said lands but also of my goodes moveable to the value of five hundreth pounds sterling which dispositions gifts & bequests by her to be made for the things & value abovesaid I promise by theis presents for me my heirs & executors to allowe ratifie & performe. In witnes whereof I have set to theis presents my hande & seale the xxv^th day of May in the xxxij^th yeare of the raigne of our Soveraigne Ladie Elizabeth. JOHN HAWKINS. Sealed & delivered in the presence of me LAWRENCE HUSE.

I KATHERINE HAWKINS wife of Sir John Hawkins Knt. do request my husband that he will be contented my corps may be buried in the parish Church of St. Dunstans in the Easte.

I bequeath the large bason & ewer of silver & gilt which was my late fathers to my brother Benjamin Gonson & to his heirs after the decease of my husband. And for default of issue to such one of my sisters or sisters children as shalbe thought most fit & convenient by mine Executors to take the use of the said bason & ewer.

To my said brothers wife my best border of pearls & gold. To my sister Marie Hawkins my other border of gold & pearle To Judith Hawkins wife of Richard Hawkins my ring with the table diamante which Sr Nicholas Parker gave me.   To my sister Peterson my great Spanische piece of golde of the value of about fifty ducats, and to Ursula Peterson her daughter £50.

To my sister Bennet Wallinger the face cloth & cushion cloth which she hath in use of mine and to Katherine Wallinger her daughter & my goddaughter £50.   And to Thomas Wallinger her son £25   To Marie Wallinger her daughter £25

To my sister Anne Fleminge 32 pieces of 10s. in gold of the mill stamp

To my sister Thomasine Fenton my pair of bracelets of gold pearle & "Agathies" and my ringe with the seale.

To my cousin Katherine Jordan 10 pieces of gold of 20s. the piece

To my cousin Marie Robinson one piece of gold of 30s.

To my cousin Margaret Huse als Roe one piece of gold of 30s.

To my cousin Anne Netmaker wife of my cousin Robert Netmaker 40s. And to Ursula Netmaker her daughter £3.

To my cousin Margaret Laurence wife of Simon Laurence one piece of gold of 4 ducats

To the wife of my cousin Michael Gonson 40s.   And to her son Benjamin his wife 40s.

Legacies to friends.

To Mr Edward Combes in consideration of his great travels in our affairs one "portague"

To my godson James Wood six angels.

Numerous legacies to friends.

To the poor of St. Dunstan's parish £5, and to the poor of Deptford £5

I ordain my good sisters Ursula Peterson & Thomasine Fenton my Executors and my Uncle Huse to be Overseer of this my will

Signed & sealed by me KATHERINE HAWKINS the xxijth day of June 1591.

On the xxiijth of June Dame Katherine Hawkins declared this to be her last will in the presence of Abraham Fleminge "preaching minister" of Deptford, Richard Chapman & William Currey.

After the delivery of the will Dame Katherine gave by word of mouth various other legacies to several people [here specified at length]

Proved 16th Oct. 1591 at Rochester.   [*Rochester Wills.*]

Will of Sir John Hawkins.

SIR JOHN HAWKINS of London Knt.

I bequeath £50 among the poor householders of Plimouth, £50 to the poor householders of the parish of St. Dunstan's in the East London where I dwell, and £50 to the poor householders of Deptford where I dwell

The sum of £2000 jointure of my wife Lady Margaret to be first satisfied by my executors, also £1000 which I bequeath to her in augmentation of her jointure & in recompense of her dower. I give to her so much of my plate as shall amount to the value of £200 to be chosen at her pleasure, also so much of my household stuff out of my house in Mincing Lane & other my houses in Deptford as shall amount to £300, also all such jewels as heretofore I bestowed upon her.

I give and bequeath to my dread Sovereign Ladie the Queen's most excellent Maiestie that now is (to be delivered by my said wife) as a testimony of my true zeal and Loyalty a Jewell of the value of 200 marks

To my very good Lord William Lord Burghlie High Treasurer of England the sum of £100

To my very good Lord Charles Lord Howard of Effingham High Admiral of England my best diamond worth £100 or so much money in gold

To Sir John Fortescue Knt. Chancellor of the Exchequer £50

To my very good Cousin Sir Francis Drake Knt. my best jewell which is a Cross of "Emorodes"

To Sir Henry Palmer Knt. a diamond worth £20

To John Heale £50, to be one of the Overseers of this my will.

To Benjamin Gunston my brother-in-law my best bason & ewer of silver & gilt, or in lieu of it £50

To Edward Fenton Esq. & to Thomasine his wife my brother & sister in law £50 which she doth owe me.

To Robert Peterson & Ursula his wife my brother & sister in law £20

[A lost list of legacies to servants and friends.]

100 marks each to every of the sons (now living) of my late brother Wm Hawkins Esq by Mary his 2nd wife, also £50 to each of the daughters of my said brother by both his wives

To my servant Roger Langforde an annuity of £20 during such term as he shall be employed going through my accounts with her Majestie which accounts I willed him to follow by the direction of my wife and of my son Richard Hawkins.

Whereas I have assured all my lands, tenements & hereditaments within the Realme of England to Sir Henry Palmer Knt. Thomas Hughs of Gray's Inn Esq. Hughe Vaughan of the parish of St. Giles without Creplegate London, and Richard Reynell of the Middle Temple Esq. I therefore will & devise them to assure unto my wife my house in London wherein I now dwell for the term of her life, the remainder thereof to my son Richard Hawkins & his heirs male; for lack of such issue to my wife the Lady Margaret Hawkins & her heirs for ever. In like manner I do devise that the said Sir Henry Palmer and his "Cobargainzees" & their heirs shall assure to my said son the moiety of the house with the appurtenances & of the garden, stable, cellars, the pallace, the

L

wharf, and forge house upon the said wharf in Plymouth that he now occupieth, to hold to him & his heirs lawfully begotten, the remainder thereof in tail to the heirs of my said brother William Hawkins by Mary his second wife, with remainder in tail to the heirs of my said brother by his first wife; with remainder to my own right heirs for ever.

In like manner Sir Henry Palmer & his Cobargainzees shall assure to the eldest son of my late brother by the said Marie the moiety of the dwelling house with the appurtenances in Plymouth wherein Warwick Heale Esq. & the said Marie now or latelie dwelt, and the moiety of the garden, the tower house to it, the shop, the "bruehouse," backehouse, the sellers upon the wharfe before the house, the moietie of the Crane, And my parte of the gardeine and Orcharde in the Howe lane, And my moitie of the stable: to have & to hold to him & his heirs, with remainder in tail to the next heir male of my said brother by the said Marie, for default of such heir, the remainder in tail to my son Richard Hawkins, with remainder to the next heir of my said brother, with remainder to my own right heirs for ever.

All the rest of my lands in Plymouth I bequeath to my son Richard Hawkins & his heirs males, with divers remainders, upon condition that my son within one year next after my death doe graunt & assure ten pounds rent charge yearly out of it to the Mayor & "Cominaltie" of Plymouth, or the Corporation of Plymouth if they may lawfully take it, if not, to the Overseers of this my last will & to their heirs, to the use & to be paid to the poor for the time being in the Almeshouses there for ever.

I will that my feoffees do go through with the erection of my hospital at Chatham & provision of living for the same according to such directions as I shall give them if during mine own life I do not perform & "parficte" that work.

I give & bequeath unto the children of my late brother William Hawkins a full fifth part of all such adventure and portion of mine as shall return to my use profit & benefit from the Seas, in mine and Sir Frauncis Drackes viage, and the like fifth part of mine adventure & portion which I have at the seas with my said son Richard Hawkins in the ship called the *Daintie*, and in the rest of his shipps. And the like fifth part of all mine adventure which I have at seas with Sir Walter Rawleighe Knt. in his ship called the *Rowbucke* or *Malecontent*, the same fifth parts to be equally divided amongst all the children of my said brother by both his wives and delivered to them within convenient time after the return of every of the said adventures. And I do referr it to the further discretion of my well beloved wife to enlarge the said portions & to bestow more on the said children as God shall bless the returns of the said adventures which I hope she will liberally do if the same adventures by the death of my said son do happen to come wholly to her.

To every child which William Hawkins the eldest son of my said brother shall have living at the time of my decease £100.

I will that my Executors do bestow £50 on a "Tumbe" over me & the said Lady Katherine my first wife (if I do it not myself).

The residue of all my lands, tenements, leases & mortgages I give to my Executors, & all my leases, goods & chattels whatsoever I give to my wife & my son Richard Hawkins "whome I doe jointlie ordaine & make my Executors."

To Judith Hawkins the wife & to Judith Hawkins the daughter of the said Ric. Hawkins the sum of £1500 to be paid to Thomas Heale Esq. of Fleete in Devonshire, to be employed by him to the best benefit of them both.

I constitute Lawrence Hussey Dr. of Civil Law, John Heale Serjeant-at-Law, & Hugh Vaughan to be Overseers of this my will.

In witness whereof I have set my hand & seal the 3ʳᵈ day of March, 37 Eliz. [1594]. Sealed & delivered in the presence of Richard Colthurst, John Wanler, Ed: Fawkner, Walther Wood, Edwa: Lawrance, John Hawkins.

[*Codicil annexed*]. Whereas by my will I have ordained my wife & my son my Executors, forasmuch as the said Richard Hawkins is supposed to be taken & detained prisoner in the Indies, therefore my mind & will is if the said Richard shall not return into this Realme of England within the space of three years to commence & immediately ensue after the xxᵗʰ day of December next coming after the date of my said will, That then and thenceforth the said Dame Margaret shall be my whole & sole "Exequutrix" & that then the executorship & all legacies of any of my goods &c. by the said will given to the said Richard shall cease & be void, saving only then the sum of £3000 I will my said Executrix shall pay for & towards his redemption and ransome "if therewith only, or otherwith together with other supply or means he may be redeemed & not otherwise."

I give to the two eldest sons of the right honorable the Lord Charles Hooward Lord High Admiral of England the debt which his Lordship oweth me being near £700

I bequeath a further sum of £50 each to the poor of Plymouth, St. Dunstans, and Deptford

To Judith & Cleere daughters of my said late brother £200 each over & above the legacies formerly bequeathed to them.

I bequeath to William Cecil son of Sir Robert Cecil £500.

All the legacies before given to my servants to be doubled.

Codicil dated 16ᵗʰ of June 1595, 37 Eliz.

Proved in London 28ᵗʰ day of April 1596 by Lady Margaret Hawkins the relict.

Will of Dame Margaret Hawkins.

23 APRIL 1619 I Dame Margaret Hawkins of London, widow. My body to
be buried in the middle Chancel of St. Dunstans in the East in London near
the monument there erected for my late beloved husband Sir John Hawkins Knt.

Funeral Charges not to exceed £700

My meaning is not to have any mourning given to any of my kindred or
friends unto whom by this my last will there is any legacy bequeathed save only
to my brothers, sisters Executors & such as shall be my household servants at
the time of my decease.

I bequeath the sum of £800 for the purchasing of Lands or Tenements
of the yearly value of £40 towards the maintenance of a learned preaching
divine to keep a free school in Keinton in Herefordshire & of a learned &
discreet Usher under him for the instructing of youths & children in literature
& good education, & the said Schoolmaster shall upon every Wednesday
morning or some other convenient day in the week preach a Sermon in Keinton
parish Church for the instruction of the parishioners. The lands aforesaid not
to be purchased for 4 years, & in the meantime any profit arising therefrom to
be used for the building of a convenient free School near Keinton Church.
£30 out of the said £40 to be paid to the Schoolmaster and £10 to the
Usher After the death of my Executors the nomination of the said Schoolmaster & Usher to be by 5 several voices or the more part of them viz. The
Owner of Hergest Court in Keinton, 2 voices; The Owner of the Manor of
West Hergest als Overhergest in Keinton, 1 voice; The Bishop of the diocese
wherein Keinton is, 1 voice; and the Lord or Owner of Earsley in Co. Hereford
for the time being, 1 voice

To the poor of the parish of Keinton where I was born £50.

To the poor of Amelly in Co. Hereford where I was nursed £10.

To the poor of the parish of Debtford where I have dwelt £10.

To the poor of the parish of Woodford in Essex where I have lived £10.
To the poor of the parish of St. Dunstans in the East in London where I do
dwell & have lived for a long time £50. To the poor of the parish of Chigwell
in Essex where I also dwell £20.

I give my dwelling house in Mincing Lane London to my brother Charles
Vaughan for life, after his decease to his daughters Margaret & Elizabeth & to
their heirs for ever. All the writings of the said house to be delivered by my
Executors to my said brother & his daughters

I devise all my other 6 messuages situate in Mincing Lane; my lease of
the Cranemead & Broomfield in Deptford or elsewhere in Kent & Surrey, and
my lease or term of the messuages, tenements & stables on or near the Tower

Hill Co. Middx unto my Executors to be by them sold for the performance of this my will

If my nephew Stephen Price of Gray's Inn Esq. shall pay to my Exec. within 6 months after my decease the sum of £600 towards the performan of my will that then the said Stephen his heirs & assigns shall have my house called the Dolphin in Tower Street & the Rectory & parsonage of North Shobery in Essex, if he do not pay the said sum, then the premises to go to my Executors to be sold towards the performance of my will, they to pay to my said nephew £300

To Mary Davies widow a yearly rent charge of £10 issuing out of my lands etc. in St. Pancras & St. Andrew's Holborn.

All my household stuff in both my houses (excepting my plate jewells apparel etc, cattle, fuel, coachs & furniture, implements of husbandry etc.) to be sold by my Executors to the uttermost worth by the help of my sister Elizabeth Pemberton my nephew John Vaughan of Hergest and my newphew Charles Price, & the money that shall be made thereof I give as follows :—To my said sister Eliz. Pemberton one 3rd part & to my two nephews aforesaid one 3rd part each.

To my niece Maud Leonard my best pair of Spanish borders enamelled black and trimmed with pearl, the upper border containing nineteen pieces & the nether border containing twenty seven pieces

To my niece the Lady St. John a pair of borders enamelled green, blue & red trimmed with pearle the upper border containing 23 pieces, the nether border 29 pieces

To my niece Mary Wilkinson my diamond ring which my niece Trevor did upon her death bed give me.

To James Vaughan eldest son of my nephew John Vaughan of Hergest all my furniture of my red chamber at Luxborowe

To my honorable Lady the Countess of Leicester wife to the Earle of Leicester my pointed Diamond ring which the Countess of Warwick gave me.

To my honorable Lady Mary Wroth a "guilded boule" of the price of £20.

To my goddaughter Margaret Hawkins daughter of Sir Richard Hawkins Knt. one Carcanett enamilled black & blue containing 11 pieces with 66 pearls having a "Tortis" pendant set with a blue sapphire

To my goddaughter Margaret Ireland 2 Carcanetts of gold, the one weighing "two ounces & half lacke pennie waight" containing 23 pieces, set with pearls with a jewell pendant of 5 Diamonds, the other containing 11 buttons being "Massy Spanish worke" enamelled & set with pearls with a jewell pendant having in it 3 diamonds, 3 rubies and one very fair pearl.

To my loving friend Sr William Killigrewe Knt. a guilded bowl of the price of £20, and to the Lady Killigrow his wife my Persian carpet.

Legacies to friends.

Legacies in money:—To my niece Anne Vaughan wife of John Vaughan £100. To my godson James Vaughan eldest son of above £400

[Mention made of late brother Walter Vaughan.]

To my nephew Thomas Vaughan £100, to my nephew Richard Wood £10. To my niece Ann Wood £100, to my goddaughter Margaret Wood £100, to my godson Baynham Vaughan £200, to my brother Ric. Llellin £10, to my sister Sibell Llellin £100, to my niece Maud Leonard £200, to my niece Ann Scandrett £100; to my niece Margaret Stephens £100. To every of the 6 sons of my sister Sibell £100; to my nephew Francis Eades £10, to my goddaughter Margaret Edes £100; to my sister Ellinor Price £100, and legacies to her children (specially named)

[A long list of legacies to cousins, friends, servants, etc.]

I constitute my worthy friends Sr Michael Stanhope Knt (to whom I leave £100), my kinsman Sir John Vaughan Knt (£100), my nephew Thomas Trevor Esq. (£100) & my servant Anthony Lewes my executors.

Signed & sealed by me MARGARET HAWKINS in the presence of Barnard Hide, Robt. Bateman, Wm Bateman, Robt. Sunderland & Ric. Davis.

Proved in London on the 4th of Jan. 1620, by Anthony Lewes. [*Dale*, 3.]

PHILIP of SPAIN SICILIE HI. KING NAPLES &c &c &c

CHAPTER IV.

The Armada.

"YOUR master would not give himself the airs he does were it not that his dominions are surrounded by a herring-pond," said Charles V. to an English ambassador in the reign of Henry VIII. But the herring-pond did not deter his son Philip II. of Spain from attacking Queen Elizabeth and the English nation, whom he hated. Accordingly, in the thirtieth year of her reign, he sent his " Invincible Armada " to overthrow England, which, contrary to his expectations, experienced a total defeat, with the result of transferring the sovereignty of the seas from Spain to England.

On Queen Elizabeth's accession to the throne, in 1558, England had no colonies; and the Queen observing the great advantages gained by the Spaniards and Portuguese in the discovery of a New World, whence they imported all their wealth, for several years encouraged her subjects in their navigating expeditions to hitherto unknown regions. These explorations greatly excited the jealousy of the Spaniards, and caused an antagonistic feeling between the rival nations, who never missed an opportunity of seizing and plundering each other's merchantmen. Philip determined to solve these difficulties by the conquest of England, which he intended to make a province of Spain.

To retard Philip's preparations, by compelling him to protect his colonies in America, in 1586, Captain Thomas Candish, or Cavendish, carried the terror of the English arms into the South Seas, and distressed the Spanish trade in America, where he was a severe scourge to the Spaniards. By the Queen's command he sailed from Plymouth on the 21st July, 1586, with three ships only—the *Desire*, of 120 tons; the *Content*, of 60 tons; and the *Hugh Gallant*, of 40 tons; 123 men in all. They arrived off the coast of America, named Port Desire after Candish's ship, passed through the Straits of Magellan, and entered the South Sea. Here they navigated along the coasts of Chili, Peru, and New Spain, or Mexico; burnt or sunk nineteen ships; surprised two rich ships at Pisco; then plundered and burnt the town of Payta, where they took great spoil; thence made an attempt on the Island of Puna, where they sunk a large ship and took 100,000 crowns, besides rich furniture and treasure, after which they fought the Spaniards. Continuing to burn and destroy, they came to San Iago, where they took the *Santa Anna*, the "admiral" of all the South Seas, of 700 tons burden, after a resistance of six hours. With her they took also £22,000, and great quantities of rich stuffs, besides other things of value. After setting the Spanish ships on fire, they returned by the Philippine Islands, China, and Cape of Good Hope; discovered the Island of St. Helena, and arrived in England 19th November, 1587, having circumnavigated the globe. Of the three ships the *Desire* alone returned, Candish, for want of hands, having early been obliged to sink his 40-ton bark; while the *Content* was lost after putting ashore the crew of the Spanish admiral's ship, before setting her on fire at Puerto Seguro. Candish then expected the *Content* would follow later, but she was never again heard of.

Meantime news came of the intended Spanish invasion, which had been so long expected, from a Venetian priest, Walsingham's spy at Rome, who bribed a gentleman of the Pope's bedchamber to take the keys out of His Holiness's pocket when asleep, open his cabinet, and send Walsingham a copy of the King of Spain's original letter to the Pope, acquainting him with the true design of his great preparations, and asking his blessing upon it.

On receipt of this letter Walsingham advised the Council to send Sir Francis Drake with a strong squadron, accompanied by a flotilla of large London merchant ships, to Spain, with orders to burn and destroy the Spanish vessels, and to do all the mischief possible to hinder Philip's preparations. Drake accordingly sailed in April, 1587, and on the way learned that the Spaniards had vast quantities of stores at Cadiz. On arriving there, without opposition, he burnt and destroyed 100 of their ships. He then sailed to St. Vincent, where he did considerable damage; and thence to the mouth of the Tagus, where lay the grand Armada, or fleet of men-of-war, under the Marquis of Santa Cruz.

Drake plundered and burnt the merchant ships that he fell in with along the coast, but was unable to provoke the Spanish admiral to give him battle; so leaving him he went in search of the *San Philip*, a rich ship expected from the East Indies, which he took. This prize contained a valuable cargo, with which he returned to England.

HAWKINS, DRAKE, AND CANDISH.

(FROM THE ORIGINAL IN THE POSSESSION OF THE MARQUIS OF LOTHIAN.

Thus the damage done to the Spaniards by Candish and Drake, together with the fact that Walsingham got all the Spanish bills protested at Genoa, that were to supply Philip with money to carry on his preparations, obliged the King of Spain to put off the contemplated invasion of England until the following year.

We now come to the memorable year 1588 (the thirtieth of Queen Elizabeth's reign), which by Regiomontanus, the celebrated astrologer at Konigsberg, was foretold about one hundred years before to be a year of wonder, and by the German astrologers to be the climacterical year of the world. Rumours of war were now daily increasing, and were not, as before, a series of variable reports, but an assured certainty.

The Pope, aided by religious and devout Spaniards, and some English fugitives, had long and diligently exhorted the Spaniards to invade and conquer England, and by the extirpation of heresy to establish the Roman Catholic religion.

The King of Spain thought he might justly claim the crown of England for these reasons : Firstly, upon the slender title of being descended from a daughter of John of Gaunt, fourth son of Edward III. Secondly, upon the conveyance and will of Mary Queen of Scots, who had given up her right to him as the only means of restoring Popery in England, because he agreed with the Church of Rome that a heretic is unworthy and incapable of reigning. Thirdly, because Pope Sextus V. had made over England to Philip, who was authorized at the same time by the Pope's bull to absolve the Queen's subjects from their oath of allegiance. Thus fortified with papal vows and prayers, the King of Spain projected the conquest of England. Of these intrigues and preparations Elizabeth was meanwhile thoroughly informed.

Although Candish, on the western coast of America, and Drake on the coast of Spain, had done King Philip great damage in the preceding year, yet so vast and universal a preparation as the latter was making against England was not easily overthrown. For three years Philip had been employed in preparations, and at length had got together the fleet, called by the arrogant name of the "Invincible" Armada, on which the treasures of the Indian mines had for these three years been spent. In the six squadrons there were sixty-five large ships, the smallest of 700 tons ; seven were over 1000 tons ; and *La Regazona,* an Italian, was of 1300. They were "built high like castles," their upper decks musket-proof, their main timbers "four and five feet thick." Next the galleons were four galleases—gigantic galleys, carrying fifty guns each, 450 soldiers and sailors, and rowed by 300 galley slaves.

M

Besides these there were four large galleys, fifty-six armed merchant vessels (the best in Spain), and twenty caravals, or pinnaces, attached to the larger ships. "Thus the Armada consisted of 129 vessels, seven of them larger than the *Triumph*, and the smallest of the sixty-five galleons of larger tonnage than the finest ship in the English navy, except the five which had last been added to it."

The fleet was manned and armed by 21,855 soldiers, 8766 mariners, 2088 galley slaves chained; it had 3165 pieces of brass and iron ordnance, with great store of ammunition, weapons of war, and instruments of torture, besides 100 monks and Jesuits under Cardinal Allen, an Englishman. Twelve ships were named after the apostles, and the daily expenditure was 32,000 ducats (the value of a ducat being nine shillings and sixpence).

The fleet was commanded by the nobles of Spain. The Marquis of Santa Cruz died while the Armada was being fitted out, and his place as Commander-in-Chief was taken by the Duke of Medina Sidonia, with Martin Recalde, an experienced sea officer and most skilful navigator, next in command. The Duke was merely selected on account of his exalted position, because there were so many volunteers of rank who would not serve under an inferior. Among the other commanders were Pedro de Valdez, General of the squadron of Andalusia, who had commanded the Spanish fleet on the coast of Holland, and knew the English Channel well; Miquel de Oquendo, who commanded the Guipuscoa squadron; Hugo de Monçada, chief in command of the galleases. Diego de Pimentel, and Alonzo de Leyva, commanded the land forces.

This fleet was got together in Portugal, at Naples, and in Sicily, and to terrify their enemies the Spaniards published an account of it in Spanish, Latin, French, and Dutch. The Spanish book soon came into the hands of the Lord Treasurer Burleigh.

For some years, however, this Spanish invasion had been expected, and now that it was on its way Elizabeth did the best she could to meet her foe.

The English navy consisted of only thirty-eight vessels carrying the Queen's flag, for economy being the order even of that day, the naval expenses had been cut down. But in 1573 Elizabeth had "placed at the head of her naval administration the fittest person in her dominions to manage it—Sir John Hawkins*—who with scrupulous fidelity threw his mind and fortune into his charge. When the moment of trial came, Hawkins sent the Queen's ships to sea in such condition—hull, rigging, spars, and running rope—that they had

* To make the narrative complete a few of the details of Sir John's services are here reprinted.

no match in the world either for speed, safety, or endurance."* Three years
before the seamen's pay had been raised by Hawkins from six and eight-
pence a month to ten shillings, but this increase cost the crown nothing, as a
smaller crew, better paid, did superior service. In 1583 five new ships, larger
than any afloat, had been added to the navy; the *Ark Royal* and the *Victory*,
each of 800 tons, the *Bear* and the *Elizabeth Jonas* of 900, and the *Triumph* of
1000. The four last had not been commissioned before 1588; and had been
constructed upon a new principle introduced by Hawkins. The high sterns
and forecastles were lowered, the keels lengthened, and the lines made finer
and sharper. Some found fault with these improvements, and foretold the
usual disasters; so much so that the Queen shrank from experiments, and

SHIP OF ARMADA PERIOD.

they were kept safe at their moorings in the Medway, until they were required
to meet the Armada, when they did more service than any other ships in the
fleet. Hawkins also fitted the vessels with nettings for the repulsion of attack
by boarders.

The chief towns sent as many ships as they were able. Howard had two
ships of his own, and Hawkins four or five. Then there were the volunteers,
who fitted out ships and joined the fleet. But it was on the Queen's ships
that the brunt of the battle would have to fall, to face the most powerful
fleet in existence. Hawkins was directed to put the whole navy, as rapidly
as possible, in condition for sea. On the 21st December, 1587, the Lord High
Admiral of England (at this time Lord Charles Howard of Effingham) received
orders "to take the ships into the Channel to defend the realm against the

* FROUDE.

Spaniards." But in January, 1588, it was announced that the fleet would be required for six weeks only, as the Queen hoped that a peace would be established before that time had elapsed.

Rumour coming from Spain that the Armada was dissolving, Elizabeth dismissed half the crews which had been collected and engaged at such expense. "Never," said Howard, "since England was England was there such a stratagem and mark to deceive us withal as this treaty." "We are wasting money," wrote Hawkins in February, 1588, "wasting strength, dishonouring and discrediting ourselves, by our uncertain dallying."

Lord Howard to Lord Burleigh.

MY VERIE GOOD LORD,—Uppon Tuesdaie beinge in the Downes the winde came to the Easte that we were fain to put over to Blacknes. This daie beinge the laste of this presente being up alongste the coaste towardes Calles I met Sᵣ Henry Palmer whoe had wafted over the Commissioners and afterwardes went to Flushinge. . . . .

I protest before god and as my soul shall answer for it that I think there were never in any place in the world worthier shippes than theise are for so many. And as few as we are if the King of Spain's forces be not hunderethes we will make good sport with them. And I praie your Lordship tell her Maᵗⁱᵉ from me that her money was well geven for the *Arke Rawlye*, for I think her the odd ship in the worlde for all conditions, and truely I think there can no great ship make me change and go out of her. We can see no sail great nor small but how far soever they be off, we fetch them and speak with them. And so I bid your Lordship most heartily farewell. From aboard her Maᵗⁱᵉˢ good ship the *Arke* the laste of Februarie 1587.

Your Lordship's most assured to command,

C. HOWARD.

[Endorsed] Ultimo Feb. 1587. L. Admiral to my L.
To the right honorable my verie good Lord, the Lord Treasurer of Englande.*

A fortnight later the ships were commanded again to sea. Men had to be collected where they could be found, and bounties and allowances were made necessary, which doubled the cost of keeping them in commission. The next difficulty to contend with was the cutting down the expense of the seamen's diet, stopping their meat, and setting them to defend their country on fish, dried peas, and oil. Still hoping for peace, the ships were kept close in harbour by a short supply of rations, served for a month at a time, and no stores; and the ships at Plymouth were often without food for days. Howard

* *Sta. Pa. Dom.* (Eliz.)

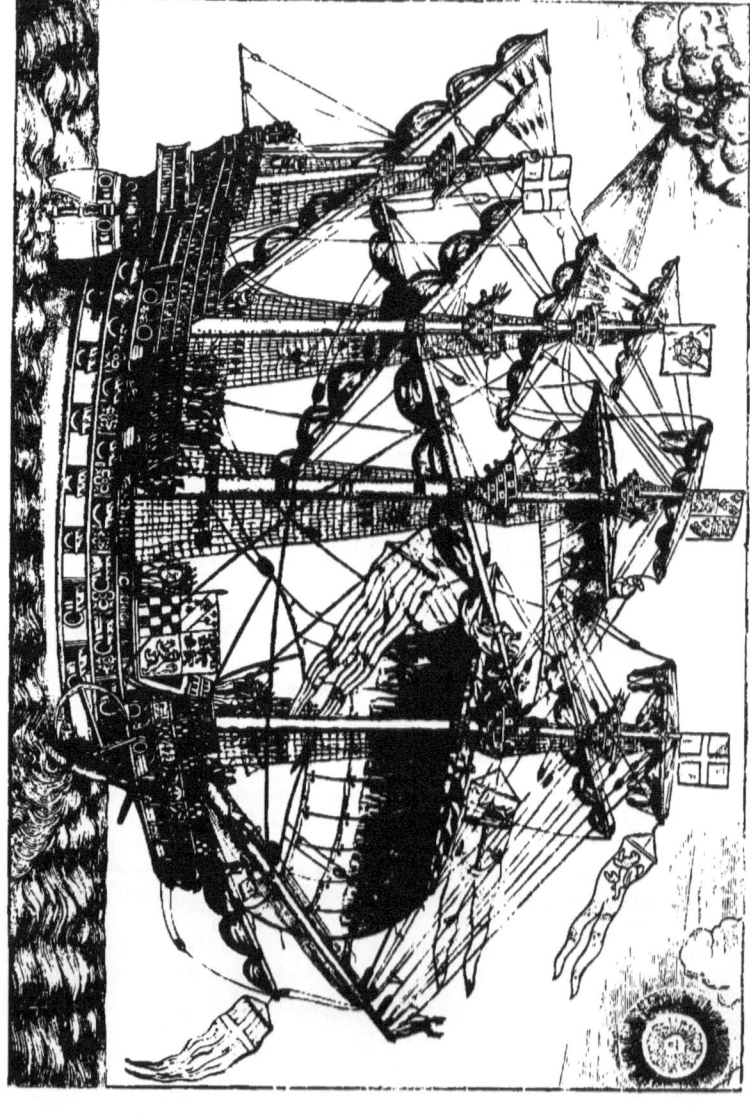

Reduced from the Original Engraving in the British Museum.

"THE ARK ROYAL," FLAGSHIP OF LORD HOWARD OF EFFINGHAM.
BY PERMISSION FROM THE "LEISURE HOUR" FOR JUNE, 1898.

wrote to Burleigh that "such a thing was never heard of since there were ships in England, as no victuals in store." ✓

The four largest ships—the *Triumph, Victory, Elizabeth Jonas,* and the *Bear*—were for weeks left behind for want of hands to man them. ✓ "Keeping Chatham Church," as Howard remarked. Upon further intelligence of the readiness of the Spaniards to put to sea, and that the Armada was really on the point of sailing, the Queen and her Council, however, ordered these ships to be commissioned, and then did the utmost in the short time left to prepare. Supplies were given out to last until the middle of June; and leaving the squadron under Seymour to guard the narrow seas, Howard and Hawkins with the royal fleet departed for Plymouth, where they were joined by Drake in the *Revenge,* a Queen's ship, together with the volunteer squadron of thirty-three sail.

Lord Henry Seymour (second son of the late Protector Somerset), with Sir William Winter, was ordered with his fleet of forty English and Dutch ships, under command of Justin of Nassau, Admiral of Zealand, to lie off the coast of Flanders, to prevent the intended junction of the forces under the Dukes of Parma and Guise, with the Armada. For the Duke, by orders received from Spain, had built ships and many flat-bottomed boats, each of✓ the latter big enough to carry thirty horses, with bridges fitted to them. He hired mariners from the east of Germany; prepared pikes, sharpened and armed with iron hooks on the sides (some may be seen at the present day in the Tower); and had also 20,000 barrels, and an infinite number of wicker baskets and faggots. In the seaports of Flanders lay his army of 103 companies of foot and 4000 horse, making together 30,000 men, and among them 700 English fugitives, under Stanley and the outlawed rebel the Earl of Westmoreland; besides 12,000 men brought by the Duke of Guise to the coast of Normandy, intended for an attack on the West of England, under cover and protection of the Armada.

The English fleet was under the command of Charles Lord Howard of✓ Effingham, Lord High Admiral of England, who, although not an experienced naval officer, having been only once previously at sea, exhibited on trial great courage, resolution, and bravery, with an affability of manner which endeared him to the sailors, and also a provident sense of his inexperience, which rendered him docile to the counsels of those excellent sea officers by whom he had the good fortune to be surrounded. "John Hawkins, one of the ablest and most experienced seamen of the age, was chiefly relied upon for the conduct of the main fleet, in which he acted as Vice-Admiral."

"The commander-in-chief, indeed, Lord Howard of Effingham, though a nobleman of high character, was of no professional experience as a seaman, but his vice-admirals, Hawkins, Drake, and Frobisher, were the most skilful and enterprising sailors in Europe. A.D. 1588."[*]

Howard, it has been observed, was not only in the entire confidence of his Sovereign, but a man of singular ability and honourable zeal, courageous, wary, provident, industrious, and active, and held in great esteem and authority by the seamen of the royal navy, "who by his prudent policy and government of our English navy, in 1588 patiently withstood the instigations of many courageous and noble captains, who would have persuaded him to have laid them aboard; but well he foresaw that the enemy had an army aboard, he none; that they exceeded him in number of shipping, and those greater in bulke, stronger built, and higher moulded, so that they who with such advantage fought from above, might easily distress all opposition below; the slaughter, peradventure, proving more fatal than the victory profitable: by being overthrown, he might have hazarded the kingdom; whereas by the conquest, at most, he could have boasted of nothing but glory and an enemy defeated. But by sufferance, he always advantaged himself of wind and tide; which was the freedom of our country, and security of our navy, with the destruction of theirs, which in the eye of the ignorant, who judge all things by the external appearance, seemed invincible; but truly considered, was much inferior to ours in all things of substance, as the event proved; for we sunk, spoiled, and took of them many, and they diminished of ours but one small pinnace, nor any man of name, save only Capt Cocke, who died with honour amidst his company.[†] The greatest damage that, as I remember," continues Sir Richard Hawkins, "they caused to any of our fleet, was to the *Swallow* of her Majesty, which I had in that action under my charge, with an arrow of fire shot into her beak-head, which we saw not, because of the sail, till it had burned a hole in the nose as big as a man's head; the arrow falling out, and driving alongst by the ship's side, made us doubt of it, which after we discovered."

Next to Howard in command of the Queen's ships was Admiral Sir John Hawkins, a Plymouth man, Treasurer of the Navy, of the Queen's Majesty's Marine Causes, and Comptroller of the Navy, "the rough veteran of many a daring voyage on the African and American seas, and of many a desperate

[*] CHARLES DUKE YONGE, *Hist. Eng.*

[†] *Observations of Sir Richard Hawkins.* Also, RALEGH's *History of the World*, book v. chap. i. sec. vi.

Charles Howard, Earl of Nottingham.

battle "*—"the most distinguished sea officer of Queen Bess."† Hawkins hoisted his flag on board the *Victory*. He was the senior officer in the fleet, and was at the beginning of the fight with Howard, who, as he had not much sea service, chiefly relied on his judgment and experience. Afterwards, when the fleet was divided into squadrons, Hawkins had the command of one of them. No English sailor bore so famous a name as Hawkins, under whom many commanders in the fleet had served as boys. He was the kinsman and patron of Drake, whom he first took to sea with him on his third voyage, in 1567. Hawkins was then an admiral, and about twelve years older than Drake, but he was twenty-five years his senior in the Queen's service.‡ Young Drake had much to thank his patron for, as he gained great advantages under so able an instructor, the terror of the Spaniards and Portuguese—"Achines de Plimua," as the Spaniards called him, and the Portuguese "Johannes de Canes."

"It is not necessary to repeat here what has been so often told, the active part taken by Hawkins on that memorable occasion. He was appointed Vice-Admiral, commanded one of the four divisions, and was distinguished by the honour of Knighthood.§ His great troubles, as treasurer, only began after the dispersion of that fleet."‖

There was no one to whom "England in her hour of peril owed more, than to her Plymouth hero Sir John Hawkins."¶ He alone had the whole control, responsibility, and anxiety of the outfit of every ship—not only being at the head of the dockyards, but employed as the collector of the ships' companies. Right well was that work done. "The royal fleet was Hawkins's work, and in preparing it he stood at the head of the naval power of the kingdom. He had also as large a share in the danger and honour of the fight as any man in the fleet."

On the 23rd May Howard ordered the whole fleet of near ninety sail to be victualled and made ready to put to sea with all expedition. He then cruised between Ushant and Scilly, to wait the coming of the enemy.

On shore preparations were also made. The militia in each county was armed; the seaports fortified, and covered with 20,000 landsmen; and orders were given, in case of the enemy landing, to lay the country waste round about, so that they might find no food.

* CREASY, *Decisive Battles.*　　　　　† BARROW.

‡ *Vide* page 25, where Hawkins is Admiral of a Royal Fleet in 1567. Drake's first command was in the same year, when he sailed with Hawkins as a volunteer, as Captain of the *Judith*, a bark of 50 tons.

§ *Harl. MSS.* Knights dubbed in the tyme of Queen Elizabeth, John Hawkins 1588.

‖ BARROW's *Naval Worthies.*　　　　　¶ WORTH.

There was a second army of 22,000 foot and 1000 horse, under command of the Earl of Leicester, at Tilbury, where the Queen reviewed her troops, and animated the soldiers by a speech.

The third army, of 34,000 foot and 2000 horse, under command of Lord Hudson, was destined to guard the Queen's person.

These preparations occupied the people, and freed them from the apprehensions of the danger they were in. They grumbled at no expense, and all were pleased with the thoughts of contributing, as best they were able, towards the defence of their country, their religion, their liberties, and their Queen.

These great preparations on both sides for war did not prevent overtures for a peace from the Duke of Parma—whether it was only to divert and deceive Elizabeth, so that she and her country might be the more easily surprised, or that Parma was persuaded that he would be unsuccessful in the Netherlands till he could deprive them of the powerful help of England. Parma, at any rate, had obtained power from the King of Spain to treat, while his master prepared with his whole strength for the invasion of England.

But Elizabeth was too watchful and jealous of her enemies to be so easily deceived by pretensions of amity; and though she thought it politic not absolutely to reject his offers, and informed the Duke that she was well-disposed to an accommodation, yet she determined to arm herself at all events, and to discuss peace sword in hand—managing the negociations so dexterously, that they were spun out in fruitless debates till she was thoroughly prepared to receive the enemy, and Philip was obliged to pull off the mask, and confess his insincerity, when his great fleet was ready for sea.

In February, 1588, the Earl of Derby, William Brook, Lord Cobham, James Crofts, Valentine Dale, and James Rogers had been sent into Flanders as commissioners to treat, but these conferences broke off abruptly in March.

Before the Armada left the Tagus the Duke of Medina Sidonia, commander-in-chief, issued his orders, in the first article of which there is a clear declaration "that before all things it was to be understood by all the officers and others, from the highest to the lowest, that the principal foundation and cause moving the King's Majesty to make and continue this journey or expedition had been and was to serve God, and to deliver a great many good people, oppressed and kept in subjection to sectaries and heretics, from eternal sorrow, and to restore them to the unity of His Church." After such a declaration, what could be expected from these Spanish missionaries, whose arguments were the ensigns of death and destruction? The bigoted adventurers, thus spirited with a notion of doing God service, as well as of enriching

SIR MARTIN FROBISHER.

themselves by the spoil of the English nation, had already conquered in their vain imagination. And so, assured of a recompense whether they lived or died in so religious and advantageous a cause, they weighed and proceeded from the Tagus on the 18th May, and bent their course first for the Groyne.

Before they had been long at sea they were scattered by a violent storm off Cape Finisterre. Two of the galleys were run into a port of France by the stratagem of David Gwynn, an English slave, assisted by some of the Moorish slaves; and fourteen of their ships were drifted on to the Chops of the Channel, between Ushant and Scilly. Then, before they were met by the English fleet, a northerly wind conveyed them back to the Groyne (Corunna), where and in the neighbouring ports they and the rest of the fleet reassembled after the storm, in a disabled condition, to take in their soldiers and warlike provisions.

This mishap proved disastrous to the Spaniards, but was nearly attended with fatal consequences to the English, by creating a report all over Europe, and a belief in the English Council, that the whole Spanish fleet had been destroyed. Walsingham, by order from the Ministry, in the Queen's name ordered four of the best ships to be sent back into port, supposing that the Spaniards could not repair their damages and proceed till the next year. But the Lord High Admiral not being so credulous, and still fearing the worst, would not agree, and retained the vessels; alleging how dangerous it was to place themselves off guard in a matter of such importance, when they had no better authority than hearsay, adding that he would rather keep the ships out at his own charge than expose the nation to so great a hazard.

On the 7th of June there was food for eighteen days only in the English fleet, and Devon could not furnish supplies: if the Spaniards had come at the end of that time the English must have gone into action starving.

On the 23rd of June the victuallers arrived at Plymouth, ten days late, bringing provisions for one month only, with orders that no more would be sent. This supply was distributed to last for six weeks. Four rations were served out to every six men; they did not complain, but many died from the effects of the poisonous beer served out. Howard ordered arrowroot and wine for the sick, for which he was afterwards called to account, when he paid the cost out of his own pocket.

On the 3rd of July Howard wrote to the Queen: "For the love of Jesus Christ, madam, awake and see the villainous treasons round about you, against your Majesty and the realm." *

* *Sta. Pa. Dom.* (Eliz.)

N

Lord Howard to Sir F. Walsingham.

I HAVE divided myself into three parts and yet we lie within sight of another
so as if any of us do discover the Spanish Fleet we give notice thereof
presently, the one to the other, and thereupon repair and assemble together.
I myself do lie in the middle of the Channel with the largest force. Sir
Francis Drake has 20 ships and 4 or 5 pinnaces which lie towards Ushant and
Mʳ Hawkins with as many more lies out towards Scilly. This are we fain to
do, else with this wind, they might pass by and we never the wiser. . . . .
    From on board Her Majestys good ship *Arke* the 6ᵗʰ of July 1588.

                        Your assured loving friend
                                C. HOWARD
    To the Right Honourable Sir Francis Walsingham Kᵗ Principal Secty
to Her Majesty.

    Howard also dispatched light vessels to spy along the coast of England,
France, and Spain; and being assured that no enemy was to be found at sea,
resolved, by advice of his council, to take advantage of the next northerly
wind, in order either to complete the destruction of the enemy's fleet, should
it be already partially disabled, or otherwise to obtain a certain account of its
condition. This Howard executed on the 8th of July; upon the 10th he had
arrived within forty leagues of the Spanish coast, where, getting good intelligence that the enemy's fleet had not sustained the damage reported in England,
and the wind shifting to the south, he, in compliance with his chief commission
to guard the English coasts, immediately returned to the Channel, lest the
same wind should give the enemy the advantage of getting there before him,
and arrived at Plymouth with his whole fleet on the 12th of July. That
the Lord High Admiral's judgment was wise appears from the arrival of
the Spanish Armada off the Lizard on the 19th of the month, having been
hastened to sea by the intelligence of an English fisherman, who, being taken
and carried into the Groyne, said that the English, upon a report that the
Spaniards were disabled from pursuing their design that year, had called home
their fleet, and discharged the sailors that manned it; which determined them
to deviate from their instructions, and to attempt, as a thing most feasible,
to surprise, burn, or destroy all our ships in harbour unawares.

    While the English fleet were at Plymouth waiting for the Armada, the
weather became very stormy, and a severe south-westerly gale set in. Plymouth
roadstead, undefended by a breakwater, was a dangerous anchorage, and to
put to sea more dangerous still. Howard with the great ships took his chance,
and lay rolling in the Sound, "dancing lustily as the gallantest dancer at Court;"

ARMADA FIRST SIGHTED OFF THE LIZARD

the smaller ships went for shelter into Cattewater. The wind and rain continued, and the "oldest fisherman could not remember such a summer season." "One satisfaction only Lord Howard found, and that a good one. 'Hawkins, at least, had done his share of the work right excellently. The English ships were 'in royal and perfect state, feeling the seas no more than if they had been riding at Chatham.' Through the whole fleet not a spar was sprung, not a rope parted, timbers and cordage remained staunch and sound within and without. The *Triumph* and her four large consorts were grounded again and again 'to tallow and to wash.' They suffered nothing from the strain, and they were dry to the keel as Arabian sand."

Lord Howard to Sir F. Walsingham.

SIR,—I have heard that there is in London some hard speeches against M' Hawkins because the *Hope* came in to mend a leak which she had. Sir I think there were never so many of the Princes ships so long abroad and in such seas with such weather as these have had with so few leaks, and the greatest fault of the *Hope* came with ill grounding before our coming hither, and yet it is nothing to be spoken of, it was such a leak that I would have gone with it to Venice, but may they not be greatly ashamed, that sundry times have so disabled her Majestys ships which are the only ships in the world. . . .

From Plymouth the 17th day of July 1588

Your very loving and assured friend
C. HOWARD.

To the Right Honourable &c. Sir Francis Walsingham K' Principal Secty to Her Majesty.*

On the 12th July the Armada, all repairs completed, had again assembled, and with a fair wind set sail from the Bay of Ferrol; but before it had proceeded far, it was overtaken by another storm, which so scattered the great Spanish fleet, that it could hardly collect again until it came within sight of England, on the 19th. This same day Captain Fleming, in his little pinnace, quickly sailed into Plymouth and informed the Admiral that the Armada had been sighted off the Lizard.

At this moment most of the commanders and officers were ashore, tradition avers, but with no definite authority, playing at bowls on the Hoe. There was an instant bustle, and a calling for the ships' companies; although it is said that Drake insisted that the match should be played out, "as there was plenty of time both to finish the game and beat the Spaniards after."

* *Sta. Pa. Dom.* (Eliz.)

Howard was somewhat chagrined by the certain intelligence of the arrival of the enemy's fleet, because the wind being at south, and sometimes shifting to south-west, almost blocked the English fleet up in the Sound and Cattewater. But "the Lord High Admiral, with great difficulty, diligence, industry, and goodwill, encouraged the seamen to labour, not only by his presence, but by setting his hand to their work among them; got most of his ships warped out into the open by next morning early, the 20th;" and there waited the approach of the enemy, whose fleet the English soon discovered to the west as far as Fowey, in the form of a half moon, the horns of which stretched out about seven or eight miles asunder, standing slowly under full sail up the Channel. The ships for size appeared like so many floating castles, under which the ocean seemed to groan.

Howard, considering it would be more advantageous to gain the wind of them, and so attack them in the rear, let them pass by.

That morning the Spaniards had captured a fishing-boat, from which they learnt that the English fleet was at Plymouth, and Medina Sidonia called a council of war, to consider whether they should go in, and fall upon it while at anchor. Philip's orders, however, were peremptory, that they should turn neither right nor left, but make straight for Margate Roads, and effect a junction with Parma. Had Medina's decision been otherwise, he would not, however, have seized the English ships; for before the Spaniards sighted the Lizard they had themselves been seen, and on the night of the 19th the beacons along the coast had told England that the Armada had come. Messengers galloped all over the country, and everywhere people armed and flocked to their posts.

It is said (but without foundation, for he had no chance of admiring it) that, when the Armada sailed past Plymouth harbour, the Duke of Medina Sidonia was so taken with the beauty of Mount Edgcumbe, that he declared that when England was conquered he intended to take it as his share of the spoil.

Next morning, Sunday, the 21st July, the English ships, about one hundred in all, being to windward of the Spaniards, two leagues west of the Eddystone, the Lord Admiral ordered his pinnace, the *Defiance*,* to advance, and declare war against the Spaniards by the discharge of all her guns. This he immediately seconded himself in the *Ark Royal*, attacking the Spanish ship commanded by De Leyva, which, on account of her bulk and station, he

---

* Another account says the *Disdain*, Captain Jonas Bradbury.

FIRST ENGAGEMENT OFF PLYMOUTH.

mistook for the Admiral, engaging her furiously, till she was rescued by several of her consorts. At the same time Hawkins, Drake, and Frobisher engaged the enemy's sternmost ships under Recalde, and threw them into such confusion as obliged Medina Sidonia to recall his scattered vessels, and to crowd all sail to continue on his course in order to join Parma, whom he expected off Calais, not knowing that he was blockaded in his ports by the English fleet under Seymour, and by the Dutch under Justin of Nassau. Nor could he do otherwise, because the wind stood fair for the English, whose light, active ships attacked, retired, and again attacked the Spaniards, on every side with incredible celerity. After two hours' running fight, Howard, however, thought good to retire, as forty of his ships had not yet come out of the haven.

On the same day a fast boat was sent on with letters to Lord Henry Seymour, reporting progress so far, and bidding him prepare in the Downs. Also an express was sent to London begging for an instant supply of ammunition.

The following night the *Santa Catalina*, a Spanish ship, being very much battered in this conflict, was received into the midst of the fleet to be repaired, and a huge Calabrian ship of Oquendo's, in which was the Treasurer to the Fleet, was set on fire with gunpowder by her Flemish gunner, in revenge for insults. The deck was blown off, and 200 seamen and soldiers were sent into the air; but the ship being strongly built, survived the shock. The fire was quenched by other ships sent for the purpose—amongst them the *Capitana*, a great galleon of 1200 tons, commanded by Pedro de Valdez, which, falling foul of the *Santa Catalina*, carried away her foremast. The night being dark and stormy, she could not keep station with the Spanish fleet; so she was forsaken, and captured by the Lord High Admiral. In this galleon were 450 men and 55,000 ducats in gold, part of which Howard took to pay the seamen their wages. Howard did not delay his pursuit of the Armada to secure his prize. De Valdez was taken prisoner. He was a great loss to the Spaniards, as he was the only officer of high rank in their fleet who was well acquainted with the Channel. The capture of this great ship was the cause of some dispute. First, Howard was charged with peculation, because, in need of money, he took gold for the men. Secondly, Drake, who took possession of the *Capitana*, conveyed her to Dartmouth; and Frobisher said, " He [Drake] thinketh to cozen us out of our share of the 15,000 ducats; but we will have our share, or I will make him spend the best blood in his body, for he hath done enough of those cozening tricks."

What Frobisher and others thought of this affair is set forth in the following report, still among the State Papers:*

A NOTE of certaine speeches spoken by Sir Martyn Frobysher at Harwiche in the presence of dyvers persons as followeth

> The Lord Sheffilde
> Sir John Hawkins with
> others whose names I
> cannot recite.

The xth daye of August *1588* I arryved at Harwich and delyvered the letter sent by the Lord Admiral unto the Lord Shefyld whome I found in his bed in the howse of Mr. Kynge.

Firste after I had delivered my Lords letter the Lord Sheffilde bade me departe and so I did according to his commandment. Then immediatlye he sent for me again at which tyme of my retorne I found there Sr John Hawkins Sr Martyn Frobysher with dyvers others whoe demanded of me in what safetye the Shipps were in and whether they were all at Margate or not.

Then Sr Martin Frobysher began some speaches as concernynge the service done in this action who uttered these speaches followinge, saying Sr Francis Drake reporteth that no man hath done any good service but he, but he shall well understand that others hath done as good service as he and better to. He came bragging up at the first indeed and gave them his prowe and his broadsyde and then kept his Lowfe and was glad that he was gone again lyke a cowardly knave or traytor I rest doubtfull but the one I will swear.

Further saith he he hath done good service indeed for he took *Don Pedro* for after he had seen her in the evening that she had spent her masts then like a coward he kept by her all night because he would have the spoil he thinketh to cossen us of our shares of xv thowsande duckattes but we will have our shares or I will make him spend the best blood in hys bellye for he hath had enough of those cossenyng cheates alreadye.

He hath saith he used certain speeches of me which I will make him eat again or I will make him spend the best blood in his bellye.

Further more he said he reporteth that no man hath done so good service as he but he lyeth in his teeth for there are others that hath done as good as he and better to.

Then he demanded of me if we did not see *Don Pedro* over night or no unto the which I answered no, then he told me that I lied for she was seen to all the fleet unto the which I answered I would lay my head that not any one man in the ship did see her until it was morning that we were within 2 or 3 Cables length of her where unto he answered I marye saith he you were within 2 or 3 cables length for you were no further off all night, but lay a hull by her where unto I answered no, for we bare a good sail all night off and on.

* *Sta. Pa. Dom.* (Eliz.) Vol. 214, No. 63.

THE CHASE UP CHANNEL

Then he asked me to what end we stood off from the fleet all night whom I answered that we had escryed three or four hulkes and to that end we wrought so not knowing what they were. Then said he Sir Francis was appointed to bear a light all that night, which light we looked for but there was no light to be seen, and in the morning when we should have dealt with them there was not above five or six near unto the Admiral, by reason we saw not his light.

After this and many more speech which I am not able to remember the Lord Sheffeilde demanded of me what I was unto the which I answered, I had been in the Action with Sir Francis, in the *Revenge* this seven or eight months, then he demanded of me what art thou a soldier, no & like your Honour I answered, I am a mariner, then said he I have no more to say unto you, you may depart.

By me MATHEW STARKE.

All this written on the other side I do confess to be true as it was spoken by Sir Martyn Frobisher and doe acknowledge it in the presence of these parties whose names are here under written.

Captain Platt, Captain Vaughan, Mr. Gray Master of the *Arke*, John Gray M^r of the *Revendge*, Captain Spindloe.

Moreover he said that Sir Francis was the cause of all these troubles, and in this Action he showed him self the most Cowarde.

By me MATHEW STARKE.

Medina Sidonia, seeing that Oquendo's ship was much damaged by the fire, and unfit for service, sent boats to save the unhurt men; but the wounded they had no means of removing, so they were left in the ship, which the Spaniards set adrift. She was picked up early next morning by the English. Sir John Hawkins and Lord Thomas Howard went in a cock-boat of the *Victory*, and boarded her. They found everything in a miserable state from the effects of the explosion; and the smell of the burnt dead bodies was over-powering. Perceiving that there was no force on board, they returned to the Admiral, who ordered a small bark to convey the wreck to Weymouth.

During the night of the 21st the enemy lay about fourteen miles off the Start, and next morning they were as far ahead and to leeward as the Berry, pursued by the Lord High Admiral with only the *Bear* and the *Mary Rose*, who kept within culverin shot all through the night; whilst his fleet was so far astern, that in the morning the nearest could scarce be seen half-mast high, and very many were out of sight. This mishap was occasioned by Sir Francis Drake's neglect to show lights for their direction, as he had been ordered the day before in a council of war, held to settle the best method of pursuing, distressing, and fighting the enemy. Drake fell into this mistake by giving chase to five German merchant ships, which he had mistaken for the Spaniards. Thus the whole fleet was obliged to lay-to all that night, having no signals for their guidance; neither could he nor the rest of the English ships come near the Lord High Admiral until the following evening, 22nd July.

"The principall Galleon of Siuill (wherein Don Pedro de Valdez, and other noble men were embarqued) falling foule of another ship, had her foremast broken, and by that meanes was not able to keepe way with the Spanish Fleete, neither would the said Fleete stay to succour it, but left the distressed Galeon behinde. The Lord Admirall of England, when hee saw this ship of Valdez, and thought she had beene voide of marriners, and souldiers, taking with him as many ships as he could, passed by it, that hee might not loose sight of the Spanish Fleete that night. For Sir Francis Drake (who was notwithstanding appointed to beare out his Lanterne that night) was giving of chase unto five great Hulkes which had separated themselves from the Spanish Fleete: but finding them to be Easterlings, hee dismissed them. The Lord Admirall all that night following the Spanish Lanterne instead of the English, found himself in the morning to be in the middle of his enemies Fleete, but when he perceived it, he clevly conuered himself out of that great danger."*

The Duke of Medina Sidonia thus finding himself unmolested, used this advantage to spend the next day in the formation and ordering of his fleet. He commanded De Leyva to bring the first and last squadrons together, assigning each ship her station in battle, as agreed on in Spain; and dispatched Ensign Glich as messenger to hurry the movements of Parma, and to inform him of the near approach of the Armada.

The night of the 22nd July was very calm, and the enemy's four galleases, separating from the main body, gave suspicion of a design on some of the smaller ships, which were still astern of the English fleet; but their courage failing they did nothing. However, on the 23rd July, off Portland, by daybreak the Spaniards tacked with the wind at north or north-east, and bore down upon the English, who also tacked and stood to the west or north-west. After several attempts to gain the weather-gage, the Spaniards at length came to another engagement, which resulted with some disorder and variety of success. In one place the English with undaunted courage rescued some ships of London, which were surrounded by the Spaniards, who with no less bravery rescued their Admiral Recalde from the hands of the English.

* PURCHAS, also CAMDEN.

ENGAGEMENT OFF THE ISLE OF WIGHT.

The guns on each side rattled pretty smartly; but the round shot from the high Spanish ships, heeled over by the breeze, passed over the heads of the English without doing much harm. Only Captain William Cocke, in a small bark of his own, was killed, fighting bravely in the midst of the enemy. "Being a cock of the Game indeed, *unus homo nobis percundo restituit rem.*"* Besides, our ships being so much smaller and easier to handle, and also better sailed, attacked and retreated, delivered their broadsides, and sheered off just as they pleased; while the heavier Spanish ships, as slow as their masters, lay like so many butts for the English, at which they could not well miss their aim. This determined the Lord High Admiral not to grapple with or to board ships which were so superior to his in bulk, number, and hands; the Spaniards having an army on board, which the English had not; but rather to advance within musket-shot and batter the hulks of those monstrous galleons. The fight on the 23rd was continued from morning till night with great bravery, Howard being always in the hottest of the engagement, during which he took a great Venetian ship and several smaller ones. The thundering of the ordnance, it is said, was so great that the volleys of small shot, though incredible in number, were hardly seen or noticed.

On the 24th neither side seemed disposed to renew the struggle. The Spaniards wanted to gain time, in order to be joined by Parma. The English were deficient in powder and ball, as Sir Walter Ralegh afterwards observed in his Essay—"Many of our great guns stood but as cyphers and scarecrows." Howard sent some ships to the shore to bring a supply of ammunition. No risk might be ventured, and the English lay now about six miles from the Armada, waiting till their magazines were refilled. Medina Sidonia, supposing them to be afraid, sent De Monçada with the galleases to engage them, and there was some skirmishing between the galleases and our ships, without any advantage to either side.

Howard, on receiving a fresh supply of powder and ball, divided his fleet into four squadrons, under himself, Hawkins, Drake, and Frobisher, and appointed pinnaces to attack the enemy in the dead of night on every side, which might have proved fatal to the Spaniards, but that, a calm following, his plan of attack could not be carried out.

On the night of the 24th Sir George Carey, who had run out from behind the Isle of Wight in a pinnace to see what was going on, found himself, at five in the morning, "in the midst of round shot, flying as thick as musket-balls in a skirmish on land."

* FULLER's *Worthies.*

O

This same calm proved the cause of the sharpest engagement on that day, July 25th, in sight of the Isle of Wight, for it prevented the *Santa Anna*, a great Portuguese galleon, from keeping up with the rest of the Armada. Sir John Hawkins contrived to lay the *Victory* alongside the *Santa Anna*, which he engaged in a single combat, and a smart engagement ensued, during which the rival fleets looked on—the Spaniards sure of their comrades' victory; for had not the storms and the difficulty of navigating the strange waters of the Channel alone prevented their conquering so weak a foe—the English proudly watching the daring of their champion. After a severe fight the English sailors boarded the Portuguese, and her brave captain yielded his sword to Hawkins. Down came the flag of Spain, and the British flag was hoisted in its place amidst a shout of triumph. The Spanish admiral seeing that Hawkins was victorious, ordered three of his largest galleases, under command of De Leyva and Diego Telles Enriques, to fall upon the *Victory*, and they were immediately taken to the spot, and poured in a broadside on the apparently-doomed Englishman. Then the Lord High Admiral in the *Ark Royal* came to the rescue of his brave officer, Hawkins, with Lord Thomas Howard in the *Golden Lion*, being towed to the galleases with their long-boats, and giving the Spaniards a warm reception.

After a most unequal fight, the Spanish ships being so much larger, and their men far outnumbering the English, they eventually drove off the galleases, and the Portuguese galleon was thus lost to Spain. One of the galleases had her lantern shot off, another lost her beak-head, and the third was terribly battered.

In the meantime Sir Martin Frobisher in the *Triumph*, to the north of the Spanish Fleet, was so far to leeward that, becoming apprehensive some of the enemy might weather her, she towed off with the help of several boats, and so recovered the wind. The *Bear* (Lord Edmund Sheffield) and *Elizabeth Jonas* (Sir Robert Southwell) perceiving her in distress, bore down to her rescue, and by their boldness put themselves in like peril, but made their party good till they had recovered the wind. With this action the battle of the 25th July, which was the sharpest of the series of engagements against the "Invincible" Armada, ended.

The next day the Lord High Admiral, in consideration of their bravery, valour, and fortitude, conferred the honour of knighthood (then prized so highly because so jealously bestowed) upon Admiral John Hawkins, on board his own ship the *Victory*, Admiral Martin Frobisher of the *Triumph*, Lord Thomas Howard of the *Golden Lion*, Lord Sheffield (the Lord High Admiral's

CAPTURE OF THE "SANTA ANNA" BY SIR JOHN HAWKINS.

nephew) of the *Bear*, and the commanders of the *Mary Rose* and the *Nonpariel.**

It is a remarkable fact that these were almost the only officers who received the honour of knighthood during the many engagements against the Armada. Even lords were knighted in those days, it being considered a mark of the greatest distinction, as while a man might be born in the peerage, his knight-hood could only come of the highest personal merit.

No decisive engagement followed this glorious fight; for it was determined at a council of war, and Howard with his usual prudence waited—as the English were short of powder and ball—to put off a general engagement until the Armada had reached the straits of Dover.

The Spanish Admiral, however, sent another messenger to hasten the junction with Parma, and to ask him to send some great shot for the use of the Armada, which continued the course up Channel, with the wind at south-west by south, closely pursued by the English.

This so animated the people on shore that many of the nobility and gentry hired ships, and in great numbers sailed to join the Lord High Admiral—as a whole country side on shore falls in at a fox hunt (or as Wotton described it, it was like "a morris dance upon the waters")—to share in the honour of the certain destruction of the "Invincible" foe. Amongst them were the Earls of Oxford, Northumberland, and Cumberland, Sir Thomas and Sir Robert Cecil, Sir Henry Brooke, Sir Charles Blunt, Sir Walter Ralegh, Sir William Hatton, Sir Robert Cary, Sir Ambrose Willoughby, Sir Thomas Gerrard, Sir Arthur Gorges, with other men of note; and this squadron proved of considerable service.

On the 27th July the Spanish fleet, lest they should be forced by the current into the Northern Ocean, anchored before Calais; and "that same night the few Flemish pilots slipped overboard in the darkness, stole the cock-boats, set their shirts for sails, and made for Flushing, leaving the Duke of Medina Sidonia dependent on the imperfect knowledge of the Spanish ship-masters, and their still more imperfect charts."

On the 28th Lord Henry Seymour and Sir William Winter joined the English fleet with their squadron, and forty London privateers were reported to be in the Thames; but ships and men were useless without food. Seymour "was victualled but for one day's full meat." Howard, with great economy, but for five scanty dinners and one breakfast. Provisions and powder had not arrived. "Burleigh tried to borrow money in the city, but with the appearance

* HAKLUYT.

of the Spaniards his credit there had sunk, and the prudent merchants had drawn their purse strings till the cloud had dispersed."

The English fleet anchored as near the Armada as convenient, being now increased to 140 sail of stout ships and good sailors; though the main stress of the several engagements was borne by no more than fifteen or sixteen ships, upon whom fell the chief weight and burden of the war. This situation showed that the Spanish expedition had come to its crisis; the Spaniards, convinced of danger, again sent to the Duke of Parma, with an urgent request to send forty fly-boats to their assistance, and to speedily forward his army. These messengers got ashore, but judged rightly that it was not in the Duke's power to join them with his army while Nassau blocked the harbours (and prevented Parma's fleet sailing).

On this day, while both fleets were then riding at anchor, Queen Elizabeth ordered the Lord High Admiral to single out eight ships (two of which belonged to Sir Richard Hawkins), and to cover them with pitch, lining them well with brimstone, and combustible matter, and also loading their cannon with destructive missiles, and to send them before the wind with a fair tide, about midnight, under the command of Captains Young and Prowse, into the midst of the Armada. This order was carried out, and the fire-ships arriving at safe distance, they lit the trains, and retired. The approach and great blaze of these ships on fire was no sooner discovered, than it threw the whole Armada into the utmost consternation. Many of the Spaniards had been at the siege of Antwerp, and seen the destructive machines used there; so, suspecting that these vessels were full of suchlike engines, in a panic they cut their cables, and put to sea in the greatest haste and confusion. Spanish authorities themselves admit that their Admiral, upon the approach of the fire-ships, gave the signal for weighing anchor, to avoid that danger; but add that he also ordered each ship, after the danger was over, to take up her former station. The Spanish Admiral, in the *San Martin*, returned, and fired a signal-gun for the rest to do the same, to which little attention was paid. Many tried to make their rendezvous off Gravelines, and some were so dispersed to sea, or among the shoals on the Flemish coast, that they could not even hear the signal. Wherever the English could sight them, they pursued and plied them so warmly with shot, that some were sunk, others ran ashore, and all were much damaged.

One of the galleases, having lost her rudder, was cast upon the sands before Calais, and was picked up next day, the 29th, by Sir Amias Preston, Sir Thomas Gerrard, and Harvey, with 100 men, in a long-boat—but not

ATTACK OF THE FIRESHIPS OFF CALAIS.

without a sharp and doubtful dispute, in which De Monçada, her captain, being struck with two musket-balls at the same moment, which pierced both his eyes, fell dead. Sir Amias, having overpowered the crew, either drove them overboard, or put them to the sword, releasing 300 galley-slaves, and taking 50,000 gold ducats. This ship was called the "Admiral," or chief galleas, and was claimed by, and left as a wreck to, the Governor of Calais.

While this was going on, Sir Francis Drake in the *Revenge*, accompanied by Captain Thomas Fenner in the *Nonparcil*, with the rest of that squadron, set upon the Spanish fleet, giving them a hot charge.

Then Sir John Hawkins in the *Victory*, with Captain Edward Fenton in the *Mary Rose*, Captain George Beeston in the *Dreadnought*, and Captain Richard Hawkins in the *Swallow*, and the rest of that squadron, put themselves forward, and broke through the midst of the Spanish fleet, where there began a vehement conflict continuing all the morning, and wherein every captain did very honourable service—Edward Fenton, Richard Hawkins, George Ryman, and Robert Crosse signally distinguishing themselves.

The Spanish ships that kept at sea, early next morning (31st July), retreated through the Straits of Dover; but the wind springing up with hard gales at north-west, forced them towards the coast of Zealand (the *San Philip* and the *San Matthew* had been taken at Flushing). The English, knowing that if this wind continued it would distribute the Spanish ships amongst the sands and shallows of that coast, discontinued the chase.

Sir John Hawkins, writing from on board the *Victory* on this day, says, "Our ships, God be thanked, have received little hurt;" and complains that "the men have been long unpaid, and need relief."[*]

But to return to the Armada. The wind had changed to the south-west-by-west, and this (by hauling their wind) carried them away from the treacherous shoals; but still the Spaniards were in the greatest distress. Without pilots; their best officers gone; De Valdez and Toledo prisoners; Pimentel left on the coast of Flanders; Monçada shot; while Diego Florez, the Castilian Admiral, had lost heart. The Duke of Medina Sidonia now asked Oquendo, "What are we to do? We are lost! What are we to do?" "Let Diego Florez talk of being lost," replied Oquendo. "Let your Excellency bid me order up the cartridges."

That evening the Dons held a council of war, to consider what was to be done with the remains of the Armada; and it was resolved that, as they were in want of necessaries, especially of cannon-ball, and as their ships were miserably

* *Vide* letter, pages 49, 50.

torn and shattered, a great number of their soldiers slain, their provisions short, and water spent, many of their men sick and wounded—further, that there were no hopes of Parma coming out to join them—they had no course left but to return to Spain by the north of the British Isles. Pursuant to this resolution, having thrown their horses and mules overboard, to save water and to lighten their ships, they made all the sail they could, followed by the Lord High Admiral till he saw them clear of the Firth of Forth, where, had they anchored, he had taken measures to destroy them entirely. But the Spaniards kept on their course round by the Orkneys, the Western Islands, and Ireland, amongst which they suffered great losses from their ignorance of the coasts and the accidents of the weather and heavy seas. Several ships were stranded on the coast of Scotland;* their men, to the number of 700, getting ashore, were by consent of Elizabeth delivered by James I. to Parma. Other ships were wrecked on the Irish coast, but the Lord Deputy, Sir William Fitzwilliam, either put their crews to the sword, or had them executed, lest they should join with his own rebellious people.

"When I was at Sligo," wrote Sir Geoffry Fenton, "I numbered on one strand, of less than five miles length, 1100 dead bodies of men which the sea had driven upon the shore. The country people told me the like was in other places, though not to the like number."

The English fleet was now short of supplies. From Dunbar an express had been sent to London, to beg that food and ammunition might be sent to Margate for the fleet. "Hunger, however, was an enemy that would not fly. Storm or no storm, unless Howard could recover the Thames, his case would be as bad as Sidonia's; and he beat back in the face of the gale, Hawkins's spars and cordage standing proof against all trials. Off the Norfolk coast the wind became so furious that the fleet was scattered. Howard, with the largest of the ships, reached Margate. Others were driven into Harwich, and rejoined him when the weather moderated."†

On the 9th August food arrived. The month's victuals served out on the 23rd June had been made to last seven weeks, and the three days' rations with which the fleet had left the Forth had lasted for eight days. The crews were starving. The excitement of the war was over, and the men were ill and dispirited; scanty food and the bad beer provided brought sickness, and

---

* At the time of the Spanish Armada the King of Scots wittily told Sir Henry Sidney, Ambassador in Scotland, "That hee expected no courtesie from the King of Spaine, but that favour which Polyphemus promised Ulysses; namely, that when he had devoured the others, he should be *his last morsell.*"

† FROUDE.

boatloads of sailors were carried ashore, and were laid down to die in the streets, there being no place in the town to receive them. The officers did their best, and some were taken to barns and outhouses. "It would grieve any man's heart," said Howard, in his letter to Burleigh, August 20th, "to see men who had served so valiantly die so miserably." And again, in a letter from Howard to the Council, dated 22nd August, he refers to the great sickness among the men. Of "present necessity there must be sent down for the payment of them unto the 25th of August, whereof I leave Sir John Hawkins to certify the Lord Treasurer in more particulars from himself." *

They sickened one day and died the next. In the battle before Gravelines not sixty in all had been killed ; before a month was out there was hardly a ship which had enough men to weigh the anchors. The disorder was traced to the poisonous beer. But this was still served out. The sick wanted fresh food, but were dieted with salt beef and fish as usual. The men's wages were still unpaid, so that they were unable to provide necessaries for themselves, and Sir John Hawkins had to remind the Government that the pay of those who died was still due to their relatives.

"Your Lordship may think that by death, discharging of sick, etc., something may be spared in the general pay. Those that die their friends require their pay. For those which are discharged, we take up fresh men, which breeds a far greater charge," writes Hawkins to Burleigh, August 26th. †

How the men were got the following entry shows :

> 1588 19 Sep' Item to John Fysher for caryinge a letter to my Lord Sheffield and Sir John Hawkins at Harwich touching the pressing of certain marryners for her Majesty's ship royall called the Whight Beare xx^d.

The greatest service ever done by an English fleet had been thus successfully accomplished by men whose wages had not been paid from the time of their engagement, with their clothes in rags, and falling off their backs. "It were marvellous good a thousand pounds' worth of hose, doublets, shoes, shirts, and such like were sent down with all expedition, else in a very short time I look to see most of the mariners go naked," wrote Howard to Burleigh, on the 20th August. And so ill-found were they in the necessaries of war that they had eked out their ammunition by what they could take in action from the enemy himself. "In the desire for victory they had not stayed for the spoil of any of the ships that they lamed." There was no prize money coming as reward. Their own country was the prize for which they had fought and conquered.

---

* *Sta. Pa. Dom.* (Eliz.)   † *Vide* letter, page 52.

They had earned, if ever Englishmen had earned anywhere, the highest honour and recompense the Government could bestow.

When the accounts were made up, Howard was obliged to defend himself against a charge of peculation brought against him for taking the 3000 pistoles out of the *Capitana*, to defray the expenses of the fleet. On the 27th August he wrote to Walsingham, "I did take them as I told you I would : for, by Jesus, I had not £3 left in the world, and have not anything that could get money in London—my plate was gone before. But I will repay it within ten days after my coming home. I pray you let her Majesty know so ; and by the Lord God of Heaven, I had not one crown more, and had it not been of mere necessity, I would not have touched one ; but if I had not some to have bestowed upon some poor, miserable man, I should have wished myself out of the world." *

The worst meanness was yet to come. A surcharge appeared in the accounts of £620 for "extraordinary kinds of victual, wine, etc., distributed among the ships at Plymouth for the relief of the sick and wounded men." Howard begged the Queen to pass this charge; but a further sum for the same purpose Howard struck out of his account-book, adding, "I will myself make satisfaction as well as I may, so that her Majesty shall not be charged withal."

Howard perhaps, as a nobleman whose father had received large benefactions from the Crown, and to whom afterwards Elizabeth was moderately liberal, might have been expected to contribute at a time of need. The same excuse will not cover the treatment of Sir John Hawkins, who owed nothing to any crowned head. Hawkins, as we have seen, had not only been at the head of the dockyards, but had collected the ships' companies, and settled their wages. No English vessels ever sailed out of port in better condition ; no English sailors ever did their duty better. But Elizabeth had changed her mind so often in the spring—engaging seamen and then dismissing them, and then engaging others—that between charges and discharges the accounts had naturally grown intricate. Hawkins worked hard to clear them, and spent his own fortune freely to make the figures satisfactory. But the Queen, who had been the cause of the confusion, insisted on an exactness of statement which it was difficult, if not impossible, to give; and Hawkins in a petition, in which he described himself as a ruined man, sued for a year's respite to disentangle the disorder.

In spite of Queen Elizabeth's careful economy in her affairs, the country's debts had greatly increased during the time of the Spanish invasion. To meet these and other charges it was necessary to raise money independently of the taxes. Howard was lamenting that the Queen had starved the seamen,

* *Sta. Pa. Dom.* (Eliz.)

and Hawkins wrote that £19,000 in arrears were actually due to the men. Lord Treasurer Burleigh was quite unable to send £8000, the amount immediately required. To meet the immediate want of money, the Queen borrowed, by way of loan, of 2416 of her subjects, as set forth in a printed list, dated 1589, out of the thirty-six counties in England, a sum approaching £75,000, a very great amount in those days, especially after the country had been put to so great an expense in preparations against the Armada. Letters were sent by the Queen to Sir Francis Walsingham, Keeper of the Privy Seal, and by him forwarded to the lieutenants of the various shires, to require the raising of the loan.

On looking over this list, which has been reprinted by Mr. Noble, it seems strange that very few if any of the chief commanders against the Armada appear to have contributed, except Admiral Sir John Hawkins, who gave £100, and his brother Captain William Hawkins £25.

The remains of the "invincible" fleet at last arrived on the coast of Spain in a most deplorable condition. Several of the ships, unable to repair the damages received in battle, had foundered at sea; many others were wrecked; and as most of the people in them perished, those who lived to return home were laden with shame and dishonour. The Duke of Medina himself was forbid the Court. He had brought back only 53, or at most 60 shattered vessels, out of the 132 he had started with, and this so enraged Philip that he would hardly have escaped with his life except for his wife's influence at Court. Some say that Philip received the news of the ill-success of his fleet with heroic patience, and thanked God that it was no greater; that he coolly said "that he had sent his fleet to fight against the English, and not against the winds." This story probably originated with the accounts given by the dispirited Spaniards on their return of the valour of the English, and the tempests of these seas.

But Anthony Coppley, an English fugitive in Spain at that time, declares that when the news was brought, Philip being at mass, as soon as it was over swore "that he would waste and consume his Crown, even to the value of a candlestick (pointing to one on the altar); but either he would utterly ruin Her Majesty and England, or else himself and all Spain should become tributary to her." He ordered Flores de Valdez, who had persuaded the Duke to break the King's instructions, to be seized, and he was carried to the Castle of Saint Andrea and never again heard of. Recalde and Oquendo died within a few days after their arrival; De Leyva, after being three times wrecked, had been drowned off the coast of Ireland.

P

Howard, on the contrary, having chased the Spaniards from the English coasts, bent his sails and steered homeward, arriving safe in the Downs with his whole fleet, to join in the acclamations and thanksgivings of the whole nation for so great a deliverance, with the loss of one small ship and 100 men; though the loss of the Spanish nobility and gentry on board the Armada was so great that there was scarcely a family in Spain but was in mourning, and Philip was obliged by proclamation to shorten the usual time.

In the several fights during July and August between the two navies in the Channel, the Spaniards lost 15 great ships and 4791 men; in September, on the coast of Ireland, 17 ships and 5394 men. Stow tells us that in all they lost 81 ships and upwards of 13,500 men.

On the 12th August victory was declared. The Queen commanded public prayer and thanksgiving to be made in all the churches of England; and on the 24th November, 1588, went herself in triumph from Somerset House, through Temple Bar, to St. Paul's to return thanks to God; listened to the sermon, and caused the Spanish colours taken in the war to be set up there and shown to the people.

QUEENE ELIZ. ROYALLE PROCEEDING IN STATE FROM SOMERSETT PLACE
TO ST. PAUL'S CHURCH. 1588. No. 24.

Messengers of the Chamber, } Servants to Ambassadors.
Gentlemen Harbingers

Gentlemen, } Her Maties Servants.
Esquires

Trumpetts.
Sewers of the Chamber.
Gentlemen Huishers.
The six Clerks of ye Chancery.
Clerkes of Starr Chamber.
Clerkes of the Signet.
Clerkes of the Privie Seale.
Clerkes of the Councell.
Chaplains haveing dignityes as Deanes &c.
Masters of the Chancery.
Aldermen of London.
Kn^ts Batchelors.
Kn^ts Officers of the Admiralty.
The Judge of the Admiralty.
The Dean of the Arches.
The Solliciter and Attorney Generall.

Serjeants at the Law.

The Queens Serjeants.

Barons of the Exchequer.

A Pursuy of Armes.	Judges of the Comon pleas.	A Pursuy of Armes.
	Judges of the King's Bench.	

The Ld Cheif Baron and the Lord Cheif Justice of the Common Pleas.

The Master of the Rolls and the Ld Cheif Justice of the Kings Bench.

The Queens Doctors of Physicke.

The Master of the Tents, and the Master of the Revels.

The Leivtenant of the Ordnance.

The Leiv^t of the Tower.

The Master of the Armorie.

Kn^{ts} that had been Amb^{rs}.

Kn^{ts} that had been Deputyes of Ireland.

The Master of the Great Wardrobe.

A Pursuy of Armes.   The Masters of the Jewell House.   A Pursuy of Armes.

Esquires for the Body, and Gentlemen of the Privie Chamber.

Trumpetts.

The Queens Cloake and Hatt borne by a Kn^t or an Esqr.

Barons younger sons.

Kn^{ts} of the Bath.

Lancaster.   Kn^{ts} Banneretts.   Yorke.

Viscounts younger sons.

Barons eldest sonnes.

Earles younger sonnes.

Viscounts eldest sonnes.

Secretaryes of her Ma^{ty}.

Knights of the Privy Councell.

Somerset.   Kn^{ts} of the Garter.   Richmond.

Principall Secretary.

Vicechamberlaine.

Comptroller and Treasurer of the Household.

Barons of the Parliament.

Chester.   Bishopps.

The Ld Chamberlaine of the House, } being Barons.
The Ld Admirall of England

Marquesses younger sonns.

Earles Eldest sons.

Viscounts.

Dukes younger sonnes.

Marquesses eldest sonnes.

Norroy King of Armes.

Earles.

Dukes Eldest sonnes.

Marquesses.

Dukes.

Clarencieux K. of Armes.

The Almoner.   The Master of ye Requests.

The Lord High Treasurer of England.

The Arch Bishopp of Yorke.

The Lord Chancellor of England.

The Arch Bishopp of Canterbury.

The French Ambassador.

Garter King   The Mayor of   A Gent Huisher

of Armes.   London.   of ye Privy Chamber.

Lord Great Chamberlaine of England.   Earle Marshall of England.

Serjeants at Armes.   Serjeants at Armes.

Gentlemen Pensioners. Esquires of the Stable. Footmen.

Sword borne by the Lord Marquesse.

The Queens Matie in her Chariot.

Her Highnesse traine borne by the Marchioness of Winchester.

The Palfry of Honno^r led by the Master of the Horse.

The Cheif Lady of Honno^r.

All other Ladyes of Hono^r.

The Captain of the Guard.

Yeomen of the Guard.

Gentlemen Pensioners. Esquires of the Stable. Footmen.

[Endorsed] Sr Wm Segar's Marshalling of a Proceeding in state in Queen Eliz. time. 1588.

An annual Thanksgiving Service for the Victory against the Spanish Armada was endowed by Mr. Chapman, *ob.* 1616. In 1877 it was held at St. Mary le Bow.

The Lord High Admiral Charles Lord Howard of Effingham was rewarded with a considerable pension. Admiral John Hawkins, Lord Thomas Howard, Admiral Frobisher, and a very few others received the honour of knighthood. For the rest, their rewards consisted more in words than in deeds. The Queen highly praised her brave sea captains as men born for the preservation of their country, and that they took as reward for their services. The wounded, maimed, and poor sailors were recompensed with pensions.

Never was collapse more complete. Not a Spaniard set foot on English soil but as a prisoner. One English ship only, of small size, became the prize of the invaders. Parma did not venture to embark a man. The King of Scots, standing firm to his alliance with Elizabeth, afforded not the slightest succour to the Spanish ships driven upon the Scottish coasts. The Lord Deputy in Ireland caused the shipwrecked Spaniards to be killed, fearing a rebellion of the Irish if the Spaniards joined them.

And so the miserable remnant of the Invincible Armada returned to Spain.

Several medals were struck in memory of this glorious victory, some in honour of the Queen, on which were engraved fire-ships among a confused fleet, and the inscription, "Une Femme a conduict ceste action" ("A woman conducted this action"), because it was said that the idea of sending the fire-ships into the midst of the Armada was the Queen's thought.[*]

Other medals had a fleet graven under full sail and hastening away, with the inscription, "Il est venu, il a vu, il a fuy" ("Hee came, Hee saw, Hee fledde").

The Zealanders, whose very existence depended upon the success of the English, also coined medals in honour of the victory, one representing the Spanish fleet in great confusion, with this motto, "Impius fugit, nemine sequente" ("The wicked fled, no one pursuing"). And, again, another memorial had the motto, "Efflavit Deus et dissipantur" ("God blew, and they were scattered)."

Among the most interesting relics of the Armada fight were the tapestries, reproduced in the accompanying engravings; made to the order of the Lord

[*] MARTIN'S *Hist. Eng.*

High Admiral, from the designs of Henry Cornelius de Vroom, born at Haarlem, 1566, marine painter, as recorded in the following note:

> The Great Earl of Nottingham Lord High Admiral of England whose defeat of ye Spanish Armada had established ye Crowne of his mistress, being desirous of preserving the detail of that illustrious event, had bespoken a suit of tapestry describing the particulars of each day's engagement; Francis Spiering, an eminent maker of tapestry, took ye work, and engaged Vroom to draw the designs.

> Abstract of King James' Revenue (p. 15), at the end of Fulk. Greville's Lord Brooke *Toutte brought to light:*

> To the Earl of Nottingham for the Hangings of the Story of the Fight in 1588, containing 708 Flemish Ells at 10^l 6^s the ell, in all 1628^l.

The hangings adorned the House of Lords, and were engraved by John Pine in 1739. They were burnt, with partial exceptions, in the fire in the Houses of Parliament, in 1834.

Appendix.

A Declaration of the Proceedings of the Two Fleets.*

1588 July 19.—Upon Friday by the 19th of the present month part of the Spanish navy, to the number of 50 sail, was discovered about the Isles of Scilly hoving in the wind as it seemed, to attend the rest of the fleet, and the next day,

20 (*Saturday*) at 3 of the clock in the afternoon the Lord Admiral got forth with our navy out of Plymouth then with some difficulty the wind being at S.W., notwithstanding through the great travail used by our men, they not only cleared the harbour but also the next day being

21.—Sunday, about 9 of the day in the morning recovered the wind of the whole fleet, which being thoroughly descried was found to consist of 120 sail great and small. At the same instant the Lord Admiral gave them fight within the view of Plymouth from which the Mayor [William Hawkins] with others sent them continually supplies of men till they were past their coast. This fight continued till one of the clock the same day, wherein the enemy was made to bear room with some of his ships to stop their leaks. The same day by accident of fire happening in one of their great ships, there were blown up with powder about 120 men, the rest being compelled to leave her, and so she was by the Lord Admiral sent into the west part of England.

* *Sta. Pa. Dom.* (Eliz.) Vol. 214, 42 I.

22.—Upon Monday the 22, one of the chief galleons wherein was Dom Pedro de Valdez with 450 men, was taken by reason of his mast that was spent with the breaking of his BOARE SPITT, so as he presently yielded with sundry gentlemen of good quality.

23.—On Tuesday the 23 the Lord Admiral chased the enemy who had then gotten some advantage of the wind and thereupon seemed more desirous to abide our force. Then fell in fight with them over against St. Albans about 5 of the clock in the morning the wind being at N.E., and so continued with great force on both sides till late in the evening, when the wind coming again to the S.W. and somewhat large they began to go roomewardes.

24.—The same night, and all Wednesday, the Lord Admiral kept very near unto the Spanish fleet and upon Thursday the 25th over against Dunnose part of the Isle of Wight the Lord Admiral espying Captain Frobisher with a few other ships to be in a sharp fight with the enemy and fearing they should be distressed did with 5 of his best ships beare up towards the admiral of the Spanish fleet, and so breaking into the heart of them began a very sharp fight by which 2 or 3 score one of the other until they had cleared Captain Frobisher and made them give peace.

26 (*Friday*).—The next day being the 26 the Lord Admiral onely continued his pursuit of the enemy having still encreased his provisions and keeping the wind of them.

27.—Upon Saturday the 27 about 8 of the clock at night the Lord Henry Seymour Admiral in the Narrow Seas joined with the Lord Howard in Whitsand Bay over against the cliffe of Callice, and anchored together and the Spanish fleet rode also at anchor to leeward of the Lord Admiral and nearer to Callice road.

28 (*Sunday*).—The 28 the Lord Admiral prepared seven ships with pitch, tar and other necessaries for the burning of some of the enemy's fleet and at 11 of the clock at night the wind and tide serving put the stratagem in execution the event whereof was done. Upon Monday the 29 early in the morning the Admiral of the enemy's Galleasses riding next to our fleet let slip her anchor and cable to avoid the fires, and driving athwart another Galleass, her cable took hold of the other rudder, and broke it clean away, so that with her oars she was fayn to get into Callace Road for relief, all the rest of the Spanish fleet either cut or let slip their anchors and cables, set sail and put to the sea, being chased from that Road.

Afterwards the Lord Admiral sent the Lieutenant of his own ship with a hundred of his principal men in a long boat to recover the Galleass so distressed near Callace, who after some sharp fight with the loss of some men was possessed of her, and having slain a great number of the enemies, and namely their Captain General of the four Galleases, called D. Hugo de Montcaldo, son to the Viceroy of Valencia, with divers gentlemen of good reckoning carried prisoners to the English fleet. In this pursuit of the fireworks by our force the Lord Howard in fight spoiled a great number of them sank three and drove four or five on the shore so as at that time it was assured that they had lost at the least sixteen of their best ships. The same day after the fight the Lord Howard followed the enemy in chase, the wind continuing at the West and South West who bearing room northwards directly towards the Isles of Scotland were by his Lordship followed near land until they brought themselves within the height of 55°.

30th (*Tuesday*).—The 30th one of the enemy's great ships was espied to be in great distress by the Captain of H.M. Ship called the *Hope*, who being in speech of yielding unto the said Captain before they could agree on certain conditions soncke presently before their eyes.

31 (*Wednesday*).—It is also advertized that the 31st two of their great ships being in the like distress and grievously torn in the fight aforesaid, and since taken by certain Hollanders and brought into Flushing. The principal person of the greatest of them is called Dom Piedmontello being also one of the Maestridel Campo.

THE ENGLISH FLEET.

The following is a statement of the English fleet against the Armada in 1588.

Men-of-war belonging to her Majesty	17
Other ships hired by the Queen	12
Tenders and store-ships or pinnaces	6
Furnished by City of London, being double the number demanded by the Queen, well manned, ammunitioned, and provisioned	16
Tenders and store-ships or pinnaces	4
Furnished by City of Bristol, large and strong . . .	3
Tender or pinnace	1
From Barnstaple, merchant ships converted into frigates . .	3
From Exeter, ships	2
A stout pinnace	1
From Plymouth, stout ships every way equal to the Queen's men-of-war	7
A fly boat	1
Under Lord Henry Seymour in the Narrow Seas, of the Queen's ships and vessels in her service	16
Ships fitted out at the expense of the nobility, gentry, and commons of England	41
One pinnace of the Lord High Admiral's, the *Defiance* . .	1
Another of Lord Sheffield	1
By Merchant Adventurers, prime and well furnished . .	10
Sir Wm Winter's pinnace	1
Total .	143 ships

LIST OF THE QUEEN'S SHIPS AND PINNACES.*

Tonnage.	Name.		Men.	Admirals and Captains.
800	The *Ark Royal*	. .	400	Carrying the flag of Charles, Lord Howard of Effingham, Lord High Admiral of England.
800	*Victory* .	. .	400	Admiral Sir John Hawkins (born in 1532), Treasurer and Comptroller of the Navy, the senior officer in the fleet. Captain R. Barker.
1000	The *Triumph* .	. .	500	Vice-Admiral Sir Martin Frobisher.
900	*Bear* . .	. .	500	Lord Edmund Sheffield. [The *Bear* was the Lord High Admiral's ship before the *Ark Royal*.]
900	*Elizabeth Jonas*	. .	500	Sir Robert Southwell.
600	*Mary Rose* .	. .	250	Capt. Edward Fenton (Sir John Hawkins's brother-in-law).
500	*Nonpareil* .	. .	250	Thomas Fenner.
500	*Golden Lion* .	. .	250	Lord Thomas Howard (born in 1561; eldest son of the fourth Duke of Norfolk).
600	*Elizabeth Bonaventure* .		250	George Clifford, Earl of Cumberland (born 1558). [*Bonaventure*, built in 1560, ran on a sandbank in 1588, but got off without hurt.]
600	*Hope* .	. .	250	Robert Cross.
500	*Revenge* .	. .	250	Sir Francis Drake, Vice-Admiral of a squadron of volunteers.
500	*Rainbow*	. .	250	Lord Henry Seymour, in command of the squadron in the Narrow Seas.
500	*Vanguard* .	. .	250	Sir William Winter, also in the Narrow Seas.
500	*Dreadnought* .	. .	200	Sir George Beston.
340	*Antelope* .	. .	160	Sir Henry Palmer.
300	*Swallow* .	. .	160	Richard Hawkins (only son of Sir John; afterwards Sir Richard Hawkins).
360	*Swiftsure* .	. .	180	Edward Fenner.
300	*Foresight* .	. .	160	Christopher Baber, gent.
250	Gally *Bonavolia*	. .	250	William Bourough, Esq.

* In addition to this list were the Volunteer Squadrons.

Q

Tonnage.	Name.			Men.	Captains.
240	*Aid*	.	.	120	William Fenner, gent.
200	*Bull*	.	. .	100	Jeremy Turner, gent.
200	*Tiger*	.	. .	100	John Bostocke, gent.
150	*Tremountain*	.	. .	70	Luke Ward, gent.
120	*George*	.	. .	30	Richard Hodges.
120	*Scout*	.	. .	70	Henry Ashley, Esq.
100	*Achates*	.	. .	60	Gregory Riggs, gent.
70	*Charles*	.	. .	40	John Roberts, gent.
60	*Moon*	.	. .	40	Alexander Clifford.
50	*Advice*	.	. .	35	John Harris.
50	*Spye*	.	. .	35	Ambrose Ward.
50	*Martyne*	.	. .	35	Walter Goare.
40	*Sun*	.	. .	24	Richard Buckley.
30	*Cygnet*	.	. .	20	John Sherrife.
	Brigandine	.	. .	36	Thomas Scott.

SIR RICHARD HAWKINS.

[FROM THE ORIGINAL IN THE POSSESSION OF R. S. HAWKINS, ESQ., WELLINGTON, NEW ZEALAND.]

CHAPTER V.

Sir Richard Hawkins, "The Complete Seaman."

DMIRAL SIR RICHARD HAWKINS was the only child of Sir John Hawkins, the great admiral. His mother was Sir John's first wife, Katherine, daughter of Benjamin Gonson, Treasurer of the Navy from 1549 to 1573.

Richard Hawkins was born at Plymouth about 1560. From a boy he became his father's constant companion, and was brought up to a sea-life, under great advantages, with his father and uncle, both renowned seamen, and then owning thirty sail of good ships.

In 1582 he made his first long voyage to the West Indies, with his uncle, William Hawkins, in which he showed the boldness and sagacity of a good officer. The following incident during the voyage is given by Sir Richard Hawkins in his *Observations*: "In the year 1582 in a voyage under the charge of my uncle Wm Hawkins of Plymouth Esquire: in the Indies, at the Western end of the Island of San Juan de Porto Rico: one of the ships called the bark *Bonner*, being somewhat leake, the captain complained that she was not able to endure to England; whereupon a counsel was called and his reasons heard and allowed." It was determined to take everything out of the ship, and to burn or sink her, to which Richard Hawkins said nothing ("it being my part to learn rather than to advise "*); but seeing the fatal sentence given, and suspecting the captain of making the matter worse than it was, so as to get into another ship which sailed better, he dissuaded his uncle privately; but not prevailing, he went further, and offered to take the ship home himself, "leaving the Vice-admiral which I had under my charge and to make her Vice-admiral." The captain, hearing this, felt his reputation at stake, and said he would not

---

* From the original edition of Sir Richard Hawkins's *Observations*, 1622.

leave his ship; and she returned safe to England, and made many a good voyage for nine years after. Thus he saved the vessel from destruction, and was esteemed for his wisdom; and from that time he was constantly employed at sea.

These *Observations* of Sir Richard were dedicated to Prince, afterwards King, Charles, in the following form:

To the

most illustrious and most excellent

PRINCE CHARLES, PRINCE OF WALES,

Duke of Cornwall, Earle of Chester, etc.

AMONGST other neglects prejudiciall to this state, I have observed, that many the worthy and heroyque acts of our nation, have been buried and forgotten: the actors themselves being desirous to shunne emulation in publishing them, and those which overlived them, fearefull to adde, or to diminish from the actors worth, judgement, and valour, have forborne to write them; by which succeeding ages have been deprived of the fruits which might have been gathered out of their experience, had they beene committed to record. To avoid this neglect, and for the good of my country, I have thought it my duty to publish the observations of my South Sea voyage; and for that unto your highnesse, your heires, and successors, it is most likely to be advantagious (having brought on me nothing but losse and misery), I am bold to use your name, a protection unto it, and to offer it with all humblenes and duty to your highnesse approbation, which if it purchase, I have attained my desire, which shall ever ayme to performe dutie.

Your Highnesse humble

And devoted Servant

RICHARD HAWKINS.

In 1585 Richard Hawkins sailed, with Drake and Frobisher, in command of the *Duck.* The fleet consisted of twenty-five ships, with 2300 soldiers and sailors, of whom 750 died, chiefly of disease, during the voyage. They took San Iago, San Domingo, Carthagena, and San Augustine in Florida.

He was admitted to the freedom of Plymouth in 1589-90 as "Ricus Hawkins gen'osus," when "he contributed towards the fund raised to reimburse Drake for bringing in the water." The previous year he provided the Corporation with a silver cup, value £12, for presentation to Sir Walter Ralegh, Lord Warden of the Stannaries, also "four demi culverins and three sakers" for the defence of the town.

Richard Hawkins commanded the *Swallow*—the ship that Howard offered.

to sail to Rio Janeiro in the wildest storm that could blow—against the Armada, and he is mentioned as greatly distinguishing himself during the many engagements which ended in the total destruction of that great fleet. The *Swallow* received more damage than any of the Queen's ships during the fight, in which she suffered severely.*

In 1590 Sir John Hawkins obtained the grant of a commission for his son Richard, to attempt, with a ship, bark, and pinnace, an expedition against Philip II. of Spain. This commission assigned to Richard Hawkins and his patrons whatever they should take; reserving one-fifth of the treasure, jewels, and pearls, to the Queen. The voyage was intended to be made by way of the Straits of Magellan and the South Sea, the object being to discover and survey unknown lands, and to report upon their inhabitants, governments, and produce; returning by way of Japan, China, and the East Indies.

"For this purpose," says Sir Richard Hawkins, "in the end of 1588, returning from the journey against the Spanish Armado, I caused a ship to be builded in the river of Thames, betwixt 300 and 400 tons, which was finished in that perfection as could be required; for she was pleasing to the eye, profitable for stowage, good of sail, and well conditioned.

"The day of her launching being appointed, the Lady Hawkins (my step-mother) named her the *Repentance;* and although many times I expostulated with her, to declare the reason for giving her that uncouth name, I could never have any satisfaction, than that repentance was the safest ship we could sail in to purchase the haven of Heaven. . . . . The *Repentance* being put in perfection, and riding at Detford, the queen's majesty passing by her, to her palace at Greenwich, commanded her bargemen to row round about her, and viewing her from post to stem, disliked nothing but her name, and said she would christen her anew, and that henceforth she should be called the *Dainty;* which name she brooked well, having taken (for her Majesty) a great Byscen, of 500 tons, under the conduct of Sir Martin Furbisher; a caracke bound for the East Indies, under my father's charge, and the principal cause of taking the great caracke, the *Madre de Dios,* brought to Dartmouth by Sir John Borrough, and the Earl of Cumberland's ships, anno 1592, with others of moment in other voyages. To us she never brought but loss, trouble, and care. Therefore my father resolved to sell her, though with some loss, which he imparted with me: and for that I had ever a particular love unto her, and a desire she should continue ours, I offered to ease him of the charge and care of her, and to take her with all her furniture

* *Vide* Chapter IV.

at the price he had before taken her of me; with resolution to put in execution the voyage for which she was first builded; although it lay six months and more in suspense, partly upon the pretended voyage to Nombre de Dios and Panama, which then was fresh a foot; and partly upon the caracke at Dartmouth, in which I was employed as a commissioner; but this business being ended, and the other pretence waxing cold, the 1st March I resolved and began to go forward with the journey, so often talked of, and so much desired.

"And having made an estimate of the charge of victuals, munition, and necessaries for the said ship: consorting another [vessel] of 100 tons, which I waited for daily from the Straits of Gibraltar, with a pinnace of 60 tons, all mine own: and for a competent number of men for them, and dispatched order to my servant at Plymouth, to put in a readiness my pinnace. And with the diligence I used, and my father's furtherance, at the end of one month I was ready to set sail for Plymouth, to join with the rest of my ships and provisions. But the expecting of the coming of the Lord High Admiral, Sir Robert Cecil, principal secretary to her majesty, and Sir Walter Rawley, with others, to honour my ship and me with their presence and farewell, detained me some days, and the rain and intemperate weather deprived me of the favour, which I was in hope to have received at their hands.

"Having taken my unhappy last leave of my father Sir John Hawkins, I tooke my barge, and rowed down the river, and coming to Barking, we might see my ship at an anchor in the midst of the channel, where ships are not wont to moor themselves. And coming aboard her, one and another began to recount the peril they had past of loss of ship and goods; for the wind being at N.W. when they set sail, and vered out southerly, it forced them for the doubling of a point to bring their tack aboard; and luffing up, the wind freshing suddenly the ship began to make a little heel; and for that she was very deep loaden, and her ports open, the water began to enter in at them, which nobody having regard unto, thinking themselves safe in the river; at length when it was seen and the sheet flown, she could hardly be brought upright. But with the diligence of the company she was freed of that danger."

Richard Hawkins now set sail, and arrived at Plymouth on the 26th April. The vessel he expected from Gibraltar not arriving, he resolved to take a smaller ship of his own instead, called the *Hawke*, only for a victualler, meaning to take out the men and victuals, and to cast her off either on the coast of Brazil or in the Straits of Magellan.

Towards the end of May all was in readiness to depart; but a westerly gale came on, during which the *Dainty* lost her mainmast, which also prevented Hugh Cornish, the master, bringing her into the Cattewater.

"Coming to my house to shift me" (wet to the skin, says Sir Richard), "I had not well changed my clothes when a servant of mine enters almost out of breath with news, that the pinnace was beating upon the rocks, which though I knew to be remediless, I put myself in place where I might see her, and in a little time after she sunk downright. These losses and mischances troubled and grieved, but nothing daunted me; *Si fortuna me tormenta; Esperanca me contenta:* of hard beginnings, many times come prosperous and happy events. And although a well-willing friend wisely foretold me them to be presages of future bad success, and so disuaded me what lay in him with effectual reasons, yet the hazard of my credit, and danger of disreputation, to take in hand that which I should not prosecute, was more powerful to cause me to go forwards, than his grave good counsel to make me desist. And so the storm ceasing, I began to get in the *Dainty,* to mast her anew, and to recover the *Fancy* my pinnace, which with the help and furtherance of my wife's father, who supplied all my wants, together with my credit (which I thank God was unspotted), in ten days put all in his former state, or better. And so once again, began to take my leave of my friends, and of my dearest friend, my second self, whose unfeigned tears had wrought me into irresolution, and sent some other in my room: so remembering that many had their eyes set upon me, I shut the door to all impediments, and mine ear to all contrary counsel, and gave place to voluntary banishment from all that I loved and esteemed in this life, with hope thereby better to serve my God, my prince and country, than to increase my talent any way.

"I set sail the 12th June, 1593, in the afternoon; and all put in order, I looft near the shore to give my farewell to all the inhabitants of the towne, whereof the most part were gathered together upon the Hoe, to show their grateful correspondency to the love and zeal which I, my father, and predecessors have ever borne to that place as to our natural and mother town. And first with my noise of trumpets, after with my waytes and other music, and lastly with the artillery of my ships, I made the best signification I could of a kind farewell. This they answered with the waytes of the towne, and the ordinance on the shore, and with shouting of voices; which, with the fair evening and silence of the night, were heard a great distance off."

They touched at Madeira, the Canary Isles, and Cape de Verdes; and approaching the equinoctial line the men "began to fall sick of a disease

which seamen are wont to call the scurvy," of which several of them died,
which together with contrary winds made them seek the shore, and towards
the end of October they sighted land—the port of Victoria on the coast
of Brazil. Richard Hawkins now sent a letter to the Governor, saying that he
was bound for the East Indies to traffic, and had been forced into port by
contrary winds, and that if he were willing they would exchange commodities.
The captain of the *Dainty* was sent with the letter; but he not returning,
Hawkins entered the harbour, when the captain returned.   They anchored
"right against the village," sending a boat for the Governor's answer, who
replied that he was sorry that he could not agree to so reasonable a request
on account of the war between Spain and England, having received express
orders from his King not to suffer any trade with the English, at the same
time requiring them to depart within three days, which he gave them on
account of their courtesy.

"With this answer we resolved to depart ; but the wind suffered us
not all that night, nor the next day.   In which time I lived in great
perplexity, for that I knew our own weakness and what they might doe unto
us if that they had known so much.   For any man that putteth himself into
the enemies port, had need of Argus eyes, and the wind in a bagge, especially
when the enemie is strong, and the tydes of any force. . . . For with either
ebb or flood those who are on the shore may thrust upon him their inventions
of fire, and with swimming or other devices may cut his cables. . . .

"In S. John de Ulloa, in Mexico, when the Spaniards dishonoured their
nation with that foul act of perjury and breach of faith given to my father,
Sir John Hawkins (notorious to the whole world), the Spaniards fired two
great ships with intention to burn my father's admiral, which he prevented
by towing them with his boats another way."

The next night the wind changing they set sail, and having refreshed
themselves at the island of Santa Anna, the men began to recover from their
sickness ; but it having lessened their number, it was determined to take
out the victuals of the *Hawke* and to burn her.   Here after a short chase
they succeeded in taking a prize ; but she had nothing of value in her,
as she had been on the great shoals of Abrolhos, and obliged to throw
everything overboard.   Directing their course for the Straits of Magellan,
they took a Portuguese ship of 100 tons bound for Angola.   They took
out of this prize a quantity of meal and some sugar, and gave the crew
their ship and their liberty, and after disarming them all, allowed them
to depart.   Then continuing on their voyage in the height of the Plate river,

some fifty leagues off the coast they were overtaken by a storm which lasted two days.

"In the first day," says Sir Richard, "about the going down of the sun, Robert Tharlton, master of the *Fancy*, bare up before the wind without giving us any token or sign that she was in distress. We seeing her to so continue her course bare up after her, and the night coming on we carried our light; but she never answered us, for they kept their course directly for England, which was the overthrow of the voyage. As well for that we had no pinnace to go before us to discover any danger, to seek out roads and anchoring, to help our watering and refreshing, as also for the victuals, necessaries, and men which they carried away with them, which though they were not many, yet with their help in our fight we had taken the vice-admiral the first time she boarded with us, as shall be hereafter manifested. For once we cleared her deck, and had we been able to have spared but a dozen men, doubtless we had done with her what we would, for she had no close-fights (barricades). Moreover, if she had been with me I had not been discovered upon the coast of Peru. But I was worthy to be deceived that trusted my ship in the hands of an hypocrite, and a man which had left his general before in like occasion and in the self-same place; for being with Master Thomas Candish, master of a small ship in the voyage wherein he died, this captain being aboard the admiral, in the night forsook his fleet, his general, and captain, and returned home."

Richard Hawkins and his men at the time believed that the *Fancy* had been lost during the storm, "for we never suspected that anything could make them forsake us; so we much lamented them." However, Robert Tharlton sailed for England, "making spoil of the prize he took in the way homewards, as also of that which was in the ship, putting it into a port fit for his purpose."

The 2nd February, 1594, they sighted land.* "All this coast, so far as we discovered, lyeth next of any thing E. by N. and W. by S."

"The land, for that it was discovered in the reign of Queen Elizabeth, my sovereign lady and mistress, and a maiden Queen, and at my cost and adventure, in a perpetual memory of her chastity and remembrance of my endeavours I gave it the name of Hawkins' maiden-land."

With a fair wind they directed their course for the Straits, passed Elizabeth Island, and in Blanches Bay they took in provisions and repaired the ship. After which, continuing their course "some four leagues to the

---

* The Falkland Islands.

R

westwards of Cape Froward, we found a goodly bay, which we named English Bay, where anchored we presently went ashore."

Soon after this the *Dainty* struck on a rock, but was got off after much labour, throwing into the sea what came to hand to lighten her, which proved fruitless until "that the flood came, and then we carried her off with great joy and comfort, when finding the current favourable with us, we stood over to English Bay, and fetching it, anchored there, having been some three hours upon the rock." Returning to Blanches Bay cold weather set in, with bitter winds, rain, and sleet, which made some of the men desire to return to Brazil; but no attention was paid to them, and Hawkins employed their spare time in gathering fruit and the bark of a tree called winter's bark, also in collecting pearls out of mussels.

Setting sail they cleared Cape Desire, and on the 19th April anchored under the island of Mocha.

Coasting Chili, in the port of Valparaiso they seized four ships laden with provisions and timber. The owners wished to redeem their ships at a reasonable price, which was agreed to, Sir Richard reserving the largest to give his men satisfaction. They also seized another vessel, in which they found some quantity of gold; and kept her pilot and part owner, Alonzo Perezbueno, to pilot them along the coast, till out of pity—he having a wife and children—he was set ashore betwixt Santa and Truxilla, Hawkins also gave them the ship. During the ransom of the ships, for about a week Hawkins and Hugh Cornish, the master, took little rest on account of the weakness of their numbers, having but seventy men and boys with five ships to guard, everyone moored separately, and fearing treachery. The Governor of Chili was there, and confessed afterwards to Hawkins that he lay in ambush with three hundred horse and foot to see if at any time they landed or neglected their watch.

From Valparaiso they sailed to Coquimbo, and off Arica took a small prize, and sighted and chased a large vessel, but as she sailed fast were unable to take her. Having examined their prizes, and finding nothing but fish in them, Hawkins returned the larger ship to the Spaniards, keeping the smaller one to make her their pinnace. But near Quilca this ship which they had brought from Valparaiso having sprung a leak they agreed to fire her, which was done accordingly; and continuing their course along the coast they anchored abreast of Chilca.

By sea and land the people of Chili had now given advice to De Mendoço, Marquis of Cañete, Viceroy of Peru, resident in Lima, of the

English being on the coast. He at once put six ships in warlike order with nearly 2000 men, and despatched them to seek and fight with Richard Hawkins, under the conduct of his wife's brother, De Castro, who departing from Callao turned to windward in sight of shore, whence they had daily intelligence of where the *Dainty* had last been discovered.

The day after Hawkins had sailed from Chilca they sighted each other near Cañete, he being some two leagues to windward of the Spanish squadron, with little or no wind. The *Dainty* was now put in the best order possible to fight and to defend herself. "About 9 o'clock," Sir Richard tells us, "the breeze began to blow, and we to stand off to sea, the Spaniards cheek by jole with us, ever getting to the windwards. The wind freshening, caused a chopping sea, which snapped the mainmast of the admiral of the Spaniards asunder, and so began to lay astern, and with him two other ships. The vice-admiral split her main-sail, being come within shot of us, and the rear-admiral cracked her main-yard in the midst, being ahead of us; and one of the armado, which was to windward, durst not assault us. . . . After much debating it was concluded that we [the English ship] should bear up before the wind, and seek to escape; and at break of day we were clear of all our enemies, and so shaped our course along the coast, for the Bay of Atacames, there to trim our pinnace, receive wood and water, and so depart upon our voyage with all possible speed." The Spaniards returned to Lima, and going ashore were "so mocked and scorned by the women, as scarce anyone by day would show his face. This wrought such effects in the hearts of the disgraced, as they vowed either to recover their reputation lost, or to follow us to England; and so with expedition the Viceroy commanded two ships and one pinnace to be put in order; and they were again despatched, and ranged the coasts in search of us." The English, who in sight of Cerro Mongon had taken and fired a ship laden with provisions, after setting the company ashore, proceeded to the Solomon Isles, and so continued on the voyage. Sighting a ship, which the captain and company wished to chase, Hawkins ordered the pinnace to do so, in which she was unsuccessful, and returned with the loss of her mainmast. So they put into the Bay of San Mateo to repair damages, resolving next morning to set sail, and to leave the coasts of Peru and Quito.

The next day, however, while weighing anchor, the Spanish squadron of eight ships, manned by 1300 men, commanded by Don Beltran de Castro, was descried coming round the Cape. Hawkins with great difficulty dissuaded his men from attacking the Spaniards before the *Dainty*, manned by only 75 men, was prepared to fight, but "to give them better satisfaction, I condescended that our captain, with a competent number of men, should with our pinnace go to discover them. In all these divisions and opinions, our Master Hugh Cornish, who was a most sufficient man for government and valour, and well saw the errors of the multitude, used his office as became him ; and so did all those of best understanding.

"In short space our pinnace discovered what they were and casting about to return unto us, the vice-admiral began with her chace to salute her, and so continued chasing and gunning at her. My company seeing this, now began to change humour ; and I then to encourage and persuade them to perform their promises and vaunts of valour. And that we might have sea-room to fight, we presently weighed anchor, and stood off to sea with all our sails, in hope to get the weather gage of our enemies. But the wind scanting with us and larging with them, we were forced to leeward. And the Admiral came upon us : which being within musket shot, we hailed with our trumpets, our waytes, and after with our artillery ; which they answered with artillery two for one. For they had double the ordinance we had, and almost ten men for one." In spite of overwhelming numbers this "worthy son of a worthy sire" fought a most gallant action for three days and nights. "Immediately they came shoring aboard of us, upon our lee quarter, contrary to our expectations, and the custom of men of war. And doubtless, had our gunner been the man he was reputed to be, she had received great hurt by that manner of boarding. But contrary to all expectation, our stern pieces were unprimed, and so were all those which we had to leeward, save half one in the quarter, which discharged, wrought that effect in our enemies, as that they had five or six foot water in hold, before they suspected it.

"Hereby all men are to take warning by me, not to trust any man in such extremities, when he himself may see it done. This was my oversight, this my overthrow. For my part, I with the rest of my officers, occupied ourselves in clearing our decks, lacing our nettings, making of bulwarks, arming our tops, fitting our wast-cloaths, tallowing our pikes, slinging yards, doubling sheets and tacks, placing and ordering our people, and procuring that they should be well fitted and provided of all things ; leaving the artillery, to the gunners dispose and order, with the rest of his mates ; which, as I said was part of our perdition. And coming now to put in execution the sinking of the ship, as he promised, he seemed a man without life or soul. So the admiral coming close to us, I myself, and the master of our ship, were forced to play the gunners. The instruments of fire wherein he made me to spend immensely,

before our going to sea, now appeared not—some of our company had him in
suspicion to be more friend to the Spaniards than to us; for that he had served
some years in the Tercera as gunner, and that he did all this on purpose. Few
of our pieces were clear, when we came to use them, and some had the shot
first put in, and after the powder. Besides after our surrender, it was laid to his
charge, that he should say, he had a brother that served the king in the Peru,
and that he thought he was in the armado; and how he would not for all the
world that he should be slain. Whether this was true or no, I know not, but I
am sure all in general gave him an ill report.

"The entertainment we gave unto our enemies, being otherwise than was
expected, they fell off, and urged ahead, having broken in pieces all our
gallery; and presently they cast about upon us, and being able to keep us
company, with their fighting sails, lay a weather of us, ordinarily within
musket shot; playing continually with them and their great artillery; which
we endured and answered as we could.

"Our pinnace engaged herself so far, as that before she could come unto
us, the vice-admiral had like to cut her off, and coming to lay us aboard, and
to enter her men, the vice-admiral boarded with her: so that some of our
company entered our ship over her bow-sprit, as they themselves reported.
We were not a little comforted with the sight of our people in safety within
our ship; for in all we were but 75 men and boys, and our enemies 1300, little
more or less, and those the choice of Peru."

In the chief of the Spanish ships was an English gunner, who, to gain
grace with his employers and preferment, offered to sink the *Dainty* with the
first shot he made. This man, as the Spaniards afterwards related, while
traversing a piece in the bow to make his shot, before he could fire, had his
head carried away with the first or second shot from the English, which also
killed two or three other men by his side.

The fight continued so hot on both sides, that the artillery and muskets
never ceased playing.

"The Spaniards towards evening determined for the third time to lay us
aboard. Their plan was that the admiral should bring himself upon our
weather bow, and so fall aboard of us, upon our broadside: and that the
vice-admiral should lay his admiral aboard upon his weather quarter, and
so enter his men into her; that from her they might enter us.

"The captain of the vice-admiral being more hardy than considerate, to
get the price and chief honour, waited not the time to put in execution the
direction given, but came aboard to windwards upon our broadside. For

although she was long . . . . what with our muskets, and fireworks we cleared her decks in a moment, so that scarce any person appeared. And doubtless if we had entered but a dozen men, we might have taken her; but our men being few, and the principal of them slain or hurt, we durst not adventure the separation of those which remained: and so held that for the best and soundest resolution, to keep our forces together in defence of our own.

"The vice-admiral (who had lost 36 men) in distress called to his admiral for succour; who laid him aboard, and entered 100 men, and so cleared themselves of us. And the admiral also received some loss, which wrought in them a new resolution, only with their artillery to batter us; and so with time to force us to surrender or to sink us; and placing themselves within a musket shot of our weather quarter, and sometimes on our broadside, lay continually beating upon us without intermission.

"In these boardings and skirmishes, divers of our men were slain, and many hurt, and myself amongst them received six wounds: one of them in the neck, very perilous; another through the arm, perishing the bone, and cutting the sinews close by the armpit; the rest not so dangerous. The master of our ship had one of his eyes, his nose, and half his face shot away. Master Henry Courton was slain. On these two I relied for the prosecution of our voyage, if God, by sickness, or otherwise, should take me away.

"The Spaniards with their great ordnance lay continually playing upon us, now and then parleyed and invited us to surrender '*a buena guerra.*' The captain of our ship now came to me, and began to relate how many were hurt and slain, and scarce any men appeared to oppose themselves for defence, if the enemy should board with us again; and how the admiral offered us life and liberty, and to send us into our own country—saying that if I thought so meet, he and the rest were of opinion that we should put out a flag of truce, and make some good composition. The great loss of blood had weakened me much. The torment of my wounds newly received, made me faint, and I laboured for life, within short space expecting I should give up the ghost. But this parley pierced through my heart, words failed me, yet grief and rage ministered force, and caused me to break forth into this reprehension following.

"'Whence is this madness? Is the cause you fight for unjust? Will you exchange your liberty for thraldom? Is not an honourable death to be preferred before a miserable and slavish life? Hold they not this maxim: that *nulla fides est servanda cum hereticis?* Have you forgotten their faith violated with my father, in S. Juan de Uloa, the conditions and capitulations being firmed by the viceroy and twelve hostages, all principal personages, given for the more security of either party to the other? Can you forget their promise broken with John Vibao and company in Florida, having conditioned to give them shipping and victuals, to carry them into their country; immediately after they had delivered their weapons and arms, had they not their throats cut? How they dealt with John Oxenham and his company, in this sea, yielded upon composition; and how after a long imprisonment and many miseries, being carried from Panama to Lima, and there hanged with all his company, as pirates, by the justice? If these motives be not sufficient, then I present before your eyes your wives and children, your noble and sweet country, your gracious sovereign; all of which account yourselves for ever deprived, if this proposition should be put in execution. And you captain, make proof of your constancy and valour.'

"Whereunto he made answer. 'My good general, what I have done, hath not proceeded from faintness of heart, for besides our reputation I know the Spaniard too well, and the manner of his proceedings in discharge of promises: but only to give satisfaction to the rest of the company. And here I vow to fight it out, till life or limbs fail me.' I replied: 'This is that beseemeth you; and this will gain you, with God and man, a just reward.' "

Richard Hawkins also exhorted the men, as true Englishmen, to sell their lives dearly, that Spain may ever record it with sadness and grief; they answering that they would continue in their duty and obedience to the last breath. In this spirit the fight was continued all that night, the following day and night, and the third day; the enemy never leaving, and continually beating upon them with his great and small shot, except at daybreak, to breathe, and to repair what was amiss, and also to consult what they should do. During which time too the English repaired, and set things in order for the day, otherwise the ship must have sunk, having many shot under water, and the pumps shot to pieces. Not any man of either part took rest or sleep, and little sustenance besides bread and wine.

"In the second day's fight, the vice-admiral coming upon our quarter William Blanch made a shot at her which carried away her mainmast, and was succoured by the admiral. All the second, and the third day our captain and company sustained the fight, notwithstanding the disadvantage wherewith they fought; the enemy being ever to windward, their shot much damnifying us, and ours little hurting them.

"The third day, the 22nd of June 1594, our sails torn, our masts all perished, our pumps rent and shot to pieces, and our ship with fourteen shot under water, and seven or eight foot of water in hold; many of our men slain, with most of them that remained sore hurt ; the enemy still offering us life and liberty; all were of opinion that our best course was to surrender ourselves before our ship sunk ; and sent Thomas Saunders, a servant of mine, to signify unto me the state of our ship. So I also gave my consent, that the captain might capitulate, and called unto one Juan Gomes, our prisoner, to go to Don Beltran de Castro from me, to tell him that if he would give us his word and oath, with some pledge for confirmation, to receive us *a buena querra*, and to give us our lives, and liberty to return to our own country, we would surrender ; otherwise that we would die fighting.

"The Spanish Admiral made answer that he received us *a buena querra*, and swore by God Almighty, to send us as speedily as he could into our own country. In confirmation whereof, he took off his glove, and sent it to me as a pledge. With this message Juan Gomes returned, and the Spaniards entered and took possession of our ship, crying, ' *Buena querra, buena querra ! oy por mi, maniana por ti.*' "

Richard Hawkins was received with the greatest courtesy, "even with tears in his eyes," by Don Beltran, who accommodated him in his own cabin, where he "sought to cure and comfort me the best he could; and truly as I found by trial a man worthy of any charge."

"While the ships were together, the mainmast of the *Dainty* fell by the board, which the people, seeking for spoils and pillage neglected, and she grew so deep with water that she hardly escaped sinking, but after much labour they succeeded in saving her." All the wounded Englishmen, nearly forty in number, were taken care of, and none of them died, although some of them had ten or twelve wounds. The English surgeons also cured the wounded Spaniards, being more numerous, as the Spanish surgeons were unskilful.

Hawkins, who could not speak Spanish, had to use an interpreter, "or the Latin or French, with a little smattering I had of the Portugal."

Arrived at Panama, the success of the Spaniards was received with great joy, with bonfires and illuminations, and guns firing.

Don Beltran showed Hawkins a letter from the King, directed to the viceroy, giving a full account of his intended voyage, saying, "Hereby may you discern whether the King my master have friends in England, and good and speedy advice of all that passeth." Don Beltran then thought it convenient that letters should be dispatched to England, and Hawkins being unable to write, by his servant wrote letters to his father, Sir John Hawkins, acquainting him with what had happened.

And here Sir Richard ends his narrative with, "What succeeded to me, and to the rest during our imprisonment, with the rarities, and particulars of the Peru and Terra Firme, my voyage to Spain, and the success, with the time I spent in prison in the Peru, in the Tercera, in Sevill, and in Madrid, with the accidents which befel me in them, I leave for a second part of this discourse, if God give me life and convenient place and rest, necessary for so tedious and troublesome a work : desiring God, that is Almighty, to give his blessing to this and the rest of my intentions : then shall my desires be accomplished, and I shall account myself most happy. To whom be all glory, and thanks, from all eternity."

There is also a Spanish account of the naval action between Richard Hawkins and Don Beltran de Castro, translated from the *Life of the Marquis of Cañete, Viceroy of Peru*, by Dr. Suarez de Figueroa, in which he says that the fisherman brought the news of the whereabouts of Sir Richard in the *Dainty*, from whom he had taken a supply of fish, and then given him his liberty ; and that during the action " the vessels came alongside each other, and were so close that the gallant Hawkins himself seized the royal standard of Spain by means of a bowline knot which he threw over it. But the attempt failed, as Diego de Avila, Juan Manrique, De Reinalte, Velasquez, and others came to the rescue, and defended it valorously. • The Englishman paid for his audacity by two wounds, one in the neck and the other in the arm, both received from gunshots. . . . . The prize was a ship of 400 tons, most beautiful in all her parts. She carried for arms [those of Hawkins] on the stern a negress with gilt ornaments. Filipon repaired her that night, lest she should go to the bottom, as she was badly damaged, for this purpose heaving her to. Ricardo was sent on board the *Capitana* with others of highest rank."

These accounts agree on all material points. Hawkins wrote from memory many years later ; while De Figueroa, although not present at the scenes he describes, had the official documents of the Viceroy of Peru at his disposal.

The Marquis of Cañete at once sent a report to the Spanish King, who replied as follows :

Philip II. of Spain to the Marquis of Cañete.

I have felt much satisfaction on receiving the news of the success which de Castro obtained over the English general Ricardo who entered that sea by the strait of Magellan. . . . . As regards the punishment of the general and others who were captured in the said ship, you inform me that they have been claimed by the Inquisition, but that as you had no instructions from me as to their disposal, you have put off compliance with the requisition of the Holy Office, and the delivery of the said general to the "auto." You understand that he is a person of quality. In this matter I desire that justice may be done conformably to the quality of the persons. From Madrid 17 Dec. 1595.

S

Doubtless it was in consequence of this letter that Richard Hawkins finally escaped the Inquisition. With the other prisoners, he was taken to Payta, and thence to Lima, receiving at the hands of the Marquis of Cañete, the Viceroy of Peru, the greatest kindness and consideration; and his servant, Saunders, says that "he was beloved for his valour by all brave men in those parts, and received by the best of the country, and carried by them to a princely house all richly hanged, the which he had to himself."

But within a few days of his arrival at Lima Hawkins was claimed by the Inquisition, which caused him much anxiety. The Viceroy, on the ground of having no instructions, did not fully comply with the request; but Richard Hawkins was taken to the "Holy House" by a Father, to remain until orders arrived from the King of Spain. Don Beltran de Castro's honour was thus compromised, as he had promised liberty before the English surrendered.

There are some interesting letters, of which Purchas gives extracts, one written by "Master John Ellis, one of the Captains with Sir Richard Hawkins, concerning the Strait of Magellan, and certain places on the coast and inland of Peru." Ellis went from Lima across the Andes to Guamanga and Cuzco, and was the first Englishman who ever visited the ancient capital of the Yncas, which he says was as "big as Bristol, having a castle on a hill with stones of 20 tons weight strangely joined together without mortar."

The other two letters were written by T. Saunders, Hawkins's servant, addressed to Sir John Hawkins from the prison of San Lucar. He mentions Master Lucas, whom the Holy Office sent to the galleys at Nombre de Dios, where he died.

Richard Hawkins was sent to Spain in 1597. The galleon in which he sailed touched at Terceira, in the Azores, where she was chased by a fleet in command of the Earl of Essex, and several Spaniards killed and wounded by the English shot; but the galleon escaped, and arrived at Seville, where Sir Richard was thrown into prison, and dishonourably detained in captivity, De Castro protesting in vain.

In May, 1598, a letter to Cecil reported Richard Hawkins in the castle at San Lucar as a hostage for Spaniards in England,* and a second letter from Lisbon reported that he escaped out of the Castle of Seville in September, 1598, but was taken, thrust into a dungeon, and great store of irons put upon him. The next year he was enabled to send word to England by Deacon, his servant, who was passed over by De Marsenal from San Jean de Luz, and got on board an English ship in the port of

* *Sta. Pa. Dom.*

Conquet, August, 1599. In April, 1600, Richard Cook, another messenger, again brought news home of the prisoner.

There are extant some most pathetic and touching letters written by Hawkins from his prison to Queen Elizabeth, and also to the English Ambassador at Paris, asking for compassion in the name of his father's services, who sacrificed his life for his Queen. That he himself had spent fifteen years in her service without pay or recompense, knowing that she had infinite charges while he had a good estate; and that he was in danger of perpetual imprisonment unless her powerful hand was reached out, expressing deep concern for the welfare of his wife and child who were living at Plymouth, and conveying to the Queen and her Council all that he could glean of the intentions of Spain towards England. At the hazard of his life, in this way, if in no other, he was determined to serve his country.

In his letter to Sir Henry Nevill, the English Ambassador at Paris, he tells him "that he is the unfortunate son of Sir John Hawkins; that he fought for three days and nights, and was wounded in six places; that most of his men were killed and wounded, and that he surrendered when the ship was ready to sink. The Spanish general sent his glove as a pledge to give life and liberty, but he had been detained lest he should return and molest the Spaniards. Most of his people had been freed long ago." He entreated the Ambassador to intercede with the Queen for him. "I and my father," he concluded, "ever since we could bear arms, spent time and substance in her service."

There is a story told of how Richard Hawkins captivated the heart of a Spanish lady during his imprisonment, and how the circumstance of the lady's attachment and of his fidelity to his wife gave occasion to the well-known ballad of "The Spanish Lady's Love" in Percy's *Reliques*—

> Would you know a Spanish lady,
> How she wooed an Englishman?

The ballad is said to have been written by Hawkins, and it is also stated that the gold chain presented to him by the lady was carefully handed down as an heirloom in the family, and was lately in the possession of Mrs. Ilbert Prideaux.[*]

At last, after almost ten years' captivity, he was set free—his ransom being £12,000, a great sum in those days, £3000 of which had been left in his father's will for that purpose—and he returned to England in January, 1603. The credit of his release is due to the Count of Miranda, who declared that if a

[*] Lysons' *Devon*.

prisoner was detained whose liberty had been promised, no future agreement could ever be made, because faith in Spanish honour would be destroyed.

"It was a sad home-coming. The brave old father gone, the estates of both ruined, and long years of the prime of life utterly wasted."

But in reward for his valour Richard Hawkins was knighted by King James I., and made Vice-Admiral of Devon and a Privy Counsellor.*

Sir Richard Hawkins to the Lords of the Council Commissioners for the peace.

1604   *June* 20.

RIGHTE honorable my singuler good Lordes, my dewtie most humblie remembred. The services of my deceased ffather, and my selfe to this Crowne are well knowen unto your honors, and our greate losses, hazardes, and expences, for which I never received anye paie or recompence neither would I sue for any yf I were able to live as my forefathers of my owne. But necessitie constrayning me I am bolde to appeale to yor Lordshippes in this occasion to crave a favor which I dare saie will stande with the honour of his Majestie, of this Kingdome, and yor Lordshippes, and the Kinge of Spayne in equitie and conscience cannot denie to be juste, and is that in the Capitulacion with Spaine the Spaniards maie yelde some recompence for the wronges done to me and my ffather in peace, in warre, and in this intermission of warre. In tyme of peace, by treacherie in Saint John de Luce the Kinge of Spaines vizroye, and Captayne generall tooke from my ffather above one hundred thousande poundes havinge given twelve gentlemen pledges of either parte, and was after borne in hande by the Kinge for the space of tenne yeres that he would make him restitution. In the tyme of the warr takinge me prisoner uppon composicion and the Kinges generalls word given to free me and all my companie presentlie, beinge helde prejudiciall for the Kinges service to accomplish with me, I was detayned almost tenne yeres a prisoner to the consuminge of all that I had, and losse of the greatest parte of my ffathers estate, which coulde not be so little domaige to me as thirtie thousande poundes. Since the comminge of th'embassador into Englande, I was a partener with Sir Thomas Midleton and others in a voyage into the west Indies in a shipp and a pynnas which went for trade, and beinge admitted to trade with the securitie of two pledges sent by the Lieutenant generall of the Island of Santo Domingo sendinge our pynnas to the porte with fifteene hundred poundes worth of goodes (our people beinge busie in their trade suddenlie were murthered) by those which came to buye and sell with them, and our pynnas and goodes surprised, which was cause of above three thousande poundes losse unto us, for that our voyage was cleane overthrowen. I desire not to drawe by suite anie thinge from my dreade

---

* Knights Bachelors made by King James—Richard Hawkins July 23 1603, at Whitehall. *Harl. MSS.*

sovereign, but my humble peticion to your Lordshipps is that you would be pleased to mediate with his Majestie : that either a clause of satisfaccion from the Kinge of Spayne unto me maie be inserted in the Articles of peace, or that I maie not be concluded by them but lefte free to seeke my remedie, accordinge as the lawe of god and natyons alloweth, And I shalbe ever bounde to praie almightie god to preserve your Lordshipps ever for himselfe and Englands good.

Your Lordshipps ever most humbly bounden

RICHARD HAWKYNS

From Plimouth the 20th
of June 1604.

Sir Richard took a warm interest in corporate affairs, and the estimation in which he was held in Plymouth is shown by the fact that he was chosen Mayor at the first opportunity after his return (1603-4). "Sir Richard came home but the year before from the South Seas, where he had been a prisoner by the Spaniards eight or nine years." The following year (1604) he was elected senior representative of the town in Parliament, with Sir James Bagge. Subsequently we find him and Sir James Bagge mulcted in 3*s*. 4*d*. each for being late at mayor-choosing, coming "tarde on St. Lambert's daye."

In 1604 one Walter Matthews was Mayor of Plymouth, and an amusing incident is reported to have taken place ; for "this Matthews was servant unto Sir Richard, as was his wife unto the Lady Hawkins, who disdaining to sit below one that had been her maid endeavoured to keep the upper hand which the other attempting, the Lady struck her a box on the ear. It made a great disturbance at the time, but at length it was composed, and Sir Richard gave the town a house somewhere in Market Street for satisfaction."

Sir Richard purchased the house and manor of Poole and Slapton from the Amerideths. It is situated between Dartmouth and the Start Point. The residence, surrounded with many fine trees, was about three-quarters of a mile from the church ; but the ruins of the old mansion were pulled down about 1880, and the site is now occupied by a modern farm-house.

No doubt Sir Richard found Slapton a convenient centre for the discharge of his duties as Vice-Admiral of Devon, in the exercise of which he was, however, constantly at his house in Plymouth, where most of his children were born. In March, 1605, we find him sequestering a Spanish prize, which was driven into Salcombe Bay. In June, 1608, he had some correspondence with the Earl of Nottingham respecting some pirates, also discussing a question of Admiralty jurisdiction ; and in the following September mention is made of his active prosecution of pirates.

POOLE PRIORY.

In March, 1614, there was a project for a new voyage of discovery, to send a ship to the Solomon Islands, and that Sir Richard Hawkins should have the command, as he was held to be of "courage, art, and knowledge," to attempt such enterprise. In a letter written by him he refers to a discovery he formerly made, and to his desire to undertake another voyage to the Straits in person; and offers to adventure £20,000 for a voyage to the South Sea. This idea was not carried out, but it serves to show that Sir Richard was still as keen as ever for discovery.

In July, 1620, he was put in command of the *Vanguard*, as Vice-Admiral of twenty ships under Admiral Sir Robert Mansell, to suppress Algerine pirates; and in October a special commission was issued to Hawkins to be Admiral in case of Mansell's death. But in 1622 (April 17th) the Lord Chamberlain wrote to Sir Dudley Carlton that "Sir Robert Mansell and his crew are ill-paid, and Sir Richard Hawkins, the Vice-Admiral, has died of vexation." "He was seized with a fit, when actually in the chamber of the Privy Council on business connected with his command." Westcote, in his *View of Devon*, noting this lamentable occurrence, says very justly of this officer and his father, "that if Fortune had been as propitious to them both, as they were eminent for virtue, valour, and knowledge, they might have vied with the heroes of any age."

ARMS OF SIR RICHARD HAWKINS.

Impaling Hele.

Sir Richard Hawkins was the sixth captain who sailed round the world, and for his skill he obtained the name of the "Complete Seaman." He was the author of an interesting account of his voyage into the South Sea (already largely quoted), which was being published at the time of his sudden death, in 1622, by John Haggard; it was afterwards reprinted in "Purchas," and again, from the original, by the Hakluyt Society. Sir Richard intended writing an account of his long imprisonment, and of Peru, Tierra Firme, Terceira, and Spain, had he lived, as a second part of his *Observations.* "Death prevented the accomplishment of this intention, and the loss of the promised second part is a serious and irreparable loss to history. For we possess no account of Peru during that period written by an observant foreigner."

SLAPTON CHURCH.

Lady Judith survived her husband, dying on 30th May, 1629; and was buried in Slapton Church. On a slate-stone slab over the vault, near the screen, on the floor by the Poole pew, to the right of the altar, is the following inscription:

The rest is obliterated.

Village tradition still tells of how Lady Judith Hawkins walked from the old house of Poole to church—a distance of nearly a mile—on a red velvet carpet, which a servant unrolled before her.

There is only one portrait of Sir Richard Hawkins known to be in existence. It was formerly in the possession of the Lords North, at Kirtling in Cambridgeshire; and on the dismantling of the house, in 1802, it was sold. In 1824 it came into the hands of Mr. Bryant, whose brother sold it, in 1866, to R. S. Hawkins, Esq., of 18, Norham Gardens, Oxford, but at present living in New Zealand, whither he removed the picture. It is a portrait on panel, kitcat size, of a man in armour, with small head, dark brown hair and yellowish beard, and the hand resting on a helmet. The face bears a strong resemblance to that of the ivory basso-relievo bust of Sir John Hawkins. Above the shoulder of the figure are reeds, a rock, and waves, and the following motto: "*Undis arundo vires reparat cædensque foventur funditus at rupes en scopulosa ruit.*"

T

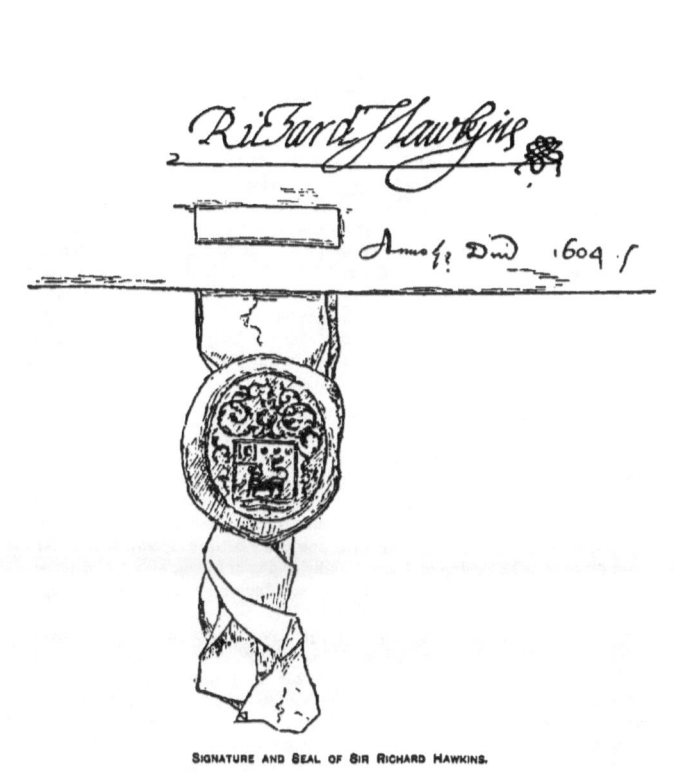

SIGNATURE AND SEAL OF SIR RICHARD HAWKINS.

Will of Sir Richard Hawkins.

IN the name of God Amen the 16th day of April 1622 in the twentieth yeare of the raigne of our Sovraigne Lord James by the Grace of God Kinge of England Fraunce and Ireland Defender of the Faith and of Scotland the fyve and fyftith I Sir Richard Hawkins of Slapton in the Countye of Devon Knight beinge sicke and weake in bodye but of pfect mynde and memory blessed be God therefore doe hereby make ordayne and declare this to be my last Will and Testament in manner and forme followinge. First and principalle I commend my soule unto Almightie God my Maker Redeemer and Sanctifier hoping and beleeving assuredly that through the only merritts death and resurrection of Jesus Christ I shall obtayne full and free remission and pardon of all my sinnes and be made ptaker of eternall life and happiness in the kingdome of heaven with God's elect for ever. And I comitt my body to the earthe from whence it came and after my bodye buried my will and minde is that all suche debts as I shall owe to any p'son or p'sons at the tyme of my deccase be first well and trulie satisfied

And touching the orderinge and disposinge of all such lands grounds tenements goods and chattells as it hathe pleased Almightie God to blesse mee with in this life I give and bequeathe the same in manner and forme following Item I give unto Judith my well beloved wife (for and duringe the terme of her natural life) all that my Mannor or Lordshipp of Poole in the Parishe of Slapton in the County of Devon with all mills lands grounds messuages cottages tenements and hereditaments with their and every of their appurtenñes to the said Mannor or Lordshipp of Poole now belonging or in any wise app'teyninge And likewise I give and bequeath unto the said Judith my wife (for and duringe the tearme of her naturall life) all other my lands and tenements cottages and hereditaments with the appertenñes situate lyeinge and being in or about Plymouth in the Countye of Devon Neverthelesse and uppon this condition followeinge that she shall yearelye duringe soe longe tyme as my sonne John Hawkins shall remaine and dwell with his said mother allowe and paie unto my said sonne twentie pounds per annum of lawfull money of England And if it shall happen that he shall hereafter be minded to lyve from her and betake himself to some other place of aboade or otherwise to travaile or to betake himself to lyve either at the Innes of Courte or at the universities of Oxford or Cambridge then to paie unto my said sonne John and his assignes during all such time as hee shall live from her as aforesaid the yearlie some of fortie pounds of lawfull money of England at fower of the most usual feests or termes in the yeare by even and equall por'cons Item I give and bequeath ymediatlie from and after the decease of my said wife Judith all the said Mannor howse

or Lordship called Poole with all mills lands grounds messuages cottages tenements and hereditaments with theire and every of theire appurten'ces in the Parish
of Slapton and all other my said lands tenements cottages and hereditaments
with th'app'tences lyeinge and being in or about Plymouth in the County of
Devon aforesaid with the reverc'on and rever'cons thereof unto my said sonne
John Hawkins with all and singular my goods chattells utensils and household
stuffe whatsoever Provided always that my said wife may have and enjoy use
occupie and possesse the same goods and chattells during her life without any
interup'con or lett of my said sonne John or of any others by his pcurement
Item I give and bequeathe to my sonne Richard Hawkins and to his heires for
ever all that messuage or tenement with th'app'tences called Pryvitt scituate
lyeinge and beinge in Alverstoke in the Countye of South' with all lands and
grounds thereunto belonginge or in any wise apperteyninge

    Item I give and bequeathe to Margaret Hawkins my daughter (over and
above a hundred pounds legacie given her by her grandmother and a jewell
of twentye pound value) the some of one hundred pounds of lawfull money
of England Item I give and bequeathe to my daughter Joane Hawkins one
hundred and twenty pounds and to my youngest daughter Mary the like some
of one hundred and twentye pounds All which said three severall legacies of
somes of money by me given unto my said three daughters as afforesaide I will
shal be paid them at sixteene yeares of age or daye of marriage which shall first
happen and to be receaved and had out of my owne entertaynmt due to me
from the King's Ma'tie for my last service and imployment don by me at
Argeire And if any of my said daughters shall happen to decease or dep'te
this transitorie lyfe before they shall happen to come or attayne to their severall
ages of sixteene yeares or daye of marriage as aforesaid then I will that the
parte and porc'on of any of them so dyeinge or deceasinge as aforesaide shall
remayne and come unto the others surviving and overlyving p'te and p'te alike
by even and equall por'cons also for the further advancement and encrease of
my said daughters porcons as aforesaide I doe equallie give to amongst my said
daughters the some of one hundred and fiftie pounds due to me by Sir Henry
Thynn Knight to be paid them when and so soone as my Executrix hereafter
named shall happen to recover and receave the same And I make and
ordayne the said Judith my lovinge wife sole and only Executrix of this my
last Will and Testament and I renounce and revoke all former Wills by me
formerly made In witness whereof I the said Sir Richard Hawkins have hereunto sett my hand and seale the said sixteenth day of Aprill 1622 in the
twentieth yeare of the raigne of our said Soveraigne Lord King James over
England France and Ireland RICHARD HAWKINS Sealed and delyvered in
the presence of us Thos Button Jo Gifford Josias Shute and Robert Holyland S'

    Proved June 13th· 1622, by Dame Judith Hawkins.

Will of Lady Judith Hawkins.

May 27. 1629.

In the name of God Amen. I Judith Hawkins sicke of body but sound and perfect of mynde and memorie, doe ordaine and make this my last will and testament in manner and forme followinge. ffirst my Soule which is heavenly redeemed through the sufferings of Christ I commend into the hands of God. ffor my bodie which is dust and ashes I commend to Christian buriall. Item I give unto my daughter Joane my two leases of Plimouth after two yeares, after my decease and in the meane while ten poundes a yeare for her maintenance, for the land (whereas my son John is at sea) if it please God he doe not returne home with life, it is my will that it should remaine unto my sonne Richard. Item I give unto my daughter Mary one hundred poundes to be paid her on her marriage daie, and ten poundes a yeare for her maintenance in the meane while. Item I give unto my daughter Margarett one gold ring. Item I give unto my son Richard one gold ringe. Item I give unto my brother Lewes Heale twentie shillinges. Item I give unto Mr John Cowte twentie shillinges. Item I give to the poor of Slopton [Slapton] ten shillinges to bee distributed at the discretion of Mr Cowte, and some one or two of the Overseers of the poor of the same parish of Slopton. ffor all the rest of my goods not given and bequeathed I give unto my sonne John whom I doe make my sole Executor. Provided allwaies that if my son John refuse to bee my Executor it shalbe lawfull for my brother Lewes Heale and my brother Nicholas Heale and my brother Nicholas Gilbert, whom I doe appoint my Overseers to sell any or all my goods and Chattells for payment of my debts and legacies, and then what remaines I doe give unto my two daughters Joane and Mary. In witnes whereof I have hereunto sett my hand the daie and yeare first written. Judeth Hawkins in the presence of Joh. Cowt. Sigñ William Bastard.

Proved at London 5th day of February 1629 by John Hawkins. [*14 Scroope.*]

CHAPTER VI.

𝔚illiam 𝔥awkins the 𝔗hird.

THE third William Hawkins laid the foundation of our Indian Empire.

He was the eldest son of William Hawkins, the elder brother of Sir John, by his first wife, and therefore first cousin and contemporary of Admiral Sir Richard Hawkins.

He was born at Plymouth about 1565, and educated to a sea life. After making some voyages to the Straits of Magellan and the West Indies in 1582, on July 21st he sailed with Fenton (who had married Tomasine, sister of Katherine Gonson, Sir John Hawkins's first wife) as Lieutenant-General of his fleet. During this voyage Hawkins and Fenton did not agree, and there were frequent disputes between them.

The following extracts are taken from the journal * of William Hawkins during this voyage, 1582:

"16th May we departed from . . .

"The 2 June we departed out of . . . into which port we came by means of a contrary . . . (wind ?) there the General . . . (Fenton ?) would have left behind him Mr. T . . . Blackoller Pilot with Capt. Drake, William . . . (Hawkins ?) and the bark *Francis;* saying that he had . better ma . . . (mariners ?) with inboard that any of those, and that if needs were . . . put in with Falmouth for as good as they."

"Because," says William Hawkins, "I left Kyrkman . . . me for quarelling I had not from that tyme till my coming . . . any good countenance."

* This manuscript is in the British Museum, and is much damaged by fire. Captain William Hawkins, jun., left three journals : I. Journal of the voyage under Captain Fenton, 1582 (MS., Otho, E. viii.). II. Journal in the *Hector,* in the third E.I.C. voyage, 1606 (MS., Egerton, 2100). III. Relation of occurrences during his residence in India, 1608 (Purchas).

It seems evident that Fenton wanted at an early period to abandon the voyage and that most of the officers protested against it.

. . . . All the men in the whole fleet, (God be praised!) are in health, only in the *Calys* 8 or 9 are sick of a fever, but all like to recover. I doubt not but you have heard of the great inconvenience which was like to have happened at Plymouth, by reason that the generall upon . . . . set sail, and left Mr Captayne Hawkyns and divers there on shore, and would not stay for them, but by the persuasion of Captain Warde and some one or two others, he cast about, after we had sailed five leagues, and met them at the Land's End in the *Francis*, which matter was like to have bred great mischief, but that we appeased it in the beginning. But now there is among us as great concord and friendly amity as may be among any people, and all things go well with us, and no doubt but God will bless us, for our people are wonderfully reformed, both in rule of life and religion towards God. In the *Edward* we have daily morning and evening prayers, besides other special prayers at other times of the day . . . .

The 14th June 1582, in latitude 35 deg.

Your hon: Lordship's humble servant and chaplain

JOHN WALKER.

"The 16th June we had sight of the Canaries and the 20th July we fell in with the coast of Guinea and on 10th August anchored off Sierra Leone." Mr. Walker now told William Hawkins that the officers were disputing as to continuing the voyage as first intended, but to make another voyage of their own devising which should be more profitable. After this controversy it was decided to return to Cape de Verde to fetch some wine, which, says William Hawkins, "was only a device to pick and steal."

The bark *Francis* was wrecked in the river Plate, and the crew were saved and kept among the savages for more than a year.

The two remaining ships—the *Calys* and the *Leicester*—entered the port of St. Vincent in Brazil, where on the 24th January, 1583, they fought an action with a Spanish fleet of three ships and 670 men, which had been sent to surprise and take the English vessels. The fight "continued very extreme till noon next day. Their vice-admiral we did sink: there were of our men slain in both ships six or eight and more than 20 hurt. They had of theirs slain above 100 men and many wounded."

The English then made the best of their way home, and the *Leicester* arrived at Kingsale on the 14th June, 1583.*

William Hawkins is next mentioned in 1607, and in the meantime he appears to have been in the Levant and to have learnt Turkish, for he could converse in that language.

The following narrative of his residence at the Court of the Great Mogul puts one in mind of the stories told in the *Arabian Nights.* The wonders and wealth of the Great Mogul; his extreme kindness to Hawkins; how the envy of his enemies, jealous of their king's favours showered upon an Englishman, gradually worked upon the mind of the Mogul, until the emperor listened to their false reports, and was persuaded by them to work the overthrow of Hawkins's project.

On the 16th April, 1607, William Hawkins sailed with a fair wind from Plymouth, bound for the East Indies, as Captain of the *Hector*, accompanied by Captain Keeling with the *Dragon*, as Admiral. Hawkins kept a journal of this voyage.

On the 30th April they sighted the Canary Islands, and continued their course for Sierra Leone, where they anchored. From thence directing their course to S.S.W., on October 28th they were nearing a colder climate, and the men complaining, a pack of clothes was opened and served out. In the morning of 12th December they put into and anchored in Saldania Bay, where they found Captain Middleton's name, who had been there a few months previously, graven upon a stone. Again setting sail on the 18th February, they next anchored in the bay of St. Augustin, Madagascar, and here took in victuals and water. Afterwards proceeding on their voyage, they touched at Socatora, and arrived at Daman, where on the "28th August I embarked myself," says William Hawkins, "for Surat in our pinnace." Captain Keeling had kept company with Hawkins until 24th June to the road of Delisa in Socatora, whence he departed in the *Dragon*. Hawkins had built his pinnace at Socatora, and received a duplicate from the General of the Commission under the Great Seal.

Arrived at the Bar of Surat, being the 24th August, 1608, William Hawkins sent Francis Buck, merchant, to make known to the Governor that the King of England had sent Hawkins as his ambassador to his King, with his letter and present. The Governor replied, that he and what the country

---

* "Written by me Wm Hawkins this vi . . . . 1583 which do not desire of myself to be justi . . . . do willingly reserve myself to the report of the Companies of the Gallion, and of the other two ships."

afforded were at Hawkins's command, and that he should be very welcome if he would vouchsafe to come on shore.

"I went accompanied with my merchants, in the best manner I could, befitting for the honour of my King and country. At my coming on shore, after their barbarous manner I was kindly received, and multitudes of people following me, all desirous to see a new-come people, much nominated, but never came in their parts. Near the Governor's house, word was brought me that he was not well, so I went to the Chief Customer, the only man that seafaring causes belonged unto. After many compliments I told him that my coming was to establish and settle a Factory in Surat, and that I had a letter for his King from His Majesty of England, tending to the same purpose, who is desirous to have league and amity with his King; that his subjects might freely go and come, sell and buy, as the custom of all nations is: and that my ship was laden with the commodities of our land, which by intelligence of former travellers, were vendible for these parts. His answer was that he would dispatch a Foot-man for Cambaya, unto his master; for he could do nothing without his order. So taking my leave I departed.

"In the morning I went to the Governor, and after a Present given him, he entertained me with great outward show of kindness; also promising to dispatch a messenger to Cambaya, and would write in my behalf. In the meantime appointed me to lodge in a Merchant's House, being at that time my Tronch-man, the Capt. of that ship which Sr Edward Michelborne took.

"It was twenty days before the answer came, by reason of the great waters and rains that men could not pass. The messengers brought answer from Mocreb-chan, with licence to land my goods, and buy and sell: but for a future trade, and setting of a Factory, he could not do it without the King's commandment, which he thought would be effected, if I would take the pains of two months travel, to deliver my King's letter. And further he wrote unto his Chief Customer, that all I brought should be kept in the Custom House till his brother, Abder Rachim, came, to choose such goods as were fitting for the King. The goods being landed, and kept in the Customer's power, till the coming of the great man, my ship not being able long to stay, I thought it convenient to send for three chests of money, and with that to buy commodities that were vendible at Priaman and Bantam, which the Guzerats carry yearly thither, making great benefit thereof. I began to buy against the will of the merchants, who grumbled and complained of the leave granted me. The great man came and gave me licence to ship it . . . . making what haste I could, and this done I called Master Marton, and all the company, willing

U

them to receive him as their commander. This done, and seeing them embark, I bade them farewell.

"The next day, I met some ten or twelve of our men very much frightened, telling me the heaviest news, as I thought that ever came unto me, of the taking of the Barks by a Portugal frigate or two; and all goods and men taken, only they escaped. I demanded in what manner, and whether they did not fight, their answer was 'no,' Mr Marton would not suffer them, for that the Portugals were our friends. I presently sent a letter unto the Capt Maior, that he release my men and goods, for that we were Englishmen, and that our Kings had peace and amity together, etc. At the receipt of my letter the proud rascal braued so much most vilely abusing his Majesty, terming him a King of Fishermen, and of an Island of no import, and a fig for his Commission, scorning to send me any answer.

"It was my chance next day, to meet a captain of the Portugal frigates who was sent by Capt Maior to say that the Governor should send me as prisoner unto him, for that we were Hollanders. I took occasion to speak with him of the abuses offered to the King of England and his subjects, 'and so tell your Captain, that he is a base villain and a traitor to his King in abusing the King of England and that I will maintain it with my sword, if he dare come ashore.' The Mores [Moors?] perceiving I was moved, caused the Portugal to depart; who soon after came and promised me that he would procure the liberty of my men and goods. I entertained him kindly, but before he departed the Town, my men and goods were sent for Goa.

"The great man came on the 3rd Oct. and two days after, the ship set sail ; I remaining with Wm Finch merchant who was sick, and not able to stir abroad, and two servants, a cook and my boy. These were the company I had to defend ourselves from so many enemies lurking to destroy us : aiming at me for the stopping of my passage to the Great Mogol. After the departure of the ship I understood that my goods and men were betrayed unto the Portugal by the Jesuit Peniero and Mocreb-chan (the great man's brother) for it was a plot laid to protract time till the Frigates came, and then to dispatch me.

"So long as my ship was at the Bar I was flattered but after her departure I was so misused that it was insufferable. Invironed with enemies, who daily did plot to murder me and cosen me out of my goods. First by Mocreb-chan, taking what he pleased, and leaving what he pleased, giving me such price as his own barbarous conscience afforded, although for three months feeding me with fair promises. All this time Wm Finch was extreme sick, and I could not peep out of doors for fear of the Portuguese who in troups lay lurking to murder me.

"The first plot laid was; I was invited by Hogio Nazam to the freighting of his ship when three gallant fellows came to the tent where I was, and forty Portuguese scattered themselves along the sea shore, ready to give an assault when the word was given. The three gallants, well armed, demanded for the English captain. I rose and told them that I was the man, and perceiving an alteration in them, laid my hand on my weapon; as did also the Captain Mogul and his followers; and if the Portuguese had not been the swifter both they and their shattered crew (in returning to their frigate) had come short home.

"Another time they came to assault me in my house with a Friar to animate and give the soldiers resolution. But I was always wary, having a strong house with good doors. The Portuguese were always coming armed into the city to murder me, which was not the custom for them to come armed as they now did, and the Governor sent them word that if they came armed again, it was at their own peril. At the coming of Mocreb-chan, with a Jesuit named Padre Pineiro, I went to visit him and for a time had many outward shows of him. After his dissembling was past he told me he would not pay for my goods but would return them. I entreated leave to go to Agra to the King, telling him that Wᵐ Finch would remain, to receive either money or wares. After license received, he gave me a letter to the King promising forty horsemen to go with me which he did not accomplish. Then the Father put it into his head that it was not good to let me pass for I would complain of him to the King. And they plotted with my Trenchman and Coachman, to poison or murder me, if one should fail, the other to do it.

"Now finding Wᵐ Finch in good health I left the trade of merchandise in his power: giving him order, what he should do in my absence. So I began to take up soldiers to conduct me, being denied of Mocreb-chan. For my better safety, I went to one of Chanchanna his captains, to let me have forty or fifty Horsemen to conduct me to Chanchanna, being then Viceroy of Decan, Resident in Bramport, who did to all in his power that I demanded, giving me valiant Horsemen Patans, a people much feared in those parts: for if I had not done it, I had been overthrown. For the Portuguese of Daman had agreed with a friend, a Raga who was absolute lord of a Province called Cruly, to stay my passage with 200 Horsemen. But I went so well provided that they durst not incounter us. That time I escaped.

"Then at Dayta, another Province, my Coachman being drunk, discovered the treason that he was hired to murder me: he being overheard by some of my soldiers, who came and told me how it should be done in the morning following when we began our travel. Upon which notice I called and examined the Coachman before the Captain of the Horsemen; who could not deny, but he would never confess who hired him, although he was very much beaten, cursing his fortune that he could not effect it: so I sent him prisoner to the Governor of Surat. But afterwards by my Broker or Trenchman, I understood that both he and the Coachman were hired by Mocreb-chan, by the Jesuit Father Penicro, the one to poison, and the other to murder me: but the Trenchman received nothing till he had done the deed, which he never meant to do, for in that kind he was always true to me: thus God preserved me.

"This was five days after my departure from Surat which was on the 1st Feb. 1608. Some two days beyond Dayta, the Patans left me, to be conducted by another Patan captain, Governor of that lordship, by whom I was most kindly entertained. His name was Sherchan. Being some time a prisoner of the Portuguese, he was glad to do me any service, for that I was of the nation of their enemies; going in person two days journey with me till he had freed me from the dangerous places; at which time he met with a troup of Outlaws, and took four alive, and slew and hurt eight: the rest escaped. He wrote a letter for me to have his house at Bramport, which was a great courtesy, the Town being full of soldiers: for then began the Wars of the Decans. The 18th of Feb. I came in safety to Bramport, and the next day I went to Court to visit Chanchanna, then the Viceroy of Decan, with a present, who kindly took it, and made me a great Feast: giving me his most kind letter to the King. This done he embraced me, and so we parted. We spoke Turkish."

After remaining a few days to exchange his money, and wait for a caravan, Hawkins took some fresh soldiers, and continued his journey to Agra, "where after much labour, toil, and many dangers, I arrived in safety on the 16th April, 1609. Seeking for a house in a very secret manner, notice was given to the King, the Emperor Jehángír, that I was come, but not to be found. He presently charged both Horsemen and Footmen not to leave before I was found, commanding his Knight Marshall to accompany me with great state to the Court, as an Ambassador of a King: which he did with a great train, making such extraordinary haste that I admired much: for I could scarce obtain time to apparel myself in my best attire. In fine I was brought before the King, with a slight present, having nothing but cloth, and that not esteemed; what I had for the King, Mocreb-chan took from me, wherewith I acquainted his Majesty. After salutation, with a most kind and smiling countenance, he bade me most heartily welcome. Having His Majesty's [King James I.] letter in my hand he called me to come near, stretching down his hand from the Seat Royal, where he sat in great majesty to be seen of the people. Receiving very kindly the letter and viewing a pretty while, both the seal and manner of making it up, he called for an old Jesuit to read it. In the mean space he spake unto me, in the kindest manner, demanding the contents of the letter, which I told him. Upon which presently promising me by God, that all the King had written he would grant. The Jesuit likewise told him the effect of the letter, but saying it was basely penned. My answer was, ' If it please your Majesty these people are our enemies : how can this letter be ill written when my King demandeth favour ? ' He said it was true. Perceiving that I had the Turkish tongue, which he well understood, he commanded me to follow him into his Presence Chamber, desiring to have further conference with me. The first thing he said was that he understood that Mocreb-chan had not dealt well with me, bidding me be of good cheer for he would remedy all. It seems that his enemies had acquainted the King with his proceedings, for he hath spies upon every nobleman. I answered, that all would go well on my side, so long as his Majesty protected me. Upon which he sent a post for Surat with his command to Mocreb-chan to deal well with the English. I sent my letter to Wm Finch. According to command I had daily conference with the King. Both night and day, his delight was very much to talk with me of the affairs of England and other Countries, also of the West Indies.

"Many weeks passed, and I now in great favour, to the grief of mine enemies, I demanded the King for his Commission with Capitulations for the establishing of our Factory to be in my power. His answer was whether I would remain with him, I replied till shipping came ; then my desire was to go home, with the answer of his Majesty's letter."

The King answered that he meant Hawkins to stay longer, while an Ambassador was sent to England. That his remaining would be beneficial to the English nation ; and if Hawkins remained he would grant articles for his factory to his heart's desire. Thus daily enticing him that he would serve his own King, and that he, the Emperor, would allow him £3200 a year with increase till he came to 1000 horse.

"So my first should be 400 Horse. For the nobility of India have their titles by the number of their Horses from 40 to 12,000, which pay belongeth to Princes. I trusting his promise, and seeing that it was beneficial to my nation and to myself, and that after six years your Worships would send another man to my place : further perceiving great injuries offered us, as the

King is so far from the Ports, I did not think it amiss to yield to his request. Then because my name was hard for his pronunciation, he called me English Chan [Inglis Khan], in Persia the title for a Duke."

Hawkins being in the highest favour, "the Jesuits and Portuguese slept not," but by all means sought his overthrow. Also the chief Mahometans were envious of a Christian being near the King. "The Jesuit Penciro, being with Mocreb-chan, and other Jesuits, did little regard their masses and church matters, for studying how to overthrow my affairs." They sent presents to Mocreb-chan, who advertised the King that suffering the English in his land would be the loss of his seaports, as Surat, Cambaga, etc.; in any case not to entertain Hawkins, for his ancient friends the Portuguese murmured at it, and that he was only laying a great stratagem.

The King replied that he had but one Englishman in his Court, and him they need not fear. At this answer the Portuguese were like "mad dogs." So I told the King what dangers I had passed, and the present danger I was in—my boy Steven Gravoner instantly departing this world, my man Nicholas Ufflet extreme sick, myself beginning to fall down too.

"The King called the Jesuits and told them that if I died they should all rue for it. This past the King was very earnest with me to take a white maiden out of his Palace, who would give her all things necessary, with slaves, and he would promise me that she should turn Christian: and by this means my meats and drinks should be looked into by them, and I should live without fear. I refused if she was a Moor, but if so be there could be a Christian found, I would accept it. At which my speech, I little thought a Christian daughter could be found. So the King called to mind one Mubarique Sha, his daughter, who was a Christian Armenian, and of the race of the most ancient Christians, who was a Captain, and in great favour with Ekbar Padasha, this King's father. This Captain died suddenly and without will, with a mass of money, all robbed by his kindred; leaving the child only a few jewels. I seeing she was of so honest a descent, having passed my word, could not withstand my fortunes. Therefore I took her, and for want of a Minister, before Christian Witnesses, I married her: the priest was my man Nicholas which I thought had been lawful, till I met with a Preacher that came with Sir Henry Middleton, and he showing me the error, I was new married again: for ever after I lived content and without fear, she being willing to go where I went, and live as I lived.

"After these matters ended, news came that the pinnace *Ascension* was cast away near Surat, upon which I told the King, having his licence and commission for the settling of our trade; which he was willing to do, limiting me a time to return. But the chief Vizier Abdal Hassan, told the King that my going would be the occasion of war and thus harm might happen to a great man who was sent for Goa to buy toys for the King. Upon which the King's pleasure was that I should stay, and sent his Commission to my chief factor at Surat, William Finch. Now the news came that the *Ascention* was cast away, and her men saved, but they were not supposed to come into Surat. I told the King, who was much discontented with Mocreb-chan my enemy: and gave me commandment for their good usage and for the saving of the goods if possible; to the great joy of Wᵐ Finch and the rest at Surat.

"And now these great favours with the King, being continually in his sight, serving him day and night: it went against the hearts of the Mahometans mine enemies to see that a Christian should be so great and near their King, the more because he had promised to make his brother's children Christians. In all this time I could not get my debts of Mocreb-chan, till at length he was sent for up to the King, to answer for many faults and tyrannical injustice to all people in those parts who petitioned the King for justice.

"To make his peace Mocreb-chan sent many presents to the King's sons, and nobles, who laboured in his behalf, but the King sent to attach all his goods, which were in that abundance, the King was two months viewing them, what he thought fitting he kept, and the rest delivered again to Mocreb-chan. Among the things were the presents that he took from me. Now being in this disgrace his friends at length got him clear, but that he pay every man his right, and that no more complaints be made of him if he loved his life. So he paid every one his due; but he put me off, delaying time till his departure, which was shortly after. For the King had restored him his place again.

"I was forced to demand justice of the King but for all the King's command he did as he listed, and do what I could he cut me off 12,500 mahmudis (a gold coin of Gujrat). For the greatest man in the Kingdom was his friend and many others, murmuring to the King, of the English being in his Country for we were at Nabion, that if once we set foot, we should take his Country. The King called me to make answer. I replied that I would answer it with my life that we were not so base a nation as these mine enemies reported.

"There were favourites nearest the King whom I daily visited and kept in with, who spoke in my behalf: and the King on my side commanded that no more wrongs be offered me. I entreated the head Vizier that he would see that I did not receive so great a loss, who answered me in a threatening manner; that if I opened my mouth any more, he would make me pay 100,000 mahmudis, which the King had lost in his Customes, by entertaining me, and no man durst adventure by reason of the Portuguese. So I was forced to hold my tongue, for I knew this money was swallowed by both these dogs. Now Mocreb-chan, being ready to depart, coming to take his leave in public; three of the principal merchants of Surat were sent for (and come to the Court about affairs wherein the King or his Vizier had employed them) to be present when Mocreb-chan was taking leave, this being a plot laid by himself, the Portuguese, and the Vizier. For some six days before, a letter came to the King from the Portuguese viceroy, with a present of many rare things. The letter saying how highly the King of Portugal took in ill part the entertaining of the English, etc.: and withal how that a merchant had arrived with a fair Ballace Ruby weighing 350 Ratis, of which stone the pattern was sent. Mocreb-chan together with Padre Pineiro saying that this and many other things he hoped to obtain of the Portuguese, so that the English were disannulled; also that it would redound to great loss if they were allowed to come into his Majesty's country. He called the merchants, who affirmed, that they were like to be all undone because of the English, nor hereafter any toy could come into the country, as the Portuguese were so strong at sea, and would not suffer them to go in and out of their ports. These speeches now and formerly, lucre of the stone, and promises by the Fathers of rare things, were the causes the King overthrew my affairs, giving Mocreb-chan his command to the viceroy to that effect that he would never suffer the English to come any more into his ports.

"I now saw that it booted me not to meddle upon a sudden, my enemies were so many, although they had eaten of me many presents. When I saw my time I petitioned unto the King, who granted my request, and commanded that it was his pleasure that the English should come into his ports. So this time I was again afloat. Of this alteration, at that instant the Jesuit had notice, for nothing passes in the Mogul's Court in secret, but it is written, and writers appointed by turns. So the Jesuit sent the most speedy messenger with his letter to Mocreb-chan and Padre Pineiro. At receipt of which they agreed not to go on to Goa till I was overthrown again. Mocreb-chan writing to the King and Vizier how that it stood not with the King's honour to send him, if he performed not what he promised the Portuguese. Again the King went from his word, esteeming a few toys which the father promised more than his honour. Now I went to Hogio Tolian, the second man in the kingdom, who very kindly went unto the King but without success. Thus was I dallied withall by mine enemies, that all the time I served in Court, I could not get a living that would yield anything; all that I received, was not fully £300, a great part whereof was spent upon charges of men sent to the Lordships. When I made petition unto the King he turned me over to Abdall Hassan; who not only denied my living, but also gave order that I was not to enter within the red rails; a place of honour where all my time I was placed near unto the King, in which place there were but five men in the Kingdom before me. Now perceiving my affairs overthrown I determined with the counsel of those who were to be trusted, either to be well in or well out.

"Upon this I had my petition made ready, which made known unto the King how Abdall Hassan had dealt with me having himself taken what his Majesty gave me, how that my charges were so heavy (being desired by his Majesty to stay in his Court) that I besought his Majesty that he would establish me as formerly, or give me leave to depart. His answer was, to give me leave, commanding his safe conduct to be made me, to pass freely without molestation through his kingdom. As the custom is, I came to do my obeisance, and to take my leave, intreating an answer to my King's letter. Abdall Hassan coming from the King, utterly denied me: saying it was not the custom of so great a Monarch, to write unto a petty Prince. I answered that the King knew more of the mightiness of the King of England, than to be a petty Governor. Well, this was mine answer, together with my leave taken. I went to my house, to get all my goods, using all speed to clear myself out of the country, staying only for Nicholas Ufflet, to come from Lahore. William Finch determined to return overland for England, being past all hope of embarking at Surat: which course I also would have taken but that for some causes I could not travel through Turkey, and especially with a woman. So I was forced to curry favour with the Jesuits to get me a safe conduct from the Viceroy, to go to Goa, Portugal, and thence to England. But my wife's kindred when they saw that I was to carry her away, suspecting they would never see her again I was forced to yield that my wife go no further than Goa, where they could visit her, and if at any time I went away, that I leave her that portion that is the custom, to which to prevent mischief I consented. But knowing that if my wife would go with me, all would be of no effect, I got the Jesuits to send for two safe passes. This and much more the Fathers would have done to get me out of the country. In the meantime news came of the return of Mocreb-chan with many things for the King, but not the Ballace Ruby, and besides he had not his full content of the Portuguese as he expected. And at this time the Vizier, my enemy, was thrust out of his place and sent to the wars of Decan. Ghiyas was made chief Vizier and his daughter married the King [the celebrated Núr Jehán.] The Vizier's son and myself were great friends, so that this alteration, and being sure of the ships comming, I sent for jewels fitting for the new Queen, and also for the Vizier and his son.

"Now after they had my gifts they began on all sides to solicit my cause; at which time news came to Agra that three English ships were at Surat. Upon which news the Vizier asked me what I had for his Majesty, and I showed him a ruby ring, who bade me go with him, and that the King was already won. So once more coming before his Greatness, my petition read he granted me the establishment of our Factory and English trade for Surat. But now what followed? A great man, nearest favourite of the king, and the dearest friend that Mocreb-chan and Abdall Hassan had, interfered, and my business was again overthrown. But for myself if I would remain in his service he would command that what he had allowed me should be given me to my content. Which I declined, unless the English might come unto his ports according to promise, and as for my particular maintenance, my King would not see me want. Again desiring answer of my King's letter, he consulted with his Viziers, and sent me denial.

"So I took my leave and departed from Agra 2. Nov' 1611. Being of a thousand thoughts what course to take; for I still had a doubt of being poisoned by the Portuguese for lucre of my goods, and by reason of the war it was dangerous to travel through Decan unto Masulipatan; by land, by reason of the Turks, I could not go; and stay I would not amongst these faithless Infidels. I arrived at Cambaya 30th Dec 1611, where I had certain news of the English ships at Surat, and departing from there 18th Jan I came unto the ships the 26th of the month where I was most kindly received by Sir Henry Middleton. He departed and arrived at Dabull the 16th Feb. In the Red Sea we found three English ships commanded by Cap' John Saris."

On the 8th December, 1612, they arrived at Bantam, where Hawkins left Sir Henry Middleton, who was not returning to England, and went home in the *Thomas* with Captain Saris, arriving at Saldanha Bay on 21st April, 1613. Here the report of Hawkins to the Company abruptly ends; for he died on the passage home, and was buried in Ireland.*

* *Calendar of State Papers*, Colonial (East India), 1608-1616.

His young wife, left alone amongst strangers, did not at once return to her own people at Agra. Possessed of one diamond worth £2000, and others to the value of £4000, in the following year she became the wife of Gabriel Towerson,* who had been in the voyage of Captain Saris, and brought home the *Hector.* In 1617 Captain and Mrs. Towerson went out to India again, and visited Agra, where the lady remained with her relations. Towerson went home, and in 1620 was appointed Principal Factor at the Moluccas, where he was the chief victim in the massacre of Amboyna.

A BRIEF DISCOURSE OF THE STRENGTH, WEALTH, AND GOVERNMENT, WITH SOME OF THE CUSTOMS, OF THE GREAT MOGUL.

By WILLIAM HAWKINS.

"As Christian Princes use their degrees by titles, they have their titles by their number of horses, except favoured by the King and honoured with the title of Chan. There are 12,000 Horsemen. Dukes 9,000, Marquises 5,000, Earls 3,000, etc. etc. The yearly income of his Crown Land is fifty Cror of Rupias, every Cror is a hundred Leckes, and every Leck is a hundred thousand Rupiæ. The compass of his country is two year's travel with Carravan. His Empire is divided into five great Kingdoms and there are five especial castles. The chief city is Delhi where he is established King. His treasure is an immense amount of gold and silver in coin. 82½ lbs weight of rough diamonds great and small, but none less than 2½ carats. Of Ballace rubies 2,000, pieces of pearl of all sorts 600 lbs, rubies of all sorts 100 lbs, of emeralds 250 lbs, of Eshime, which comes from Cathaya 100 lbs. Of stones of Emen, a red stone 5,000 pieces. Of other sorts as coral, topasses, etc. there is an infinite number. Of the jewels wrought in gold. Of swords of Almaine blades, with hilts and scabbards set with stones of the richest sort 2,200. Of Saddle Drums used for Hawking 500 ; brooches for their heads, wherein their feathers be put 2,000. Saddles of gold and silver set with stones 1,000. Of Teukes 25 ; a great lance which instead of colours, are carried, when the King goeth to the wars. Of Quilasoles—state umbrellas—for to shadow him 20. None in his Empire dareth have any of these carried for his shadow but himself. Five chairs of state ; three of silver, and two of gold : of others 100 of silver and gold. Of rich glasses 200 ; vases for wine very rich set with jewels 100 ;

* The Company presented Mrs. Hawkins with a purse of 200 Jacobuses, as a token of their love, upon a general release being given by her.

X 2

500 drinking cups but 50 very rich, made of one piece of Ballace ruby, and other stones. Of chains of Pearl and precious stones, rings with jewels an infinite number which only the keeper knoweth. Of all sorts of Plate of silver wrought 100,000 lbs. of wrought gold plate 50,000 lbs. weight.

"There are 12,000 horses, whereof 4,000 are Persian, 6,000 Turkish, and 2,000 of Kismire. Of elephants there are 12,000, camels 2,000, oxen for carts and other service 10,000, mules 1,000. Of deer for sport 3,000, of dogs for hunting 400. Tame lions 100. Of buffaloes 500. All sorts of hawkes 4,000. Pigeons for sport of flying 10,000, and 4,000 singing birds.

"Of armour of all sorts, at an hour's warning, in readiness to arm 25,000 men.

"His daily expense for his own person, feeding his cattle, apparel, victuals, and house amount to 50,000 Rupias a day. The daily expenses for his women is 30,000 rupias. All this written concerning his treasure, expenses, and monthly pay is at his Court or Castle of Agra; and all his Castles have their several treasure, especially Lahore, which was not mentioned above. The custom of this Mogul Emperor is to take possession of his Noblemens' Treasure when they die, and to bestow on his children what he pleaseth; but commonly he dealeth well with them. Also his custom is, that all his treasures and things are divided into 360 parts so that he daily seeth a certain number; for what is brought to him to-day is not seen again, till that day twelvemonth. He hath 300 Elephants Royal which he rideth; when they are brought before him they come with great iollitie [jollity] with 30 or 40 men before them with small Stremers. These elephants eat 10 rupias every day in sugar, butter, grain, and sugar canes: they are tame, and so well managed, that I saw with mine eyes, when the King commanded one of his young sons (a child of seven years of age) to go to the Elephant to be taken up by his snout: who did so, delivering him to his keeper that commanded him with his hook: and having done this to the King's son, he afterwards did the like to many other children. When he rideth on Progress of Hunting the compass of his tents is as large as London and more for of all sorts of people that follow the camp, are 200,000 for he is provided as for a city. This King is thought to be the greatest Emperor of the East. As for elephants of his own, and those of his nobles there are 40,000, of which one half are trained for war; they are of all beasts the most understanding; and many strange things are done by them. He hath also infinite numbers of Dromedaries, which come with great speed to give assault to any city, which the King uses to unexpectedly surprise his enemies. Myself at the time I was one of his Courtiers have seen many cruel deeds done by him. Five times a week, his Elephants fight before him, during which many men are killed; but if a man be badly hurt that man is cast into the river, the King commanding it, saying: dispatch him, for as long as he liveth he will curse me. Again he delighteth to see men torn in pieces by Elephants. In my time he put his Secretary to death only upon suspicion, with his sword giving him a deadly wound. Likewise it happened to a nobleman and a great friend of mine, that a fair China dish which cost 90 rupias was broken by a mischance being packed amongst other things on a camel, which fell and broke the whole parcel. The nobleman knowing how dearly the King loved this dish sent a trusty servant overland to China to seek for another. Two years after the King remembered the dish but the messenger had not come back. Now when the King heard that the dish was broken, he was in a great rage, commanding the nobleman to be brought before him and almost beaten to death. After two months, he was reasonably recovered; when he was commanded to depart the Court and go to China in search of a such like dish. In my time a Pattan, a man of good stature, proudly demanded 1000 rupias a day for his services of one of the king's sons. The Prince asked him the reason of so great a demand: he replied make trial of me with all sorts of weapons, and if I do not perform as much, let me die for it. At night the King's custom being to drink the Prince seeing his father merry told him of this man and he was brought before him. Now while he was sent for, a wild lion was brought in, a very great one, and strongly chained. The Pattan came in, and the King asked what valour was in him that he should demand so much wages. He asked the King to make trial. That I will, said the King, go wrestle with this lion. The Patton answered that it was a wild beast and to go upon him without weapon, would be no trial of his manhood. The King again commanded him to wrestle with the lion which he did for some time: and then the lion got the poor man between his claws, and tore his body and the one half of his face, so that this valiant man was killed. The King not contented sent for ten of his horsemen being that night on the watch: who one after another, were to buffet with the lion; all were badly wounded, and it cost three of them their lives. The King continued in this vein, for whose pleasure many men were killed and hurt. Also he cannot abide that any man should have any precious stone of value, for it is death if he know it, not to have the refusal thereof. Every day he weareth a diamond of great price, also a chain of pearls, another of Emeralds, and ballace rubies: and another jewel in his turban, he does not wear the same again for a year: all his things are divided into proportions for every day of the year. It is not to be wondered that he is so rich in jewels, gold, and silver when he hath heaped together the treasure and jewels of so many Kings as his forefathers have conquered. Again all the money and jewels of his nobles when they die come unto him. India is rich in silver, for all nations bring coin, and carry away commodities : the coin is buried in India, and every 20 years it is thought comes into the King's power. All the lands are at his disposing, who giveth and taketh at his pleasure.

"The manner of the praying of the Great Mogul is first, in the morning about break of day he is at his Beades which are of precious stones, at the upper end of the Jet is a picture of our Lady and Christ.

"The custom of the Indians is to burn their dead and at their burning many of their wives will and voluntarily burn alive with them because they will content themselves to live no longer than their husbands."

Judith, eldest daughter of Captain William Hawkins, of Plymouth, by his first wife, married Henry Whitacre, of Westbury, co. Wilts, and had issue William and others. "Judith Whitaker widowe . . . tennte . . . etc. of the heirs and assignes of William Hawkins Esq. deceased." So named in the indenture of composition of the Plymouth Water Act, July 5th, 34th year of Elizabeth (1592).

ARMS OF WHITACRE, IMPALING HAWKINS.

Clare, second daughter of William Hawkins by his first wife, married Robert Michell, July 3rd, 1587, at St. Andrew's, Plymouth.

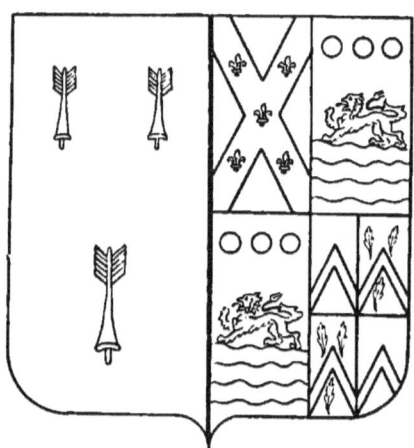

ARMS OF RISDON, IMPALING HAWKINS.

Mary, third surviving daughter and co-heir of William Hawkins by his second wife, married (at Modbury, in 1601) Thomas Risdon, of Sandwell, near Totnes, a learned Bencher of the Inner Temple in Elizabeth's reign. He is the Thomas Risdon mentioned in the Plymouth Receivers' Accounts (1637-8) as handing over to the Corporation "such writings as concerned Vauters Fee lately bought by the Town of Mr John Hawkyns"—John Hawkins being Sir Richard Hawkins's eldest son, then living at Poole, in Slapton.

Thomas Risdon died at the advanced age of 100 years, in 1641 (?), without children, leaving his estates, which were very considerable, to his nephew, Francis Risdon, of Bableigh.

Thomas Risdon, of Sandwell, was a younger son of Thomas Risdon, of Bableigh, near Bideford, by Wilmot, daughter of . . . . . Gifford, of Halsbury. The Risdons lived at Bableigh *temp.* Edward III., and were descended from the Risdons of Risdon, in Gloucestershire.

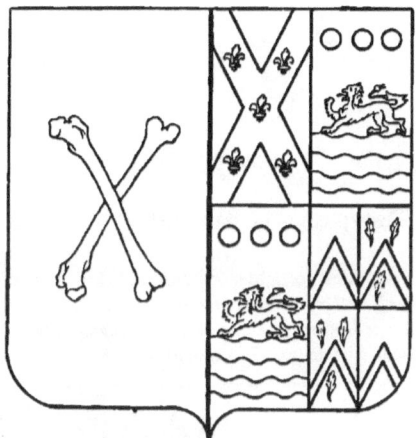

ARMS OF NEWTON, IMPALING HAWKINS.

Frances, fourth daughter and co-heir of William Hawkins by his second wife, married (about 1608) John Newton, of Crabaton, in Deptford, Devon (age 36 in 1620). He was son of William Newton, of Somerset (died at Crabaton 1618), and Grace, daughter of Philip Sture, of Bradley, North Huish.

William Newton, son and heir of John and Frances, was aged 11 in 1620; and had six sisters: Maria, aged 10; Grace, 9; Francisca, 8; Judith, 7; Philippa, 6; Elizabeth, 5. The last-named married Walter Fursland; and Elizabeth Fursland, their daughter, in 1660 married Francis Calmady, fourth son and heir of Sir Shilston Calmady. Anna, her sister, died unmarried.

CHAPTER VII.

Descendants of Sir Richard Hawkins.

UDITH, eldest daughter of Admiral Sir Richard Hawkins, was baptized at Deptford, November 7th, 1592—before her father was a prisoner in Spain—and was eleven years older than the five other children. She married Tristram Sture, of Marridge House, Ugborough.

ARMS OF STURE, IMPALING HAWKINS.

John, eldest son of Admiral Sir Richard Hawkins, was baptized March 16th, 1604, at St. Andrew's, Plymouth. In 1627, the year his mother died, he was at sea; at her death he inherited the manor of Poole, in Slapton, with the

Y

Plymouth estates.   In 1637–8 he appears to have parted with his Plymouth property; for in the Receiver's Accounts for that year we find:

> Itm for a present given M' Risdon [Thomas Risdon, of Sandwell, who had married Mary Hawkins, his father's first cousin] to procure out of his hands such writings as concerned Vauter's Fee lately bought by the Town of M' John Hawkyns and a man and two horses two journeys to fetch the said writings v^{li} iiij^s.

John Hawkins resided at Poole until he sold it, or the manor went, to the Luttrells.   They sold the estates to Mr. Nicholas Paige, the daughter of whose son, William Paige, married Mr. Bastard.

ARMS OF HAWKINS, IMPALING RICHARDS.

John Hawkins, of Slapton, married Hester Richards, of Dartmouth, in 1636, by whom he had—

Judith, baptized June 27th, 1639.
Hester   „   1640 ; *ob.* 1644.
Richard   „   January, 1641.
John   „   September 21st, 1643 ; *ob.* 1670.
William   „   November 6th, 1644.
Hester   „   November 19th, 1647.

All baptized at Slapton as the children of John Hawkins, Esq., and Mrs. Hester his wife.   Their other children were Robert, Mary, Thomas, and Nicholas.

Hester, the wife of John Hawkins, was buried at Slapton, July 23rd, 1660.

Richard, born in 1641, married Tomasine, daughter and heiress of John Sloley, Esq., of Fremington; *ob.* 1680, and left his property to Dorothy, daughter of his brother Nicholas.

John, born in 1643, died and was buried at Slapton, May 12th, 1670. He appears to have lived in his father's house. Administration granted, May 12th, 1671, to his sister Hester. The inventory of his things in his room was rather over £100; clothes, £20.

Robert married Jane . . . . and lived at Bideford; *ob.* 1680. In his will he names his wife Jane, his brothers Thomas and Nicholas, and his sister Mary.

Thomas Hawkins married Sarah, daughter of John Crocker, vicar of Stokefleming; *ob.* at Stokefleming, 1695. In his will he left everything to his daughter Judith,* who, in 1702, married Peter Creed.

The old Church Register at Stokefleming is very imperfect.

ARMS OF HAWKINS, IMPALING CROCKER.

Nicholas married, at Fremington, Ann Manning, by whom he had an only daughter, Dorothy.

* The grandmother of Mary Creed, who married Richard Hawkins. (See page 170.)

John Hawkins the father, the eldest son of Sir Richard, died at Stoke-fleming, near Slapton, where he lived after he sold the estate of Poole; but he was buried at Slapton. Administration granted, December 20th, 1678, to his daughter Hester. The inventory is lost.

Richard, the second son of Admiral Sir Richard Hawkins, according to his father's will, inherited Pryvitt, in Alverstoke, Southampton; but lived at Slapton. He married Elizabeth . . . . . by whom he had:

               Elizabeth, baptized October 18th, 1635.
               Nicholas   „   March 31st, 1639.
               Jeremiah   „   June 12th, 1642.

All baptized at Slapton as the children of Richard Hawkins and Elizabeth his wife.

Elizabeth, the wife of Richard Hawkins, was buried at Slapton, January 27th, 1666.

Richard Hawkins was buried at Slapton, November 22nd, 1667.

Robert Hawkins was buried at Slapton, March 8th, 1644.

Joane Hawkins was buried at Slapton, April 1st, 1698.

The old Register at Slapton is much worm-eaten, and many pages are missing.

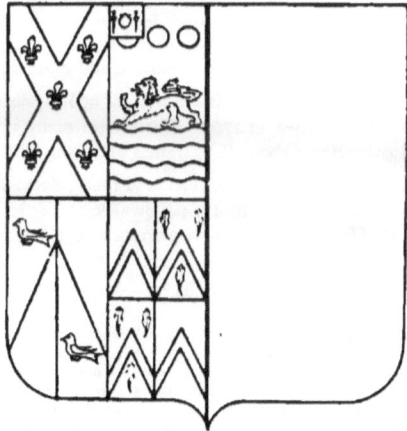

ARMS OF HAWKINS, IMPALING · · · ·

Nicholas, the eldest son of Richard Hawkins, left Slapton, and went to live at Kingsbridge, a few miles distant. He married . . . . . and had a son John.

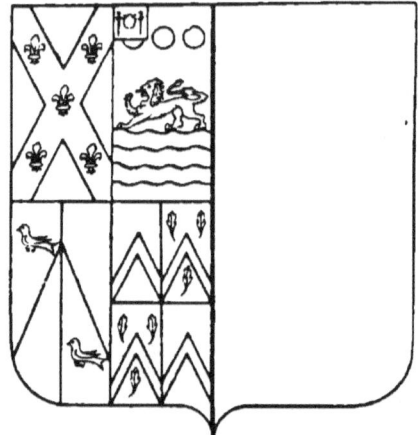

ARMS OF HAWKINS, IMPALING · · · ·

The Kingsbridge Registers are very imperfect, and much cut out in places.

John, the eldest son of Nicholas Hawkins, lived at Kingsbridge. He was a Captain of the Militia, and died in 1700. There were many stories told of his quarrelling with Justice Beare about King James and King William.

Justice Beare lived at Bearscombe, Buckland-tout-Saints; he was the local Church champion of the day. "In 1684 a justice called John Beare keeps Friends out of their House." On the weathercock of Kingsbridge Church is "I. Beare."

John Hawkins married Elizabeth Lane,* by whom he had:

* William Lane, B.D., Rector of Aveton Gifford and Ringmore, was educated at Oxford, and possessed the living of Ringmore before he obtained that of Aveton Gifford, to which he was admitted about the beginning of the Rebellion, and was unable to settle in it or remove his goods from Ringmore when Plymouth declared for the Parliament. At which time the garrison "came out with their boats and plundered those parts and took off the most valuable goods in the house and took [so says Mr. Lane's son] two of my brethren Richard and John to Awmar. They imprisoned them in Plymouth some time, where they suffered greatly. All which time my father was active with Sir — Champernoun and other gentlemen for raising succours for His Majesty. Then did the champions vaunt about the country and make deligent enquiry after Bishop Lane the Traytor, at which time he hid in the Church Tower 3 or 4 months. He was then disposest of both livings Ringmore being given to Ford, and Aveton Gifford to Francis Barnard.

ARMS OF HAWKINS, IMPALING LANE.

Richard.

Honour. Married William Saunders, Esq. (of Quay House, West Alvington, in 1707), July 22nd, 1706, at Aveton Gifford, near Kingsbridge. Issue three daughters. The eldest married Wheatley, and left no children; the second married Grove, of Plymouth, issue a son, Thomas Grove, R.N., *ob.* 1822; the third daughter married . . . . . Fountain, of London, issue a daughter, who married Rev. Charles Ed. de Coetlogon.

His 'temporal estate' at Aveton was also sequestered except a 'sett of mills' where Mrs. Lane with 5 children took up their abode. The eldest son Richard went to New England and Mr. Lane to France where he remained till he could 'buy his peace.' Afterwards Mr. Lane returned from France and removed with the second son John, third son William and daughter ELIZABETH to a place in Torbay called 'Hope's Nose' where he employed himself in drawing Lyme Stones." That did not succeed ; so he returned to his mills, and found the water supply cut off by Barnard, and his family in a miserable condition. He then determined to lay his case before "Cromwell's Council board," so in his sixty-third year walked to London. "It being discovered and proved, he had orders to dispossess Barnard and named another person (one John Martin) for Aveton Gifford." On his way home he caught cold, and died at the King's Head, in High Street, Exon, and "lieth interred under the Chancel Table in Alphington Church."

"Mr. Lane is certainly the first instance in all English History of a Bachelor of Divinity who was forced to turn miller and dig in a quarry for a livelihood."—WALKER's *Sufferings of the Clergy.*

Richard Hawkins, of Kingsbridge, eldest son of John Hawkins, married Dorcas Knowling at Aveton Gifford, July 22nd, 1706, by whom he had:

John,	baptized November 9th, 1708. Of Norton.	
Richard	„	June 9th, 1710; *ob.* October, 1712.
Mary	„	March 3rd, 1712; married, in 1755, Barton Land, Esq., of Hayne.
Elizabeth.		Married, in 1736, Thomas Cornish,* of West Prawle, Portlemouth.
Richard	„	April 14th, 1717. Of Kingsbridge.
Knowling	„	February 7th, 1719; married, in 1749, Mary Hemmings.

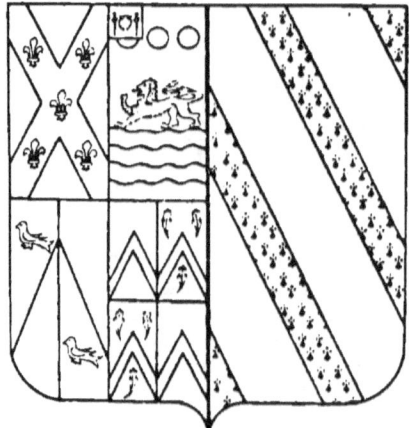

ARMS OF HAWKINS, IMPALING KNOWLING.

John, the eldest son of Richard Hawkins and Dorcas Knowling, born 9th November, 1708, married first, Sarah, daughter of William Gilbert, of Long-

* A daughter of Thomas Cornish, by Elizabeth Hawkins his wife, married Richard Lake, Esq., of Scoble, South Poole, whose daughter and coheiress married Roger Ilbert Prideaux. She was the Mrs. Ilbert Prideaux mentioned by the Lysonses, the Devonshire historians, as having in her possession the gold chain given to Sir Richard Hawkins by the Spanish Lady. This gold chain, on the death of Mrs. Ilbert Prideaux, went to the Lightfoot family.

brook, by whom he had a son (John) and six daughters.   He married, secondly, Elizabeth, daughter of Abraham Gilbert, of Holwell, July 23rd, 1751, by whom he had a son, Abraham, and a daughter, Elizabeth.   John Hawkins lived at Norton, parish of Malborough, near Kingsbridge.   He commenced to build the Moult in 1764, but did not live to finish it, as he died a few months later.   The Moult was sold to S. Strode, Esq., in 1785.

ARMS OF HAWKINS, IMPALING GILBERT.

His eldest son, John Hawkins, married Judith Hayne, of Kingsbridge, by whom he had four sons, John Gilbert Hayne, born 1771; William, born 1772; Samuel Holditch, Captain Royal Marines; William Gilbert; and a daughter, Letitia.

Their eldest son, John Gilbert Hayne, married Jane Souter, by whom he had two sons, John Gilbert Hayne, Royal Navy; William Gilbert; and a daughter, Jane.

Second son, Samuel Holditch, married Letitia Isabella Hayne, of London. Issue, a daughter, Louisa Fountain Trafalgar Hawkins.

Third son, William Gilbert Courtenay Hawkins, married Sarah Ashe, of Langley, by whom he had one son, William Gilbert Courtenay, born 17th November, 1807; lived at Chippenham, Wilts.

Abraham, son of John Hawkins of Norton, by his second wife, married Harriet Hamilton, daughter of Petre, of Mawnan, Cornwall, by whom he had two daughters. Henrietta Hamilton Hawkins, the elder, who lived at Alston, unmarried, drove a four-in-hand, and had her pew painted to match her livery! Miss Elliot, of Tresillian, Kingsbridge, has a doll which belonged to this old lady. Stephana, the second daughter, married Captain E. M. Bray.

Abraham Hawkins, F.R.S., J.P., of Alston, near Kingsbridge, was the author of the *History of Kingsbridge*. He translated the works of Claudian, and helped Polwhele with his *History of Devonshire*. "Justice Hawkins" was the terror of Kingsbridge in those days. He was a Captain in the North Devon Militia, and a Deputy Lieutenant for Devon.

ARMS OF HAWKINS, IMPALING PETRE.

Richard, second son of Richard Hawkins and Dorcas Knowling, lived at Kingsbridge, and married Elizabeth, daughter of Alexander Wills, of Kingsbridge, and Mary, his wife, daughter of Thomas Wyse, Esq., of Harburton, by whom he had two sons, Richard and John, and five daughters.

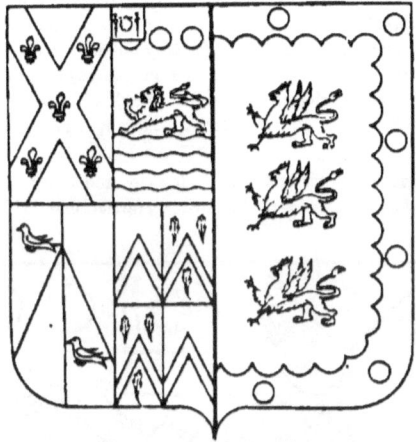

ARMS OF HAWKINS, IMPALING WILLS.

Richard, eldest son of Richard Hawkins and Elizabeth Wills, married Mary, daughter of William Creed, by whom he had two sons and two daughters. Mary Creed's grandmother was Judith Hawkins, daughter of Thomas Hawkins,* Esq., of Stokefleming (by his wife Sarah, daughter of John Crocker, rector of Stokefleming), who was a son of John Hawkins (by his wife Hester Richards), son of Admiral Sir Richard Hawkins. She was the wife of Peter Creed, who was the grandson of Francis Rous, Provost of Eton and Speaker of the House of Commons, and one of Oliver Cromwell's lords. He was Provost of Eton, and the founder of Pembroke College, Oxford. Joan Rous, daughter of the Provost, married the Rev. Wm. Bailey, rector of Stokefleming, in 1641, and their daughter, Joan Bailey, married Peter Creed, of Coombe, Stokefleming, in 1678.

John	baptized April 19th, 1782.
Abraham Mills	„ August 13th, 1784.
Charlotte	„ January 1st, 1786.
Harriet	„ February 11th, 1787.

* See page 163. By this marriage the lineal descendants of the *two* only sons of Admiral Sir Richard Hawkins were continued in one line.

Major John Hawkins, E.C.I. Engineers, elder son of Richard Hawkins and Mary Creed, married Frances Schutz, daughter of Richard Vere Drury, of Shotover House, Oxford, by his first wife, only child of Sir George Vandeput, Bart., by whom he had a son, Richard George, *ob.* 1832, unmarried, and two daughters—Caroline Charlotte, married General H. Blois Turner, Royal Engineers; and Stephana Mary, married Captain Conrad Owen, C.B., 1st Lancers (Bombay).

Charlotte, elder daughter of Richard Hawkins and Mary Creed, unmarried, lived at the Knowle, Kingsbridge. Her sister, Harriet, married Thomas Harris.

ARMS OF HAWKINS AND CREED.

Admiral Abraham Mills Hawkins, born 13th August, 1784, of Butville, Kingsbridge, married, in 1819, Mary Wise, only daughter of Christopher

ARMS OF HAWKINS, IMPALING SAVERY.

Savery, Esq., of Shilston and South Efford, by Mary, daughter of John Wise, Esq., of Wonwell, by whom he had two sons. He died November, 1857, and was buried at Dodbrook, Kingsbridge.

"Rear-Admiral Abraham Mills Hawkins entered the Navy in March, 1798, and after serving as volunteer and midshipman in H.M. Ships *Barfleur, Prince, Lancaster, Rattlesnake,* and *Trident,* under the late Admirals Dacres, Sir Roger Curtis, Capt. Roger Curtis, and Admiral Rainier—on the Channel, Cadiz, Cape of Good Hope, and East India Stations—was, in 1804, appointed acting-Lieut. of H.M.S. *Sheerness;* on her wreck, in 1805, of the *Psyche;* and in Jan., 1806, first-Lieut. of H.M.S. *Duncan,* Capt. Lord George Stuart; but towards the end of that year ill-health, contracted from a service of seven years in hot climates, obliged him, by invaliding, to quit the East Indies for England; and it was only on his arrival that the Lords of the Admiralty were pleased to confirm him a Lieut., by commission dated 11th June, 1807, thus losing three years of acting-Lieut.'s time, the greater part of one having been served as first-Lieut. of a frigate. He was then appointed to H.M.S. *Amiable,* on the North Sea Station, commanded by his former Captain, Lord George Stuart, becoming about the end of the year her first Lieut.; and on his Lordship's removal to the *Horatio,* in 1810, first of that ship, and served in her till his wounds obliged him to go to the hospital for cure, in Sept., 1812 ; and he was promoted for his services to the rank of Commander on the 11th Dec. of that year. During the period above mentioned he participated in all the services of his gallant Captain (and for which that officer received the Order of the Bath, on its extension in 1814); but was severely wounded, the following account showing how it occurred. In August, 1812, he was sent by Lord George Stuart, with the *Horatio's* barge and three six-oared cutters, to attack some enemy's vessels at Trompsen, on the coast of Norway, and succeeded in boarding and bringing out all that were in that port ; viz., a schooner and cutter of His Danish Majesty's Navy, and a ship of 400 tons, their prize, after a most determined resistance. His right hand was shattered by a grape-shot as the boats he commanded were advancing to the attack, and he received a pistol-shot in his left arm when in the act of boarding the enemy's second vessel of war, after having carried the first, as is detailed in a letter from Lord George Stuart, published in the *Gazette* of Aug. 25th, 1812.

"In 1813, shortly after his promotion, he was informed at the Admiralty, by Admiral Domett, that he had been elected for the command of gunboats intended for a particular service on the North Sea Station ; but circumstances arising from which this expedition was not carried into effect, Lord Melville was pleased to appoint him to H.M. Sloop *Conflict*, which vessel he commanded on the Home Stations till she was put out of commission, in Sept., 1815, at the conclusion of the war.

"Unsuccessful in his endeavours to procure employment during the earlier part of the peace, he, in 1819, accepted the appointment of Inspecting Commander of the Coast Guard, under a constitution from the Lords of the Treasury, and then considered permanent ; but on transfer of these appointments to the Admiralty, they becoming triennial, he was superceded ;* and without entering upon the particulars which called forth the approbation of Comptrollers-General Shortland and Bowles, the following letter was addressed to him by the heads of department :

"'I cannot allow you to quit the command you have so long held, and the duties of which you have discharged with so much credit to yourself, without expressing in the strongest terms the sense I entertain of the zeal, activity, and ability you have uniformly shown in the performance of a very arduous and harassing service, and I shall feel great pleasure in representing your merits to the Lords Commissioners of the Admiralty in any way which may tend to your advancement in His Majesty's Service. Dated 2nd July, 1824.

"'Signed WM. BOWLES, Compt.-Gen.'

* The present arrangement for promotions from the Coast Guard did not then exist.

"His appointment to H.M. Sloop *Raleigh*, in July, 1830, was given with a view to promotion, in consequence of his services, he has reason to know ; for both Lord Melville and Sir George Cockburne did him the honour to tell him so previous to his sailing for the Mediterranean.   The opinion of the late Sir Henry Hotham as to the efficient state of that sloop was well known throughout the Fleet, of which he was Commander-in-Chief.   Sir Pulteney Malcolm, his successor, on Sir Henry's lamented sudden death, was pleased to express himself publickly on the *Raleigh's* quarter-deck in most gratifying terms, and did him the honour to state his intention of bringing before Sir James Graham the sense he entertained of his deserving promotion on his last inspection at Malta, and he has reason to believe that he did so.   In May, 1834, he paid off the *Raleigh*, having commanded her nearly four years ; and on the 6th Feb. following, then more than 22 years a Commander, was promoted to the rank of Captain, his several steps of promotion having been earned by service.   He stands on the list of Captains within one of an officer on whom it (the good service pension) has been bestowed, and he further ventures to state that his Commander's commission is of previous date to that of 18 of the 21 now enjoying it.

"Dated at Kingsbridge, Devon, March 10th, 1837."*

We also read in JAMES'S *Naval History :*

On August 1st (1812), as the British 38-gun frigate *Horatio*, "Capt. Lord George Stuart, was in latitude 70° 40″ north, running down the coast of Norway, a small sail was seen from the mast-head close in with the land; and which, just before she disappeared among the rocks, was discovered to be an armed cutter. Considering it an object of some importance to attempt the destruction of the enemy's cruisers in this quarter, Lord George Stuart despatched the barge and three cutters of the *Horatio*, with about 80 officers and men, commanded by Lieut. Abraham Mills Hawkins, assisted by Lieut. Thomas James Poole Masters, and Lieut. of Marines George Syder, to execute the service.   Lieut. Hawkins, gaining information on shore that the cutter had gone to a village on an arm of the sea, about 35 miles distant over land, detached one of the cutters, under master's mate James Crisp, to disperse some small-armed men collected on the shore, and proceeded with the remaining three boats for the creek in which the Danish cutter lay.   On the 2nd Aug., at 8 o'clock in the morning, Lieut. Hawkins discovered the vessel, which was the Danish

---

* Taken from the Memorandum of Capt. Abraham Mills Hawkins, submitting his name as a candidate for the good service pension (which he obtained).

King's Cutter No. 97, of four 6-pounders and 22 men, lying at anchor with the Danish King's Schooner No. 114, of six 6-pounders and 30 men, commanded by Lieut. Buderhorf, of the Danish Navy, the Commodore, and an American ship of 400 tons, their prize. On the approach of the British boats, the Danish vessels presented their broadsides, with springs on their cables, and were moored in capital defensive position. The British nevertheless advanced to the attack, and at 9 a.m. received the fire of the Danes, whom however Lieut. Hawkins and his party, assisted towards the end by Mr. Crisp's boat, completely subdued, after a most sanguinary combat. The British lost 9 killed, including Lieut. George Syder, of the Marines, and 16 wounded, including Assistant-Surgeon James Larans and one seaman mortally, Lieuts. Hawkins and Masters, the boatswain, and one midshipman, Thomas Fowler, severely. The loss on the Danish side was also very severe, amounting to 10 killed and 13 wounded, including the commanders of the schooner and the cutter severely, and some other officers. Both the British and the Danes fought in the bravest manner, and between them sustained a loss for which the prizes were a poor compensation. As a reward for his gallantry Lieut. Hawkins was made a commander in the ensuing December."

ARMS OF HAWKINS, IMPALING PONSFORD.

John Mills Hawkins, eldest son of Admiral Abraham Mills Hawkins, born July 22nd, 1821, lieutenant 52nd Light Infantry. Died, February 22nd, 1846, unmarried, from the effects of yellow fever.

Christopher Stuart Hawkins, second and only surviving son, born September 9th, 1823. Member of Lincoln's Inn and a magistrate for Devon. Married, January 30th, 1857, Elizabeth Richardson, daughter of the late James Ponsford, of 24, Kensington Palace Gardens, and has one surviving son—John Servington; and three daughters—Mary Wise Savery, Florence Elizabeth, and Blanche Stephana.

awkins of Devon.

A Genealogical Table of the Family of Hawkins of Devon.

Arms.—Sable, on a base wavy argent and azure, a lion passant or; in chief, three bezants. First augmentation, granted by Queen Elizabeth for Admiral Sir John Hawkins's exploits: On a canton or, an escallop between two palmers' staves of the field. Second augmentation. Crest upon his helm, a wreath argent and azure; a demi Moor proper bound and captive, with annulets on his arms and in his ears, or; mantled gules doubled argent. Motto, "Nil Desperandum."

Arms of Hawkins or Nash Court, Kent.—Argent; on a saltire sable five fleurs-de-lis or.

A branch of the Hawkinses of Nash Court settled in Devon.

APPENDIX.

THE following papers relating to the Hawkins family have been calendared by the Historical Manuscripts Commission from the collections named:

MARQUIS OF SALISBURY.

1580.	Aug. 27.	Sir John Hawkins to Burghley.
1598.	April 1.	Capt. R. Hawkins to the Earl of Essex.
,,		Fourteen items connected with Earl of Essex. Examination of Thomas Graye taken in the South Sea with Richard Hawkins.
,,	Aug. 1.	Richard Hawkins to Earl of Essex.
,,	Nov. 14.	Richard Hawkins to Earl of Essex.
,,	,,	Richard Hawkins to Earl of Essex.
,,		Mrs. Judith Hawkins (wife of R. Hawkins) to the Queen.
,,	Dec. 5.	Lady Mary Hawkins to the Queen.
,,	,,	Lady M. Hawkins to Earl of Essex and Earl of Nottingham.
1601.	May 20.	Richard Hawkins to Cecil.
,,	June 30.	Richard Hawkins to the Queen.
,,	,,	Richard Hawkins to the Privy Council.
1602.	Jan. 8.	Richard Hawkins to the Queen.
1604.	Jan. 4.	Sir R. Hawkins to Cecil.
,,	Feb. 1.	Sir R. Hawkins to Cecil.
,,	Mar. 22.	Sir R. Hawkins to Cecil.
,,	June 20.	Sir R. Hawkins to Cecil.
,,	July 6.	Sir Richard Hawkins to Julius Cæsar, Judge of the Admiralty.
1605.	Sept. 16.	Sir Richard Hawkins to Cecil.
1606.	Aug. 28 (?).	Sir R. Hawkins to Cecil.
,,	Oct. 3.	Sir R. Hawkins to the Privy Council.
1609.	May 25.	Sir R. Hawkins to Cecil.

MARQUIS OF ORMONDE.

1629.	Dec. 4.	Receipt for money from Walter, Earl of Ormonde, for use of Earl of Holland, by Jo. Hawkins.

2 A

ALFRED MORRISON, ESQ.

1581. July 11. Sir John Hawkins to Robert Peter, Auditor of the Receipt
of the Exchequer, "touching a warrant for the supply of cordynge
and canvas, w^h was taken out of her Maties storehouse at Dedeford
the last year for extraordinary service."

F. B. FRANK, ESQ.

1604. Sir Richard Hawkins is stayed from his journey, being ready to go forth.
[One and three-quarter pages.]

LORD LECONFIELD.

1595. A fleete to the Indies, Sir F. Drake and Sir John Hawkins Generals,
when they ventured deeply, and dyed in the journey. [Fol. 59, p. 24.]

,,   Jan. 29. Copy of Sir John Hawkins and Sir F. Drake's Commission
to go anywhere against the King of Spain. The names of the
Garland, Defiance, Bonaventure, Hope, Foresight, and *Adventure.*
[Brief Sheets 37 Eliz.]

HOUSE OF LORDS.

1645. Petition of John Packer and Will: Hawkins, two of the clerks of H.M.'s
Privy Seal.

1646. June 23. Annexéd certificate signed "Will: Hawkins Sec^ry to Committee."

W. M. MOLYNEUX, ESQ.

1586. Sept. 16. Letter by John Hawkinges and William Holstocke to the
J.P.s of the Counties of Surrey, Sussex, and Kent.

TRINITY HOUSE PAPERS.

1664. June 1. £10 ordered towards the repair of Sir John Hawkins's
almshouses at Chatham.

Extract from a letter written by Wm. Hawkins, of Plymouth, to Cromwell in 1536.

I DURST never sue to your Lordship for any help till I had first put my ship
goods in adventure to search for the commodities of unknown countries and
seen the return thereof in safety, as has metely well happened unto me
albeit by four parts not so well as I suppose it should be if one of my pilots
had not miscarried by the way. I beg to have of the King four pieces of
brass ordnance and one last of powder on good sureties; and also on security
of 100*l.* a loan of 2,000*l.* for seven years towards equipping three or four ships,
and I doubt not to do such feats of merchandise as shall be of great advantage
to the King's custom.

In the MS. Collection of Earl Cowper, K.G., at Melbourne Hall, Derby-shire, are some interesting letters from Sir John Hawkins.

In October, 1588, he writes to Burleigh:

> I HUMBLY pray your lordship to be favourable to me that I may end some part of my life in some quietness. The matters in this office are far out of order and far behindhand, which I shall never overcome unless I be sequested from this new business.

Again, he writes that divers payments may be secured to his wife in London.

Once more, on 15th January, 1590–1, he prays for a settlement of £4,385. A few days later he begs that his account may be settled. "I do not desire," he says, "to better my estate, my brother being deceased and my wife in such an extreme sickness as not like to recover; myself in years, and subject to sickness and infirmities. I desire not to be made rich, but that I may by your lordship's honourable favour have an honest reputation of my charge and former life, and that travail which I may hereafter take for her Majesty's service shall be faithful without corruption, and my poor advice wherein experience hath taught me shall be without spot or any covetous desire."

Seventeen days later he writes again that he has used his credit for wages and victuals, and for repairing and new rigging of the *Rainbow:*

> TRULY my very good lord, necessity doth force me to trouble your lordship to do me some favour, for my poor ability is not able to bear so great a burden.

The conclusion of this correspondence has its own pathos:

> I HAVE sent the note which your lordship willed me to make. Humbly desiring your good lordship to pardon mine attendance, for it hath pleased God to take my wife to His mercy, Godly in her life and Godly in her death.

The final letter of the whole series is one in which Sir John asks to have somebody joined with him to do the work, "so that with a quiet mind he may leave the cares of this world and prepare for the time to come." It is dated 28th August, 1594.

*Extract from a letter of Sir Wm. Winter to Sir John Hawkins,
28th February (9th March), 1588.*

OUR ships do show like gallants here, it would do a man's heart good to behold
them. Would to God the Prince of Parma were on the seas with all his forces,
and we in sight of them. You should hear that we would make his enterprise
very unpleasant to him.

Howard to Walsingham, $\frac{11}{21}$ March, 1588.

LET me have the four great ships and twenty hoys, with but twenty men
apiece, and each with but two iron pieces, and her Majesty shall have a good
account of the Spanish forces, and I will make the King wish his galleys home
again. Few as we are, if his forces be not hundreds we will make good sport
with them.*

Page 17.

Previously to the negro slaves being brought from the coast of Africa,
Irish Redshanks, or Wild Irishmen, who had been driven into the bogs, were
used for the purpose of slavery.

Page 65.

In the possession of the Plymouth Corporation is an original Hawkins
portrait, in oils (which hangs in the Mayor's parlour), framed, restored to its
present size, and presented to the Corporation, by Dr. F. W. P. Jago, of
21, Lockyer Street, Plymouth, on 16th February, 1881. This picture, although
it bears a striking resemblance to other portraits of Admiral Sir John Hawkins,
is more probably a portrait of his elder brother, William Hawkins, and thus
accounts for the greater age—seventy-four years—as Sir John was sixty-three
in the year he died, 1595. The head, face, ruff, and the following words,
" . . . . EÆ 74 Añº Dñi 1596," are the only remains of the old portrait, painted
on panel, the head of which appears to have been cut out from the original
picture. Dr. Jago tells me, that twenty years ago, when visiting a patient, the
wife of a dairyman, named Cotton, who is since dead, he noticed the portrait
hanging on the wall. The vigour with which it was painted attracted him, and
in answer to his enquiries he was told that it was some old picture that had
been picked up in a house in Stonehouse Lane, and that if Dr. Jago liked he
might have it.

Page 93.

"Hawkins and Frobisher cannonaded the *Capitana* at a distance,"† but

---

* *Sta. Pa. Dom.*　　† MOTLEY, *Herrara III.* iii. 100–102; *Bor.* iii. 322, *seq.*

Drake, disregarding the Lord High Admiral's order to show a light for the guidance of the English fleet, had "dowsed his glim" to chase some Flemish traders, mistaking them for stragglers from the enemy, and stood after possible plunder. Returning from this pursuit he lingered behind to make a prize of the *Capitana*. This explains Frobisher's speech against Drake.

Page 98.

"The 25th the English kept their division, and, as they had been directed, watched the motions of the enemy. Towards noon a vast galleon, too unwieldly for sailing well, fell behind the rest. Vice-admiral Hawkins saw her, and, running in between that vessel and the rest of the enemy, attacked, boarded, and, after a desperate resistance, took her."*

The Spanish accounts also tell of the capture and recapture and subsequent fate of the "urca" *Santa Anna.*

Page 136.

There is a legend of how, when Sir Richard Hawkins returned to England after his long captivity, he came to Slapton. There was a great gathering of people in the streets, and much preparation for rejoicings. On enquiring the cause, he was told that his faithful Judith, supposing him dead (he had been ten years a prisoner) was that very day about to console herself with another husband.

Page 137.

The arm in the portrait of Sir Richard Hawkins has a yellow silk scarf round it. The hair is dark brown; the beard and moustache light brown; the eyes bluish-grey. The reeds, rock, and waves are on the proper left.

Page 154.

The will of Sampson Mannaton, Esq., of Stokeclimsland, Cornwall, proved in 1627, names his wife, Judith; charges his sons Pierse, Edward, and Richard Mannaton to be dutiful to their mother; names his son William Whitaker, his son-in-law Henry Whitaker, his daughter Elizabeth Smythe, and nephew Ambrose Mannaton. Inventory taken by John Harris and William Whitaker, Esqs. This will proves that Sampson Mannaton married Judith, widow of

* BERKLEY's *Naval History*, book xvi. cap. cxxxiv. page 383.

Henry Whitaker and daughter of Captain William Hawkins, of Plymouth, and not Judith, daughter of Richard Hawkins, as stated in the *Visitation of Cornwall.*

Page 171.

A chevron between three swans were the arms of the Creeds of Coombe, Stokefleming, not those of Creed as on pages 171-2.

LIST OF SUBSCRIBERS.

Adkins, Dr. Joshua . . . Yealmpton.
Alger, W. H., Esq. . . . The Manor House, Stoke Damerel, S. Devon.
Alexander, Colonel . . . Late Duke of Cornwall's L. I.
Allen, George, Esq. . . . Wickeridge, Ashburton.
Allin, Rev. A. . . . . Holbeton, Ivybridge.
Appleton, Dr. . . . . 33, Half Moon Street, W.
Archer, Miss Constance . . . Penlee, Stoke.
Arnaud, J. B., Esq. . . . 135, Ebury Street, S.W.
*Arthur, R. F., Esq. . . . Wellsbourne, Compton.
Arthur, Richard W., Esq. . . Slade, Kingsbridge.
Aspinwall, J., Esq. . . . 8, Hyde Park Square, W.

Baker, R., Commander R.N. . . Broom House, Southmolton.
Barton, Benyon, Esq. . . . 20, Onslow Gardens, S.W.
Bastard, B. J. P., Esq. . . Buckland, Ashburton.
Bate, C. Spence, Esq., F.R.S. . . The Rock, South Brent.
Battams, G. B., Esq. . . . Kilworthy, Tavistock.
Baxter, C. E., Lieutenant R.N. . . 24, Ryder Street, S.W.
Beer, W., Esq. . . . . Buttville, Kingsbridge.
Bewes, C., Esq. . . . Hillside, Plympton.
Bewes, Charles, Esq. . . . Gravesend, Torpoint.
Bignold, W., Lieutenant R.N. . .
*Birch, W. M., Esq. . . . Exeter.
Blachford, Lord . . . Blachford, Cornwood.
Blennerhasset, Commander R.N. . .
Bradshaw, F., Esq. . . . Lifton.
Bradshaw, J. B., Esq. . . . Scots Guards.
*Brendon, Mr. W. T. . . . Woodbine Villa, Mannamead.
*Broadley, A. M., Esq. . . Cairo Cot., Beta Place, Regent's Park.
†Brutton, Major and Mrs. Edward . . 48, Emma Place, Stonehouse.
Buller, Alex., Rear-Admiral, C.B. . . Erle Hall, Plympton.
Bulteel, John, Esq. . . . Pamflete.
Burnard, C. F., Esq. . . . Chatsworth Lodge, Mannamead.
Burton, General Fowler . . 2, Osborne Villas, Stoke.

Caldwell, R. Townley, Esq. . . . Cambridge.
†Calmady, Miss L. . . . Knighton.
Campbell, Sir Duncan, Bart. . . . Scottish Club, W.
Carden, Major H. P. . . . Duke of Cornwall's Light Infantry.
Carew, Rev. R. B. . . . Bickleigh Rectory.
Carew, Miss . . . . Haccombe.
Carew, Rev. Henry W. . . . Rattery.
Carew, A., Lieutenant R.N. . . .
Cary, Robert, Esq. . . . Torr Abbey.
Cary, Stanley, Esq. . . . Follaton.
Caunter, Mrs. . . . . Ashburton.
Cavaye, Alex., Captain K.O.B.'S . . . The Citadel, Cairo.
Chaloner, Mrs. Richard . . . Sedgehill, Sealey, Wilts.
Champion, Colonel P. R. . . .
Chichester, W. H., Esq. . . . Grenofen, Tavistock.
Christian, Arthur, Lieutenant R.N. . . .
Clarke, H., Esq. . . . Efford Manor.
Clay, Dr. . . . . Roborough House.
Coddington, F. H., Commander R.N. . .
Coham-Fleming, B., Esq. . . Coham, Highampton.
Colborne, Hon. and Rev. Graham . . Dittisham.
Collier, W. F., Esq. . . . Woodtown, Horrabridge.
Collier, Mortimer, Esq. . . . Foxhams, Horrabridge.
Collins, Rev. J. A. Welsh . . . Burrington, near Saltash.
Collins-Splatt, W., Esq. . . . Brixton House.
Collins-Splatt, Hawtrey, Esq. . . . Brixton, Plympton.
Coney, Rev. T. . . . Wingfield Villas, Stoke.
Cornish-Bowden, Admiral . . . Newton Abbot.
Cornish-Bowden, F. J., Esq. . . . Blackhall.
Coryton, Colonel A. . . . Pentillie Castle.
Cranford, Mr. R. . . . Dartmouth.
Cumberlege, Miss E. . . . 21, Princes Gate, S.W.
†Cumming, W., Captain R.M. . . .
Cunningham, Captain W. . . . County Constabulary Barracks, Exeter.
Curtis-Hayward, Colonel J. F. . . . Quedgeley, Gloucester.

Dalgety, F., Esq. . . . Lockerly Hall, Romsey.
Daubeney, Colonel . . . The Beacon, Kingswear.
Davey, Sidney, Esq. . . . Bochym, Helston.
Davies, Dayrell, Lieutenant R.N. . . .
Dawson, Hon. R. . . . Holne Park, Ashburton.
Dawson, Ralph, Esq. . . . Wembury House.
Deacon, Barrington, Esq. . . . 12, Osborne Place, Plymouth.
†Deane, H. Pollexfen, Esq. . . . Cliff Cot, Torcross.
De Lacy, Mrs. . . . The Island, Waterford.
Derry, W., Esq. . . . Houndiscombe House, Plymouth.
*Dockyard Library . . . Devonport.
Drury, Charles, Captain R.N. . . .

Duntze, Lady . . Exeleigh, Starcross.

Earle, Miss Louisa A. . . 13, Vicarage Gate, Kensington.
Eden, F. Morton, Major R.M. . Royal Marine Barracks.
Elliot, Mrs. . . . Tresillian, Kingsbridge.
Elliot, Richard, Esq. . . Tresillian, Kingsbridge.
Elliot, J., Esq. . . Leigham.
Evans, Miss Jane M. . . Eton College.
Evans, Major H. . . 73, Warwick Square, S.W.

Farquhar, Sir Arthur, Admiral, K.C.B. . Drumnagesk, Aboyne, N.B.
Farquhar, Arthur M., Lieutenant R.N. .
FitzGeorge, Adolphus, Captain R.N. .
Fitzroy, General George . . Guards' Club.
Fleming, J., Esq. . . Bigadon, Buckfastleigh.
Fortescue, William B., Esq. . . Octon, Torquay.
Freake, Dowager Lady . . 11, Cranley Gardens, S.W.
Freake, Lady . . . Warfleet, Dartmouth.

Gatty, Alfred Scott, Esq. (York Herald) . . Heralds' College.
Glegg, E. Maxwell, Esq. . . Backford Hall, Chester.
Goodeve, Colonel H. H. . . Wingfield House, Stoke.
Graham, Mrs. T. . . . Wolston Heath, Rugby.
Gribble, W., Esq. . . . 12, Abchurch Lane.
Guthrie, James, Esq., and Mrs. . . 13, Ennismore Gardens, S.W.
Gye, H. F., Commander R.N. . . 4, Boulevard des Italiens, Paris.

†Hallifax, A. P., Esq., and Mrs. . . Halwell, Kingsbridge.
Hamilton, A. H. Kelso, Esq. . . The Retreat, Topsham.
Hamilton, Henry, Esq. . . Fenwick Chambers, 292, High Holborn.
Hamilton, G. de Courcy, Esq. . . Pennsylvania Park, Exeter.
Hannay, Mrs. . . . 33, Porchester Terrace, W.
*Hannay, J. Lennox, Esq. . . .
Hannay, J. P. K., Esq. . . .
Hare, Fred, Esq. . . Berry Pomeroy.
*Harris, Augustus, Esq. . . Theatre Royal, Drury Lane.
*Harris, Miss C. . . . 7, Leinster Square, W.
Harris, T., Esq. . . .
Hawker, W. H., Esq. . . Burleigh, Devonport.
*Hawkins's (Admiral Sir John's) Hospital . Chatham.
*Hawkins, J. Servington . . Hayford Hall, Buckfastleigh.
Hawkins, Mrs. C. Stuart . .
†Hawkins, Rev. B. R. J. . . Crowfield Parsonage, Needham, Suffolk.
*Hawkins, R. S., Esq. . . Wellington, New Zealand.
Hawkins, J. Staples, Esq. . . St. Fenton's, Baldoyle, Co. Dublin.
Hewett, Colonel H. . . 5, Elliot Terrace, Plymouth.

2 B

Higgins, G. C., Lieutenant R.N. . . .
Higgins, L., Esq. . . . . Castle Close, Bedford.
Higgins, C., Esq. . . . . Bedford.
Hillyar, Sir Charles, Admiral, K.C.B. . . Torpoint.
†Hillyar, Henry, Admiral, C.B. . . . Plympton.
Hoare, Mrs. C. Hugh . . . . 102, Eaton Place, S.W.
Holland, P., Esq. . . . . South Brent.
Hopkins, J. O., Rear-Admiral, Comptroller of the Navy.
Hopwood, Surgeon-Major R.A., and Mrs. . 18, Gloucester Terrace, W.
Hornby, Mrs. . . . . . 11, Hyde Park Terrace, W.
Horndon, David, Esq. . . . . Pencrebar, Callington.
†Houldsworth, Arthur, Esq. . . . Widdicombe, Kingsbridge.
Hurrell, J., Esq. . . . . Manor House, Kingsbridge.

Ilbert, W. Roope, Esq. . . Boweringsleigh, Kingsbridge.
Ilbert, A., Esq. . . 67, Gloucester Place, Portman Square, W.
Irwine, Mrs. . . . Buckland Tout Saints.

Jackson, Sydney F., Esq. . . . United University Club, S.W.
Jago, Edward, Esq. . . . . Coldrenick.
Jerram, Martyn, Lieutenant R.N. . . .
*Jewers, Arthur F., F.S.A. . . . Wells.
Johnstone, Rev. R. . . . . Moreton Say, Market Drayton.
Joliffe, Hon. W. Hylton, Lieutenant R.N. .
Jones, Colin H., Lieutenant R.N. . . .
Jones-Vaughan, Colonel H. T. . . . Stoke.

Kekewich, Trehawke H., Esq. . . . Inner Temple, Peamore, Exeter.
Kelly, Mrs. . . . . . 3, Windsor Villas.
Kelso, B., Commander R.N. . . .
*Keltie, J. Scott . . . . Librarian Geographical Society.
Kemball, C., Esq. . . . . 15, Cranley Gardens, S.W.
Keppell, Hon. Sir H., G.C.B., Admiral of the Fleet.

Lambe, Rev. G. . . . Highlands, Ivybridge.
†Laughton, Professor J. K. . . 130, Sinclair Road, West Kensington Park, W.
Liddell, Hon. Athole C. J. . . Winter Villa, Stonehouse.
Lidderdale, W., Esq. . . 23, Cambridge Square, W.
Lidderdale, F. F., Esq., and Mrs. . 59, Porchester Terrace, W.
Lindesay, Colonel H. R. P. . . Donmore, Cornwood.
Legge, Colonel Hon. Edward . . Holmwood Lodge, Dorking.
Llewellyn, Evan, M.P. . . .
Lloyd, Captain H. . . Langdown, Hythe, Southampton.
*Longman, T. Norton, Esq. . . 18, Thurloe Square, S.W.
Lopes, Sir Massey, Bart. . . Maristowe.
†Lovett, Captain H. . . . Somersetshire Light Infantry, Colchester.

Lovell, Mrs. . . . . Llanerchydol, Welshpool.
Lowdell, Edward, Lieutenant, R.N. .

MacAndrew, J. C., Esq. . . . Lukesland, Ivybridge.
*Macaulay, Dr. J. . . . . Editor of *Leisure Hour.*
†McGhee, Miss . . . .
Maire, Mrs. Peter . . . . 4, Bayswater Hill, W.
Mallock, Richard, Esq., M.P. . . . Cockington Court.
Mansell, Mr. W. A. . . . . 271, Oxford Street.
Margary, P. S., Esq. . . . 6, Wingfield Villas, Stoke.
*Markham, Clements R., Esq., C.B., F.R.S. . 21, Eccleston Square, S.W.
Marlborough, Bishop of, and Mrs. Earle . . 13, Vicarage Gate, Kensington.
*Martin, Mrs. . . . .
Matthews, G., Lieut. R.M. .
Maurice, Mr. . . . . . 34, Bedford Street.
Michell, W. Pryce, Esq. . . . Holwell, Tavistock.
Michelmore, Jeffery, Esq. . . . Bridgetown, Totnes.
Mildmay, H. Bingham, Esq. . . . Flete, Ivybridge.
Mildmay, F., Esq., M.P. . . . Flete, Ivybridge.
Monro, E. Hale, Esq. . . . . Ingsdon, Newton.
†Morgan, Mrs. Delmar . . . . 15, Roland Gardens, S.W.
Moore-Stevens, R. A., Esq. . . . Speccott, Merton.
Morley, The Earl of . . . . Saltram.
Mortlock, Mr. J. . . . . Oxford Street.
Mount Edgcumbe, The Earl of . . . Mount Edgcumbe.
Myers, A. B. R., Brigade-Surgeon . . Foot Guards.

Napier, Macvey, Lieutenant R.N. .

Orpen, Rev. E. Chatterton . Bigbury.
Owen, Mrs. Conrad . . 40, Warwick Road, S.W.

Page, Mr. James H. . . . . George Street, Plymouth.
Page, Thomas, Esq. . . . . 12, Brookside, Cambridge.
Parker, George, Rear-Admiral, and Mrs. . Delamore, Ivybridge.
Parker, John, Commander R.N. . . . Ware Park, Herts.
Parsons, Major Charles, R.A. . . . Colchester.
Pearce, Mr. S. . . . . Royal Hotel, Plymouth.
Pethick, J., Esq. . . . . Norley House, Plymouth.
Phillpotts, A., Commander R.N. . . . Bronwylfa, Exmouth.
Pitts, N., Esq. . . . . Wympston, Modbury.
Pitts, Thomas, Esq. . . . . Hoe Place House, Plymouth.
Ponsford, Captain H. . . . . Newland House, Swimbridge.
Ponsford, W., Esq. . . . . Essex House, Brondesbury.
Pooley, Rev. J. G. . . . . Stonham, Aspal.
†Powning, Rev. J. . . . . Dart View, Totnes.
Prance, W. H., Esq. . . . . 12, The Crescent, Plymouth.

Radcliffe, Walter, Esq.	Warleigh.
Radcliffe, Mrs.	Derriford.
Radcliffe, John A., Esq. . . .	39, Cambridge Terrace, W.
Radcliffe, Rev. Raymond . . .	Eton College.
Reiss, Mrs.	Jodrell Hall, Cheshire.
Revelstoke, Lord	Membland.
*Robinson, Charles N., Commander R.N. .	*Army and Navy Gazette*, London.
Rogers, Miss Katherine . . .	Moor Cross, Cornwood.
Rogers, H. Montague, Esq. . .	Helston.
Romanes, Captain R. J. . . .	King's Own Scottish Borderers.
*Rosebery, The Countess of . .	38, Berkeley Square, W.
*Sailors' Rest	
St. Aubyn, Rev. William . .	Stoke Damerel.
*St. Aubyn, Rev. Edmund . .	Stoke Fleming.
St. Clair, A. F., Commander R.N. . .	
St. Germans, The Earl of . .	Port Eliot.
Salmon, Mrs.	Borringdon Terrace, Plympton.
Scott, Mrs.	38, Green Street, W.
*Seale, Sir Henry, Bart. . . .	Norton, Dartmouth.
Seale-Hayne, C., Esq., M.P. . .	3, Eaton Square, S.W.
Sherard, Hon. Mrs. . . .	Gurrington, Ashburton.
Short, F., Esq. . . .	Bickham, Alphington.
†Shortland, P. F., Vice-Admiral . .	6, Hoe Villas, Plymouth.
Simpson, C., Esq. . . .	Chilworth Court, Romsey.
*Soltau, John T., Esq. . . .	Little Efford.
Soltau-Symons, G., Esq. . .	Chaddlewood, Plympton.
Sommers, Mrs. . . .	Mendip Lodge, Langford, R.S.O., Somerset.
Sommers, E. B., Esq. . . .	Clandon, Guildford.
*South Devon and Cornwall Hospital . .	
Southey, Mrs.	Eastleigh Court, Warminster.
Square, W. J., Esq. . . .	Plymouth.
Square, W., Esq., F.R.G.S. . .	Plymouth.
*Stacey, Mrs. . . .	
Steer, Rev. H. Hornby . . .	33, Mount Sion, Tunbridge Wells.
Stevens, Robert, Esq. . . .	St. Stephen's, Plympton.
Stewart, Mrs.	Mendip Lodge, Langford, Somerset.
Stirling, J. Wilfred, Captain R.A. . .	Dublin.
Symonds, Sir Thomas, G.C.B., Admiral of the Fleet	Sunny Hill, Torquay.
Tanner, F., Esq. . . .	Hawson, Buckfastleigh.
Tanner, C. F., Esq. . .	Stowford, Ivybridge.
Tayleur, John, Esq. . . .	Buntingsdale, Market Drayton.
Taylor, Colonel A. . .	The Rosary, Ashburton.
Toll, H. L., Esq. . .	Street.
Toms, Major H. . . .	Kingswear.
Trafalgar, Viscount . . .	Cole Park, Wilts.
Trelawny, Sir William L. S., Bart. .	Trelawne, Cornwall.

Trelawny, General Jago	.	. Coldrenick.
Trood, Colonel R.	.	. Matford, Exeter.
Turner, General H. Blois	.	. 131, Harley Street, W.
Turner, Henry B. H., Esq.	.	. 4, Calverley Terrace, Tunbridge Wells.
Turner, Miss Emily	.	. Coombe Royal.
Turner, A. F., Lieutenant R.N.	.	
Twysden, S., Commander R.N.	.	. Kingsbridge.

Vyvyan, Sir Vyell, Bart.		. Trewan, St. Columb.

Wade, Mr. W. C.	.	.	. 5, Portland Square, Plymouth.
Waldy, W. T., Esq.	.	.	. 9, Ashburn Place, S.W.
Waldy, Miss G.	.	.	. 9, Ashburn Place, S.W.
*Walford, Miss Emma	.	.	.
Waring, H., Esq. (Mayor of Plymouth)	.		. Osborne House.
*Warner, Rev. H. G.	.	.	. Slapton.
Watt, R. W., Lieutenant R.N.	.	.	
Wells, Major H. L., R.E.	.	.	. Teheran, Persia.
West, Mrs. Thornton	.	.	. Streatham Hall, Exeter.
†Weymouth, T. Wyse, Esq.	.	.	. Woolston, Kingsbridge.
J. Whidborne, Esq.	.	.	. Gorway, Teignmouth.
†White, Arthur, Esq.	.	.	. Wrangaton Manor, Ivybridge.
*Whitmarsh, Mr. J.	.	.	. Librarian, Plymouth Proprietary Library.
Whipple, Dr. Connell	.	.	. St. Andrew's Lodge, Plymouth.
Williams, John, Esq.	.	.	. Scorrier.
Wills, Mr. T. G.	.	.	. St. Mildred's, Compton Gifford, Plymouth.
Wippell, P. H. Pridham, Esq.	.	.	. Goldsmith, Building Temple, E.C.
Wood, C. R., Commander R.N.	.	.	
Woodley, James, Esq.	.	.	. Halshanger, Ashburton.
*Worth, R. N., F.G.S.	.	.	. 4, Seaton Avenue, Mutley.
Wrey, R. B. S., Lieutenant R.N.	.	.	
*Wright, Mr. W. H. K.	.	.	. Librarian, Free Library, Plymouth.
*Wymper, E., Esq.	.	.	. St. Martin's House, 29, Ludgate Hill, E.C.
Wyndham, Mrs. F.	.	.	. 10, Hyde Park Street, W.

Yonge, James, Esq.	. Brixton.

ARMS OF QUEEN ELIZABETH.

www.ingramcontent.com/pod-product-compliance
Lightning Source LLC
Chambersburg PA
CBHW030817020726
47499CB00006B/1951